FOOL ME ONCE

MARK GILLESPIE

INKUBATOR
BOOKS

Published by Inkubator Books
www.inkubatorbooks.com

Copyright © 2024 by Mark Gillespie

Mark Gillespie has asserted his right to be identified as the author of this work.

ISBN (eBook): 978-1-83756-443-9
ISBN (Paperback): 978-1-83756-444-6
ISBN (Hardback): 978-1-83756-445-3

FOOL ME ONCE is a work of fiction. People, places, events, and situations are the product of the author's imagination. Any resemblance to actual persons, living or dead is entirely coincidental.

No part of this book may be reproduced, stored in any retrieval system, or transmitted by any means without the prior written permission of the publisher.

PROLOGUE

'Get back here, you little bitch!'

The man's voice is a furious roar, and it's catching up with me. He's right to be angry, of course, but it's all part of the game. Nothing personal. I have to ignore the screaming child too and the shrill racket of the woman shouting from inside the house. They'll get over it. People do.

For now, I have to run. I have to survive. And it's the thought of the rewards that keeps me going.

Most of all, it's the thought of *her*. Seeing. Acknowledging what I do.

I wonder if she's scared when she does this.

I run and feel the blood pumping in my arms and legs. My breathing is heavy and ragged. I'm no longer filming – I got all the footage I needed back in the house. But this is new. No one has ever chased me before like this guy is chasing me now. That's not how it's supposed to go, and all the others were so stunned to see me in their house that I was long gone before their legs started working.

Not this guy. He's running like an Olympic sprinter. Can't he take a joke?

'I said get back here, you little bastard!'

Run, Zara. Run.

Do the stunt. Get out of the house and then bask in the glorious aftermath and hope that she'll see me. Hope that she'll reply to one of the many messages that I've sent on her website and social media channels. I know she's read them – or at least some of them. She must know by now that I'm not just another fan.

Like her, I'm something special.

Like her, I'm one of the greats.

I race down the garden path. Wrestle with the gate, which I thought I'd left unlatched on the way in. I'm sure I did. That's common sense, for God's sake. An unlatched gate (assuming there is a gate, of course) is necessary for a quick getaway.

Note for the future – double-check the gate.

'What the bloody hell are you thinking?' the man's voice bellows in my ear. He's big and fast, and if he gets his hands on me, he'll snap me like a twig. And why wouldn't he? I waltzed into his house without knocking. Performed the stunt and then abandoned it when it was clear this guy wasn't messing about.

The child is still screaming inside the house. I can hear her. Four years old, that'd be my guess. Looked like she had Down syndrome or something like that.

My clumsy fingers find the latch. I lift it and jerk the gate open. Now I'm running in the middle of the road, trapped in this suburban nightmare. I can't feel my legs, but I know they're turning over faster than they've ever done before. I've never been much of a runner, and I realise that's something I'll have to fix.

Note for the future – join a running club.

'Get back here!'

We're on the road, and he isn't giving up. I'm nowhere near his property or his wife or his kid anymore, and still he isn't giving up. But then why would he? Why and when did I get so sloppy? The first few times I did this, I scouted out the houses in advance. I saw the people who lived there, and whether I thought about it consciously or not, they weren't the type who'd chase me down the street. And even if they did, they wouldn't get very far.

Now I'm just showing up at their front doors blind. Doing it the way she does it or at least the way I think she does it.

Sloppy.

Stupid.

Subpar.

I keep to the middle of the road as I make my escape. Fortunately, I *did* plan my escape route. Past the junction straight ahead, there's a narrow lane that winds left and leads into a crummy old playpark with rusting swings and a slide and not much else. Beyond the park, a stretch of dense woodland that leads away from suburbia. That's the way I came in. That's the way I'm getting out. I can be there in three minutes and lose him in the woods. I just have to hope that whatever speed is left in my legs is enough to carry me there.

But he's gaining on me. I can hear him blowing in my ear. There's no way to explain it, but I sense myself outrunning this guy. I can do it. He's still yelling. Still cursing. I'm almost there. Just need to get myself across the junction, turn down the path without slipping or losing my balance and—

The blaring horn is there as soon as I try to cross the junction. A siren in my left ear. The piercing shriek of screeching brakes and, amid all that, just enough time for me to realise that there's a car on the road. There's a sudden thud that feels like the earth flinching. No pain, just the sensation of flying. Falling. A whooshing noise, followed by stillness.

How did this end up so badly?

What would she do now?

Die, I guess.

I know right away that I'm not going to make it. Something warm is washing over me, and I'm not actually sure that I want to make it. The darkness that's coming is far from unpleasant. There's no feeling anymore and certainly no feeling of inadequacy or never being quite enough. There's just a faint hope of something better in that warm dark void that I'm now floating in.

A group of people stands over me. Someone kneels down beside me, and I think she has my hand in hers. I'm not sure. She's talking to me in a soothing voice, but her face is a blur. Everything, faces and voices, is slipping further and further away. Just can't feel it anymore. Can't feel ... light is fading, and it's okay. It's nice.

Still, there's one good thing that might come from dying. At long last, she might notice me.

Please, for the love of God. Notice me.

Notice, please.

I've earned it.

PART I
KATE

1

'What the—?'

I open my eyes and sit up too fast. All I see are flashing pinpricks of white light, and after that, I'm trudging through a thick blanket of fog. I push myself up a little further, and it feels like I'm stepping off a rollercoaster.

Where am I?

I come back to my surroundings. I'm on the couch in the living room, and it's ... it's night-time because the curtains are drawn. It's dark inside except for the hazy, sluggish light of a solitary lamp and the TV. There's a sci-fi horror movie on low volume. At a glance, it looks like it's about a monster going apeshit on a spaceship. Eating up the crew. I have no idea what's going on.

'Kate,' a voice yells from upstairs.

I stare at the ceiling.

'You okay?'

Good question. Glancing left, I see a bottle of wine and a tube of salt and vinegar Pringles sitting on the coffee table.

There's one glass, empty except for a little red splotch at the bottom. The bottle's almost empty too.

'Kate?'

'Umm, Tommy?'

'Kate, can you turn down the TV, please? You know I need to sleep before rugby in the morning.'

I'm still staring at the ceiling. That's right. Tommy, my boyfriend – my *fiancé* – plays rugby every Sunday morning. It's a ritual. No more Saturday-night fun for Tommy. I drink alone on the couch these days. Rugby – what a stupid thing to do on a Sunday—

'Kate?'

'The TV isn't even that loud.'

God, my head is throbbing, and talking makes it worse. I reach over the coffee table and pick up the remote control. I hit the mute button, and that's when I hear a noise coming from outside on the street.

I look at the window. *That's* what Tommy could hear.

'What the hell is that?' I say.

I kick a tartan blanket off my lap and launch a meteor shower of Pringle crumbs into the air. Quickly, I spin my legs over the edge of the couch. I'm still looking over at the window. Listening to the racket outside.

It's a car. Racing towards the street at high speed by the sound of it. All I can hear is a revving engine, and for a second it feels like I've woken up in the middle of a Formula 1 racetrack. There's a loud pop and a throaty growl. I can almost smell the exhaust fumes from inside the house.

'Tommy, do you hear—?'

A loud *vroom-pop-pop-bang* cuts me off. It feels like the floor is shaking under my feet, and maybe it's the wine, or maybe it's the boy racer out there living out his own *Fast &*

Furious movie on a Saturday night. Killing small-town boredom with a dose of good old motorised masturbation. But that's the last thing my head needs right now.

I stagger towards the window where headlights shimmer on the back of the curtains. The light burns inside the living room. It feels like there's a giant spotlight trying to claw my eyes out. I blink. I wince and keep moving forward. Another high-pitched roar. That car is moving *fast*, and I can only hope that it'll move on and the screaming engine will fade into the distance. Maybe it was a wrong turn. Why else would someone come here?

Go away, I think.

Another look at the empty bottle of wine on the table. Am I really at the point where I'm drinking full bottles by myself? And even worse, forgetting that I've done it.

'Tommy?'

I pull back the curtains and see a car fishtailing its way up the road.

'Bloody hell.'

The vehicle lurches back and forth yet somehow keeps moving at a ferocious speed. It's getting closer to the house now. Either it'll pass, or my head will explode. It jerks suddenly to the left, and the dazzling white headlights point towards our house. That car is looking at me, I swear to God. Its full-moon eyes are coming straight for me. In a split second, I envision what's about to happen next: the car crashing through our fence, still picking up speed, ploughing through the living-room window, an explosion of glass and the crunch of my bones under its hungry wheels.

The shriek of rubber versus asphalt is pure torture. The car spins back towards the right, away from our house, and there's a jolt of acceleration that makes me gasp. What the hell is the driver thinking? And what's that other noise? Is that someone screaming inside the car?

There's no last-second reprieve this time as the car races towards the other side of the street. Only a bone-jarring crunch as it rams the metal fence that belongs to our neighbours. The fence holds up, but it's all bent and twisted out of shape. Smoke billows from the car tyres. The engine cuts off after impact, and for a second, everything is silent.

I hear Tommy cursing upstairs. His feet thumping on the floor like a silverback gorilla giving plyometrics his best shot.

I glance at the other houses up and down the street. Lights flicker on, both inside and outside. The street is waking up, and no wonder after that racket. We just had ourselves an overdramatic car crash in the most boring street in the most boring town imaginable. I see curtains pulled back and blinds opening at frantic speed. Silhouettes at the windows. Dogs barking as if in chorus. And then I see the first of the neighbours stepping outside, an elderly couple wrapped in their dressing gowns. A quick shuffle down the garden path. Crumpled, disbelieving faces looking at the car that hit the fence. The other neighbours follow. Some venture out of their homes slowly. Others rush out like their living room's on fire.

All are gawping at the car.

I hear the toilet flush upstairs. All that excitement must have gone straight to Tommy's bladder. He's still cursing. Calling down to me about the state of Jack and Sarah's fence across the street.

'Be there in a second,' he says.

I'm at the window, watching the action unfold. There's movement at the car. The driver's side door opens, and a young man who looks to be in his early twenties falls through the gap and onto his knees. He looks around with a thousand-yard stare. Then he picks himself up off the pavement and staggers away from the car, wafting the endless smoke from his face. He's got a straggly brown beard, and he's wearing a dark red Adidas tracksuit zipped to the neck. The man is as skinny as a rake.

I feel a jolt of electricity and press my face against the cold glass. There's something familiar about that man. I've seen him before.

I'm sure of it.

All of a sudden, he snaps out of the shock that envelops him. Now he's jumping around with his hands on his head. Screaming. Freaking out. His voice is cartoonishly high-pitched, but it's probably just the horror of what's happened. He does hurried laps around the mangled car, which looks like a Subaru.

'Oh fuck!' he yells. 'Oh ... oh fuck!'

My head's still pressed tight against the glass. I'm looking at the Subaru, and if I had to guess, I'd say there are at least two other people in the car. One in the passenger seat and another in the back. I don't know if they're hurt or not. Only the driver has come out so far.

Tommy hurries through the living-room door in his shorts and a faded Homer Simpson T-shirt. As he arrives, he's wrapping his caramel-coloured dressing gown around his thick frame.

I stare at him.

'What the actual—?' he asks.

He looks at me.

'Kate!'

'Hmm?'

His eyes are bleary, and I feel them zoning in on me. 'Are you alright?'

'I'm fine.'

He glances at the wine bottle on the table.

'Did you see it?' I ask.

'Eh?'

'Did you see the crash?'

'Boy racer. Slammed right into Jack and Sarah's fence.' He nods and points at the window. 'What's happening now?'

I give him a summary from my vantage point. 'Lots of people have come out. The driver's out of the car too, and he's going nuts. Looks like he's having some kind of breakdown, if you ask me. I suppose we should go out there, eh? See if there's something we can do.'

I look at Tommy, and he's frowning in my direction. Yet again, he glances at the empty bottle, and I feel a pinprick of irritation. Is he judging me?

'Are you okay?' he asks. 'Don't take this the wrong way, but you sound a little out of it.'

'I'm fine,' I say. 'Just tired.'

'Had a few drinks?'

Bastard.

'I suppose.'

He smiles, but it's not a comforting gesture. *That's just like you.*

Screw it. We've got bigger things to worry about right now. There's a frigging car crash on the street outside, and for all I know, two people inside the car might be seriously hurt. Who cares if I've had a few glasses of wine or not?

I hurry past Tommy, into the hallway and towards the front door. 'C'mon. We need to show our faces.'

'You're in your pyjamas, Kate.'

'So are half the people out there. C'mon, will you?'

He protests, but it's too late. I've opened the front door, and oh my God, it's a cold night. But that's not enough to stop me. Now I'm shuffling down the garden path in my pyjamas and fluffy socks, one of many neighbours riding to the rescue.

2

We're outside, and I hear the frantic sound of sirens wailing in the distance. I hope it's an ambulance on the way because now that Tommy and I are out on the street, I know for sure there are two people still inside the Subaru. It's just like I thought – there's one in the back and one in the passenger seat. I see their heads moving, but I don't know why they're still in there. Don't know if they're okay. At least the smoke billowing off the front of the car has eased off. Not that I thought it was going to blow up or anything. But then again, what do I know?

My head is rough. Falling asleep on the couch has kick-started my hangover. All the excitement on the street is distracting me, for now at least. It's going to be rough later – but I guess that's what painkillers are for.

The street is overflowing with neighbours in their dressing gowns and pyjamas. Some of them are buried under long coats and rubbing their hands together for warmth. Hair sticking up. Standing on the road, on the pavement. Always that expression of pronounced bewilderment on their faces.

Cold air snaps at my legs. Trying to steal my warmth.

I look at the car, still keeping my distance, with Tommy beside me. Why won't the other two passengers come out? Maybe they're in shock. Maybe they're ashamed or embarrassed about what just happened, and who can blame them?

The driver's still bouncing around like a hyperactive puppy. Shouting. Pointing at the car like everyone on the street can't see what's happened for themselves. It's exhausting just looking at the guy. I notice a diamond stud in his left ear. The more I look at him, the more convinced I am that I've seen this man's face before. I know I have. He's young and skinny. Razor-sharp cheekbones and hollow eye sockets. My guess is he's on drink or drugs. Probably both.

A handful of the neighbours shadows his every move like parents watching their kids take their first baby steps. They talk in soothing voices. They're trying to calm him down, but he's too fast, too twitchy, too full of nervous energy. He shakes them off and continues circling the car, hands clamped on top of his head.

'No,' he yells. 'This isn't happening.'

The little jewel in his ear sparkles as he laps the car again.

I feel myself inching closer.

'Where are you going?' Tommy asks.

'I recognise him.'

'Him? From where?'

'I don't know.'

I stop my approach when the passenger door opens. A long leg in blue jeans swings through the gap, followed by the other. A pair of shiny black Dr Martens hits the road. A young woman steps out, and she's about the same age as the driver, early twenties, dressed in a red Fred Perry shirt with braces. She's got short hair, shaved at the sides. Quite fashionable, if you like the skinhead look.

She looks dazed. Frightened. Very slowly, she sits down on the pavement, and an old woman wrapped up in a pink dressing gown goes over and asks if she's okay. The girl nods but can't meet the woman's eyes.

The sirens are getting louder.

I take another step towards the car and stare at the outline of a head in the back seat. Right now, it's perfectly still. Like there's a mannequin in there. What about this third person? Won't they ever come out?

The driver is still hyper while the girl remains seated on the kerb, flanked by kindly neighbours trying to get information out of her. She's not talking. Just shaking her head over and over in a disbelieving manner. Staring into space.

A fresh cluster of neighbours has gathered around the back of the car, peering through the window at the mystery third passenger. They're talking to him or her. I want to go over and take a look, but my legs hold me back. I can hear them encouraging the passenger to come out. One man decides to bypass conversation and tries the door handle. It's locked.

'Won't you come out?' he asks, peering in.

No response.

'The police are on their way.'

Nothing.

'Why don't you unlock the door? We just want to help you.'

I'm distracted when the driver stops pacing, and for a brief second, we make direct eye contact. It's like a cold hand grabbing my wrist. Where have I seen that face before? Is he famous, like an actor or something? Is he in a band? Have I seen him on TV, or is he just someone local whom I've seen around?

I grab Tommy by the arm. So far, we've done little to help anyone around here. We're just standing at the edge of the road like useless spectators.

'We need to do something,' I say.

'Like what?'

'I was hoping you could tell me.'

Tommy puts a hand on my shoulder and grins. 'I dunno. It was your idea to come out here.'

'I feel like we should do something.'

'We *are* doing something.'

'What?'

He hesitates. 'Umm, waiting for the police.'

I can still hear the crash in my head. The bone-jarring crunch of the Subaru hitting the metal fence is still there, replaying over and over again. And just before the crash itself, I recall the icy-cold horror I felt when I thought the car was coming for our house. That feeling of helplessness. It's a miracle that no one was killed or badly injured.

Then again, maybe someone is.

'You okay?' Tommy asks, nudging me with his pointy elbow. 'You wanna go back inside?'

'Hmm?'

'I can hear your teeth chattering. Wanna go back in?'

'I know *you* do.'

He looks at me in that probing way again, and the half-smile on his face dissolves back into a frown. 'How much wine did you drink tonight?'

'What the fuck?'

'C'mon, Kate. It's just a question.'

I shrug off his bullshit question. But there's a nagging voice at the back of my mind, a voice that sounds more like my own than Tommy's, and it's telling me that I *have* been drinking too much. Why else would I feel so crappy right now?

Just admit it, I tell myself. *You're a social drinker who doesn't wait to socialise anymore.*

Jack and Sarah are standing on the pavement outside their house. Looks like they're examining the damage to the gate or as much of it as they can with the Subaru still wrapped around it. They're talking to a silver-haired woman whose face doesn't ring any bells. Modern life, I guess. Tommy and I know nothing about most of the neighbours. Their names and stories are a mystery to me. We only know Jack and Sarah because they're in the house directly opposite from us. And when I say *know*, I mean I remember their names. They're about twenty years older than us, as are most of the people who live on this street, come to think of it, and most often it's a quick hello, a few pleasantries, and then we move on.

Still, we should go say something.

'C'mon,' I say, grabbing Tommy by the arm. It's like dragging a polar bear across the road. 'We'd better show our faces.'

We wait until there's an opening. After about three minutes of non-stop chat, the silver-haired woman says her goodbyes to Jack and Sarah and then shuffles along the pavement in her pink dressing gown and tartan slippers. Clearly making for home and the comfort of central heating.

I let go of Tommy's hand. Then I approach Jack and Sarah with what I hope is a look of concern on my face. It feels more like a grimace thanks to the worst hangover of my life. I'm hanging on, but it feels like I actually might be dying.

'How are you both?'

Jack and Sarah look like they're waking up from a dream. There's a dazed look in their eyes, and I can only imagine what the crash must have been like from inside their house. Were they both asleep at the moment of impact? They must have thought the house was crashing down with them inside it.

Sarah wrestles a tired smile onto her face. Jack's arm is wrapped around his wife's shoulders, and both have thick coats on over their striped pyjamas. I think they *were* asleep when it happened. Poor buggers.

'Got a bit of a shock,' Sarah says. It's an understatement, but I hear the wobble in her voice. 'I suppose it could've been a lot worse.'

I get the feeling she's said that a lot since it happened.

Jack nods. 'Crazy kids.'

'As long as no one's hurt,' I say. 'That's the important thing.' It's lame, and we all know it, but what else can I say? What can anyone say to make it better?

Good job they didn't go through the fence and through the front window, eh? Could've gone right through you.

'If there's anything we can do,' Tommy says in a calm, reassuring voice. 'Anything at all, please let us know.'

Jack and Sarah both thank us, and the awkward silence that follows is our cue to get the hell out of there. We'll give them space, that's what we say. I'm relieved when we start walking across the street. But I still feel like shit, and I don't want to bang on about the mother of all hangovers because I get the feeling that Tommy will say I told you so.

I just want to curl up in a ball and sleep. For a month.

We're back on our side of the street when a police car pulls up near the mangled fence. The flashing red and blue lights conjure up a stabbing pain behind my eyes. The siren makes a whooping noise. Fuck this. I'm shivering, and Tommy flinches when I take his hand.

'You're cold,' he says.

'I know.'

We stand at the gate for a few minutes.

The ambulance shows up a few minutes later. That's followed by some sort of recovery vehicle with an orange flashing light at the back. *More lights*, I think. *Great*. The breakdown vehicle pulls up at the side of the road, and a couple of guys in high-vis get out, talk to the police officers and look over the crashed car.

The third passenger still won't get out. There are people talking to him, but whoever's in the back of that car, they're ignoring everyone. The police are ignored. Ambulance personnel, ignored. Breakdown-truck guys, ignored.

'Why won't they come out?' I ask.

Tommy shakes his head. 'Probably just a kid. Scared out of his mind.'

'Or embarrassed?'

He nods. 'Wouldn't you be? C'mon, that's enough excitement for one night. Let's go back in the house.'

Tommy steers me towards the gate, and I don't resist. I hear him tell me that I need to get warm, but I don't listen. My head is fuzzy. Feels like I'm out on my feet.

'You alright?' I hear him ask.

'Good. I'm good.'

We go inside and close the door. That pushes at least some of the noise away, just enough to make it bearable.

Tommy gives me a peck on the cheek, goes upstairs, and I hear the hallway creak under his rugby-player weight.

I need something to drink, and although it's tempting to consider a hair of the dog, I'll steer clear of the wine. I walk into the kitchen, let the tap run cold and pour myself a glass of water.

'Where's the paracetamol?' I yell up to Tommy.

'Kitchen cupboard.'

A pause.

'Headache?' he asks.

No, I just love taking paracetamol.

'Bit.'

I find the pills, take a couple, and without thinking about it, I'm back at the living-room window. Tired but not sleepy anymore. Staring through a narrow gap in the curtains, doing the nosy-neighbour thing. It's busy on the street with emergency services and neighbours, and I guess it'll be like that for a while.

As for me, I can't take my eyes off the Subaru. There's *still* someone in the back seat, and they won't get out of the car for anyone.

I tap my finger on the glass. Point it towards the car.

'Who are you?' I whisper. 'And what are you hiding from?'

3

It's Sunday morning, and it feels like there's a bus parked on my chest.

What the hell is wrong with me? Barely in my mid-twenties and I can't handle a bottle of wine? Or two? I'm too young to have hangovers this bad, aren't I? I should be able to get up easily the next day, shake it off and have a clear head. Not feel this ... *heaviness*. Maybe I'm not built for drinking alcohol. There are people like that, aren't there? People who just can't take it. Lightweights.

I feel more like a flyweight this morning.

It's hard work, but I push the sheets back and get up. The house feels cold, but despite being tempted, I don't dive back into bed.

I stop for a moment. Whoops, I'm a little off-balance, but that's okay. Slowly, I walk out of the bedroom with what feels like kettlebells hanging off my quads. The house is so quiet, and that's partly because Tommy left for rugby a couple of hours ago. I must have been out of it because I've got no recollection of hearing him get up this morning. Didn't hear his alarm go off. Didn't hear him leave the house.

Something comes back to me. The way he looked at the empty wine bottle last night. That look of *oh shit, not again.*

I'm barely past the bedroom door when I stop and lean my back against the wall. Beads of sweat form on my forehead. This feels like more than a hangover. A simple thing such as walking shouldn't feel this hard, and a voice in my head tells me to go back to bed. Write the day off and rest before I have to go to work tomorrow.

C'mon, I tell myself. *Get a grip.*

I trudge downstairs to make coffee. The stairs creak under my feet, and it's only when I'm at the bottom that last night comes back to me in fragments. The space horror film. Pringle crumbs all over the blanket, headlights and—

'Shit.'

The crash. There was a huge car crash last night.

How could I forget that?

Suddenly I'm wide awake. I rush into the living room and over to the window, where I pull back the curtains. The daylight stings, but it's pretty out there, like a scene from a springtime calendar. I wince. I squint as I look over the street, wondering what I'll see first in terms of leftovers. I envision thousands of shards of glass and metal scattered all over the road. Blood, maybe? Or is that too gruesome? Is the car still there? What about Jack and Sarah's fence? How bad does it look in broad daylight?

My heart is thumping as I press my forehead against the glass. I look outside, then take my head off the window. I squint harder.

'What the—?'

There's nothing out there. The street looks normal, as in Sunday-morning normal. I don't see any people, and I imagine most of them are tucked up inside, still in bed or sitting at the kitchen table, having Sunday breakfast. All the cars are parked in their respective driveways or tucked in tight at the side of the road. A few are propped up on the kerb while a small transit van sits on the nature strip a few doors down from us. Across the street, a ginger cat strolls along the pavement without a care in the world. I can hear the bell jingling on his collar until a dog barks in response to the cat's presence.

Jack and Sarah's fence is untouched.

That can't be right, but it is. I can't see a single dent from where I'm standing. That's not possible. I saw the crash last night, and even though my head is a total shitshow right now, I remember that part clearly enough. A Subaru sped down the street and, after almost hitting our fence, went through *that* fence. Jack and Sarah's fence. The sound of it is still ringing in my head. I can still feel the shudder of impact like it happened a minute ago. Yet to look outside this morning, there's nothing. Not a trace of a car crash.

But it happened.

Or was it a dream?

No, I know it happened.

There's no debris. No glass. No metal fragments. Okay, so the mess has been cleaned up, and I guess that's possible if enough people were out on the job, right? Must have been a rapid-fire and well-organised clean-up job this morning. But the fence – not a mark on it? Am I supposed to believe they have put up a new fence already?

I look at the clock.

It's 9.09 a.m.

I let go of the curtains, and the living room dims. My headache is a constant, gnawing sensation, and I decide to eat something even though I'm not in the slightest bit hungry. But food might help. Still thinking about what I just saw outside, I walk into the kitchen and put the kettle on. Two slices of wholegrain bread go into the toaster. While I wait for the bread to toast, I return to the window. My finger opens a tiny gap in the curtains, and I stare across the road again.

'Seriously?'

Am I overthinking here? Maybe the crash wasn't as bad as I thought. Maybe I was tipsier – okay, *drunker* – than I thought.

'That's the same fence,' I say, as if to convince myself. 'That's the exact same fence.'

What are the chances of Jack and Sarah finding and putting up an identical replacement overnight?

Something isn't right here.

The kettle pings, and I ignore it. I don't want coffee or tea anymore. The toast pops up, and that's ignored too. Instead of sitting down to breakfast, I hurry upstairs, grab my dressing gown from the bedroom and then walk downstairs to the front door. I slip my feet inside a pair of trainers next to the mat. Then I open the door, and the cold pinches my face with its sharp claw. As I walk further out, I can't take my eyes off Jack and Sarah's fence.

I stop for a second. Tighten the belt on my dressing gown, still staring at the fence.

'What the hell is going on here?'

Just being outside brings the events of last night back to

life. Suddenly everything is so vivid again. That was no dream – there is no way it was a dream. The hyperactive driver jumping around and the skinhead girl and the mystery passenger who stayed inside the car. The neighbours standing on the pavement and on the road, the wailing sirens that went on for ever and sounded like they were trapped inside my head.

I look at the road, searching for a hint of glass or metal in the morning sunlight.

Nothing.

I'm about to look closer when I hear the sound of a door opening. I look across the street, and Sarah's walking outside, carrying a yellow binbag in her left hand. She looks fresh – much fresher than I feel. Pink sweater, blue jeans and there's a healthy glow to her face like she hasn't got a care in the world. Shouldn't she appear exhausted right now?

She walks to the end of the garden path, opens the lid of a small wheelie bin and drops the yellow bag inside. The lid slams shut. That's when she spots me standing in the middle of the street. I must look pretty weird (and pretty rough), but nonetheless she gives me a smile and a wave. Like this little exchange is something we do every morning.

'Morning, Kate.'

I wave back and realise my arm is shaking. I lower it quickly. 'Morning.'

Sarah maintains that neutral smile as I approach. Is that a flicker of apprehension in her eyes? Or am I overthinking everything again?

'That was quick,' I say.

'What was quick?'

'The clean-up. Did you guys even get to bed last night?'

What follows is the longest pause I've ever experienced.

'Clean-up?'

'Yeah. After the crash.'

Another long pause.

'Crash?'

My dumb grin is hanging on by a thread. Looks like there's someone in the world who's slower than me on Sunday mornings, even if she does look raring to go. Already, this conversation is too weird.

I talk slowly to the point of being patronising. Just in case she's hard of hearing because, truth be told, I know nothing about this woman even if she has lived across the street for ... God knows how many years?

'The car crash,' I say. 'You know – the one that went through your fence.'

I point at the fence as if some kind of visual cue is needed.

Sarah's face takes on a troubled expression. She looks the fence over on both sides, searching for something out of the ordinary.

'Crash? Here?'

Another examination of the fence. Then she shakes her head.

'I'm sorry, Kate. I don't know what you're talking about. There was no car crash last night – certainly not one that involved our fence. Is it possible you've got us mixed up with someone else?'

I feel panic bubbling up, but I tell myself it's okay. It's all a big misunderstanding.

'No,' I answer. 'I ... I don't think so.'

Why are you adding that? I don't think so? Just say no and leave it at no.

Be certain.

Sarah talks in a quiet voice. It's the sort of voice that people use on the village idiot to stop her doing something stupid. And there was me thinking I was being patronising a few seconds ago.

Sarah's blushing. To my horror, she looks embarrassed for me. 'Umm, I'm quite sure Jack and I would've heard a car going through our fence.'

She has a nervous laugh.

My tongue feels like a swollen lump that's forgotten how to do its job. 'Sarah ... we stood right here ... we had a conversation. The police were here.'

'Kate, are you okay?'

Me? Am I okay?

What the fuck?

Is she on meds? I don't know this woman. Maybe she thinks *I'm* on meds, but whatever's going on here, I find it deeply unsettling that she's standing in front of me telling me the crash didn't happen. Is she suffering from some kind of degenerative brain disease?

'If this is a joke ...'

She gives me a stern look. 'I beg your pardon?'

Screw it. I'm getting out of here before she starts foaming at the mouth. For whatever reason, she can't or won't remember the crash. Or the subsequent clean-up. Okay, fine – whatever helps her sleep at night.

'Don't worry about it,' I say. 'You're right. It's, umm, my mistake.'

Sarah nods, her face kindly again. 'Are you sure you're okay?'

'Yep.'

I back off as I'm saying it, and we even exchange another

quick wave like we didn't just have the weirdest conversation ever. 'Have a nice Sunday, Sarah.'

I turn around, but, man, I can feel her eyes on my back. She really thinks it's me, the poor thing.

I hurry back to the house. I don't think I've ever walked so fast in all my life.

4

I'm lying on the couch when Tommy comes home from rugby practice.

It's been a lazy morning for the most part. I've been trying to read, but every time I get through a paragraph of the mystery novel I chose at random off the bookshelf, my eyes grow heavy. Then it's a twenty-minute nap, and still I can't shake off the tiredness. Wake up. Rinse and repeat. So far, I've covered a grand total of five pages in two and a half hours. And I've no idea what's happening.

At least the headache has eased off. Just a little.

Tommy dumps his sports bag in the hallway. There's a loud thud like he's carrying half a dozen rugby balls around in that bag. Then he walks into the living room, leans over the couch and gives me a peck on the cheek. I nearly retch.

'You stink,' I say. 'Don't they have showers at the pitch?'

'You have to pay for them.'

'Worth it.'

He laughs. 'Hangover that bad, is it?'

I put the book on the floor face down, then sit up on the couch, yawning to the point where it feels like my jaw is about to lock. 'What hangover? I'm fine.'

Tommy backs off. He leans against the doorway, a smug grin on his sweaty face. 'Whatever you say, honey. You had a good morning?'

I shrug. 'Not really.'

'Something happen?'

'That's an understatement.'

'What?'

'You won't believe it.'

'Let me guess,' he says, taking his back off the doorway. Now he's walking through the living room towards the kitchen. 'You won the lottery? You finally started to write that novel you're always banging on about? Greta Gerwig called, and she wants to cast you as the lead in her next movie? Am I getting close?'

I scratch my head and growl.

'Whatever.'

Tommy's in the kitchen for about a minute, making a racket. I hear the pantry door open and the sound of a bag rustling. He walks back into the living room with a packet of pickled onion crisps and a can of Coke. He flops into the armchair, pulls the tab on the Coke and drinks like he's been living in the desert for a week.

'Ahhhhh.'

'I thought you were taking a shower,' I say.

With a grin, he adjusts the sweaty cap on his head. 'Recovery first. Gotta get the nutrition in.'

I point at the crisps and Coke. 'Is that what that is?'

He nods. 'So, what happened?'

'What?'

'What happened that I wouldn't believe?'

I lower my voice, which is ridiculous because we're alone in the house.

'Tommy, do you know if Sarah is on meds or something like that?'

He wrinkles his face in confusion. Unable to hear me over the sound of his own crunching. 'What's that, honey?'

My thumb points at the window. 'Sarah, across the street. Do you know if she's on some kind of medication? Is there something ... is there something *wrong* with her?'

Tommy looks at the window, then back at me. 'How should I know?' He shovels crisps into his mouth like it's a race. Crumbs disappear down the side of the chair. Some onto the floor. Has he always been this much of a messy eater?

'Well?' I ask.

'I don't know, Kate. What happened?'

'I had this really weird conversation with her this morning. Like *really* weird.'

'With Sarah?'

'Yep.'

'Okay,' he says, still talking with his mouth full. 'About what?'

I put a finger to the side of my head.

'Headache?' Tommy asks.

I nod.

'You want some paracetamol?' He's halfway off the chair, looking over at me with a concerned expression. 'That's one hell of a hangover you're nursing this morning.'

'I've already taken some.'

I take my finger off my head.

'Did you notice anything weird when you walked out to the car this morning? Anything weird on the street?'

Tommy flops back into the chair. He's chewing in slow motion now. 'Weird? Like what?'

I sigh. 'Like Jack and Sarah's fence, for starters.'

Tommy glances at the window again. Eyes narrowing in confusion. 'Jack and Sarah's ... *fence*?'

'Yes, their fence, for God's sake! Didn't you notice? It hasn't got a mark on it.'

'Umm ... okay.'

'But here's the really weird thing,' I say. 'And this is going to *freak* you out. I spoke to Sarah this morning, and she flat out denied it happened.'

I pause to wait for an immediate reaction. But Tommy's face is blank, and I figure he's processing. So I continue.

'She said there was no car crash. Looked me straight in the eyes and without any hesitation tried to convince me that all that stuff last night didn't happen. I mean, can you believe that? It's pretty scary when you think about it.'

I'm still waiting for the appropriate reaction, but Tommy's sitting as still as I've ever seen him. He's no longer eating, and there's a silly smile on his face.

'I don't follow.'

'You don't follow?'

His dumb grin gets bigger.

'What do you mean? I'm trying to tell you that Sarah doesn't remember the crash last night. She said it didn't happen. Did. Not. Happen.'

The living room is cold and deathly silent. When Tommy finally speaks, his deep and gruff voice is soft like a boy's.

'What crash?'

I stare at him.

'Fuck off, Tommy.'

Tommy's sitting up straight now. Looking at me like there's a third eye sprouting on my forehead. 'I'm serious, Kate. What crash?'

I respond with a manic smile. It feels like my face is having a wrestling match with itself. 'I said—'

He holds up a hand and cuts me off. 'Kate, I don't get it.'

'What?'

'The joke.'

My voice rockets up an octave. 'Joke? I'm not joking. This isn't funny, Tommy. I'm talking about the Subaru that went through Jack and Sarah's fence – THAT'S what I'm talking about. Isn't it obvious?'

Oh shit. The look on his face.

It feels like I'm being sucker punched in the stomach. No, it's much worse than that. He's serious, for God's sake. Just like Sarah was serious earlier. This isn't the conversation I was expecting to have with Tommy when he got back from rugby. I was expecting a bit of back-and-forth banter on the merit of Sarah's memory, her sanity, her reliance on prescription medication, but instead, it's my sanity that's in the spotlight.

I can't breathe. It's like there's a tight knot in my stomach, and it's getting tighter with every word that Tommy says.

This is a misunderstanding.

'Last night,' I say, my voice cracking despite my efforts to sound calm. 'The crash. It woke you up. It … it was a Subaru, and it went through Jack and Sarah's fence. We went outside, and everyone in the neighbourhood was out there. What the fuck, Tommy?'

I've never wanted someone to burst out laughing so much in all my life. Even if it is at my expense. *Gotcha!* But

Tommy doesn't laugh. He's looking at me like I'm nuts. And when he talks, he lowers his voice, like he's afraid of setting me off or something. It's similar to the way Sarah was talking to me earlier.

'Honey, listen to me. There was no car crash. You had a dream – that's all.'

I study his face. 'You're scaring me, Tommy.'

He sighs, then flicks a few crumbs off the armrest. Straight onto the floor.

'Kate—'

'Don't *Kate* me. This isn't funny.'

He shakes his head, and I hate him for the way he's looking at me right now. Like I'm a child who needs a soothing voice and a back rub. 'This isn't a joke, honey. It was just a d—'

'We were outside,' I say. 'All the neighbours were outside.'

'No,' he repeats in a firm voice. 'We weren't outside. I went to bed early, and you were in here watching TV until about one o'clock in the morning. Just like every other Saturday night. C'mon, hon. Sounds like a vivid dream, doesn't it? And ... you *were* drinking a lot last night.'

'Stop talking to me like I'm a headcase, will you?'

'You drank almost two bottles of wine by yourself. Two bottles, Kate. The other empty was in the kitchen before I binned it.'

I don't actually remember drinking two bottles of wine, but I'm in no position to deny it.

'Did you go online?' Tommy says. 'Did you check the news or local Facebook pages for anything about a crash?'

I nod.

'And?'

'Nothing.'

'You had a dream,' Tommy says again, leaning forward. 'That's all, honey. And by the sound of it, you owe Sarah one hell of an apology.'

This is beyond messed up. This was no dream. It *did* happen, yet what are the chances of Sarah and Tommy both being wrong? And me, off my face on two bottles of wine, being right?

'Kate?'

Tommy's perched on the edge of the armchair, and if he comes forward another inch, he'll fall off. His expression is serious. It feels like the sweaty rugby player is gone and there's a thoughtful psychiatrist across the room in his place. '*Did* you have a nightmare last night?'

I shrug. 'I don't know.'

Yet I remember the look on Sarah's face this morning when I spoke about the crash. The shock and confusion were unmistakable. It's the same look on Tommy's face right now. Looking at me like I'm batshit crazy. Well, I guess that settles it.

I *am* batshit crazy.

I let out a spurt of nervous laughter.

'Oh shit.'

Tommy's eyes light up, and his face relaxes. He laughs with me, and I keep laughing even though none of this is funny. What the hell must Sarah think of me? What have I done? Never in all my life has a dream been so vivid, yet two people with no reason to lie have made it clear that there was no car crash last night. And the scene outside certainly backs their claim up too.

'That must have been some wine,' I say.

Tommy nods. He's still looking at me kind of strange.

Like he's not quite convinced that I'm convinced by the dream story. 'You always did know how to pick the good stuff.'

I laugh again, but it sounds demented. Like someone forced to laugh at gunpoint.

5

I walk to work on Monday morning like I always do. My shift at Little Market starts at nine, and that's me until five o'clock. Five days a week. Monday to Friday, as regular as clockwork.

It's only a short walk from the house. The walk itself is unspectacular, almost a straight line over the pavement that leads through the heart of our little town centre with its shops, the one decent café and a couple of pubs and restaurants that never seem to fill up. There's a hairdresser too and a second-hand book shop. And Little Market, of course.

It's not much, yet it's home. Walking to work and seeing the same old sights, I'm often struck by the thought – why didn't I get out after school? And come to think of it, why don't I even consider the possibility of getting out now? I'm only in my twenties. Life isn't over yet, is it? Yet, it sort of feels like it is. Tommy and I hooked up in school, and we stayed hooked up, and that's our story. Safe and predictable. We've settled, and I suppose the longer we stay here, the harder it becomes to leave.

Someone has to work the little jobs, don't they? Lead the unspectacular lives that never get noticed. We can't all be headliners and rock stars and CEOs. Those people thrive because of what we, the little people, do in the shadows. There's no floor under their feet without us. Without us, they fall.

I've settled. And that's fine with me.

I pass through the sliding doors of Little Market, an affordable supermarket in the town centre. The lighting is horrendous. Harsh yellowy light trickles down like a violation. The sort of light that exposes all the flaws on your face, it's one that's usually confined to tacky hotel bathrooms. Muzak plays through speakers that crackle and hiss. A hideous version of a Tom Jones song. Everything about Little Market screams cheap and temporary. There are only a handful of shoppers in the building at this time of morning, many of them picking up sandwiches and other bits and pieces for lunch later in the day.

Here we go again.

I take the stairs up to the staff room. Despite everything, I'm still thinking about the crash or, as I should call it, the crash I dreamed up. I kept a low profile after talking to Tommy yesterday. And I've never walked so fast down our street as I did this morning, fearful that I'd bump into Sarah and then have to deal with my performance yesterday at her gate. I blush just thinking about it. I've never experienced a dream like that before. Most are a vague, disjointed recollection of images that evoke sensations but tell no stories. They slip away, but not the crash. It's not going anywhere.

Thankfully, the staff room is empty. I smell coffee and the faint stink of aftershave. I take off my coat, drop my bag off and then use the toilet before starting my shift.

I'm on the stairs when I stop.

What exactly is it that I do here?

I ... work ... the ... shop floor. Stock ... shelves.

How could I forget? Then again, nothing is clear today. My head is still painful, and on top of everything else, I'm feeling sorry for myself. Feeling heavy. Not only that, I'm worried. Considering what happened yesterday, I wonder if there's something wrong with me. Some sort of alcohol-related damage going on upstairs? I worry about degenerative brain disease. About forgetting.

No, it's nonsense. There's nothing wrong with me.

I go back down to the shop floor. As I close the staff door behind me, I see Donna working at the customer assistance desk near the checkouts. She lives on the same street as I do. Or maybe it's the next street along, but I know she's close to Tommy and me. That much I remember.

I'll just go over there and ask. One last time to make sure no one else heard anything on Saturday.

I wipe a smidge of dirt off my name badge as I walk past the staffed and self-serve checkouts. The latter chirp and beep without pause. I hear someone swear in frustration as they try and fail to scan a bag of sugar. That awful Muzak feels like it's following me around like a bad smell.

This'll just take a moment. A quick word with Donna and then I'll check in with the boss, what's-her-name, and see what needs doing on the shop floor.

The customer assistance desk is located beside the front window, and although Donna is managerial, she's around my age and has a friendly face. Approachable – that's the word for her. Maybe I need to make more of an effort to be approachable too. Maybe Donna is someone I could get to know outside work.

'Hey,' I say.

I lean my elbows on the desk.

Donna smiles and drops the pen in her right hand. It looks like she was scrawling numbers into a notepad, and I've no idea if it's work-related or some sort of life admin she was doing to pass the time. She's a good-looking woman – lean with toned arms, a great smile, and not even the dowdy Little Market overall can take the shine off her.

'Hi, Kate – how are you?'

'Good. You?'

'Same old, same old.'

'Quiet morning?'

She nods. 'I'm enjoying it while it lasts.'

'It won't last?'

She points at the sliding doors.

'As soon as we put up the Beer Week signs on the front windows, they'll be here in busloads. Thirty per cent off. That's a discount most people around these parts can't ignore. Small-town drinkers are the worst, you know?'

I nod.

'Good weekend?' she asks.

I hate that question. Always makes me feel like I'm supposed to have some exciting, well-prepared narrative planned for Monday. With slides. *No, I'm boring, and I like it that way. Okay?*

'Quiet. You?'

'Yeah, really good, thanks. Took a nice wee road trip yesterday, just me and Carl. We travelled up the west coast for the afternoon and left the kids with Mum, and oh my God, I love them to bits, God knows I do, but I love the breaks. Does that make me a bad mother?'

I smile. 'That sounds nice.'

I take my elbows off the desk.

'So that was your Sunday?'

'Yep.'

'What about Saturday?' I say, trying to sound like we're still exchanging chit-chat. 'Were you guys at home on Saturday night or—'

'Oh yeah – it was a quiet one. Wanted to be fresh for the road trip.'

I'm tempted to end the conversation here. To walk away and get on with things, but I know I'd never forgive myself if I did that. I look at Donna over the customer assistance desk, and for now at least, I don't hear the Muzak. I can't imagine what the smile on my face looks like right now. It sure is hard work to cling on to.

'Did you hear anything ... *weird* ... on the street?'

'Weird?'

'Yes.'

'On Saturday?'

'Saturday night.'

'Weird, you say?'

I nod.

There's a brief moment of hope. I swear to God there's some kind of understanding in her eyes, but then Donna shrugs, and I realise I'm imagining it. I'm seeing what I want to see, and in reality, she has no idea what I'm talking about.

'Like what?' she asks.

'Like cars. Boy racers. Maybe ... did you hear a crash or something?'

Her face is blank. That settles it. I'm an idiot, and as Tommy put it, I owe Sarah one hell of an apology. That's an apology I'd better get on with fast. Today, after work. Oh shit. That's something to look forward to all day.

Fuck. Fuck. Fuck.

'Didn't hear anything out of the ordinary,' Donna says, picking up her pen off the desk. 'But then again, I sleep like the dead.'

She laughs, and as a customer approaches the desk, I mumble a quick, 'See you later,' and get the hell out of there.

I walk past the beeping checkouts again.

Well, if there was any doubt left, it's gone. That's three-one to the side that says the car crash didn't happen. And no matter how real it seems in my mind, I guess that's that – it didn't happen. I had a dream, and it fooled me into thinking I was awake. Turns out I'm so desperate for excitement that I'm letting my dreams make an idiot of me. Wow, what a mind-bender. I'm almost ready to burst out laughing.

But I don't.

I think I've got a drinking problem.

6

Walking home from the supermarket is one of life's small pleasures. It's been a crappy day, but nonetheless, the cool evening breeze revives me. Work is done. My legs feel unshackled, and putting one foot in front of the other feels easy – like floating. I follow the street that leads straight through the town centre and towards home. There are lots of commuters on foot, in cars and on buses. It feels busy.

The smell of vinegar wafts out the doorway of Michael's Superchippy. I glance inside, and there's a long line of people waiting to be served. I hesitate. My pace slows, and my stomach rumbles. A bag of hot chips doused in salt and vinegar would be lovely right now, but that's not on this evening's agenda. I'm making dinner for Tommy. Wholegrain pasta, that's what he requested this morning before he left for work. Nice and healthy, with chopped veggies and tomato sauce. I could've picked out a bottle of wine in Little Market to go with it (they have quite a decent choice), but I guess that's not a good idea after the events of Saturday night. It's certainly not a good idea after talking to Donna. I need to leave off the drinking for a while.

'Hey!'

It's a man's voice calling to someone over the traffic. It sounds far off, nothing to do with me. But I glance over my shoulder anyway.

There's no one there.

I keep walking, and now I'm thinking about the apology I owe Sarah. The *big* apology. Oh man – this sucks. I have to do it, but does it have to be now? I don't think I can face it, face *her*, not tonight. To distract myself, I think about cooking dinner. I think about what time Tommy said he'd back from work and what we'll watch on TV while we eat.

Sarah.

Fuck.

I feel myself blushing. But it's getting dark, and the last thing she wants is me knocking at her door, especially after my performance yesterday.

I'll do it tomorrow. Tomorrow for sure.

'Hey!'

I walk under the streetlights. There's a faint crackling noise, and one of the lights flickers on and off. A white van whooshes past.

'Hey!'

It's that same voice. But I keep walking because it has nothing to do with me.

I need a holiday, I tell myself. That would do me the world of good. I can't even remember the last time I went on holiday. If only there were a travel agent on the main street so I could gawp at the pictures in the window: Caribbean beaches, majestic city skylines and snowy mountain escapes in Europe. I need a world that isn't mine. And even if there were a travel agent within a short walking distance? Would I have the nerve to go in and do something about it? Something like booking two weeks away for Tommy and me? Do we have the money to spare? Do we have an excuse? Do we *need* an excuse? Well, how about this – I'm conjuring up car crashes in my sleep and acting like they are real.

'Hey ... Kate!'

I stop. Turn around again, but there's no one standing behind me. Did I just hear someone call my name? I stay right where I am. Waiting for God knows what to happen. Then something stirs the hairs on the back of my neck. I look across the street.

There's a man staring at me.

I catch glimpses of him in between the slow-moving traffic.

We didn't just catch each other at an awkward moment. This guy is watching me. What the hell? Even from across the street, I see him twitch with nervous energy as the cars and buses momentarily block our view of one another. He's gone; then he's back. Still there, still staring at me with that intense look. He's short, no more than five feet seven, with a scruffy mop of black hair and a stocky, welterweight build. Looks like he's wearing a black trench coat. Blue jeans, white trainers.

There's a gap in the traffic now. I notice his body leaning forward from the ankles. He's taut, like he's about to burst into a sprint.

'Oh my God,' I say.

I'm walking away at a speed that's just shy of a run. *A misunderstanding*, I tell myself as I keep under the safety of the streetlights.

'Kate!'

I freeze. Turn around just in time to see him cutting across the street. Weaving his way in and out of traffic as he tries to reach the opposite pavement. He's got a limp on his left leg, and it's slowing him down. Every step looks painful, especially when he's trying to build up speed. There's a loud shriek as a taxi skids to a stop inches in front of him, but the guy in the trench coat doesn't seem to care.

He's still looking at me. Still coming.

He makes it across the street, arms swinging furiously. Ignoring the yells and insults of angry drivers behind him, and despite his limp, he picks up the pace. Staggering along the pavement towards me. There's a shimmering madness in his eyes that makes my blood run cold.

'Kate! Stay there.'

I can't move.

He's coming straight for me.

7

He shouldn't be this fast, not with that limp, but my God, the man is determined. It's early evening on the main street, and we're surrounded by cars and people travelling in both directions, yet now that he's on my side of the street, it feels like it's just me and him out here.

His eyes reach for me. No, they're not reaching. *Grasping.*

The obvious (and courageous) thing for me to do is stay put. Stand my ground and stay under the lights. It's not dark yet, and there are no alleys at my back for him to drag me down and mug me, if that's what this is all about. Or something much worse. Is that, I think, what he sees when he looks at me? A victim?

He labours his way down the pavement towards me. He's about to say something when survival instinct kicks in and I abandon the option to stand my ground. Fuck it. I turn and explode into a sprint, passing a blur of shocked faces coming towards me. Clearly, they weren't expecting to see someone running this fast along the pavement, dressed in a jacket and jeans with a Little Market badge pinned on their top.

I turn my legs over like my life depends on it. His voice is still there behind me. Thinner. More desperate.

'Kate! My name is—'

A bus speeds past, drowning out his words. I glance to my left for a second and see a row of deadpan faces pressed against the windows of the bus. All watching me with that single uniform expression. They see it. They see what's happening, don't they? But they're gone already. The bus has sped away.

I look ahead and almost bowl over an old woman in a mobility scooter. I make a yelping noise, leap out of her way and ignore the insults. Somehow, I'm still on my feet.

'Kate! STOP!'

I've gone out too hard and too fast. The adrenaline dump can't prevent the lactic acid building up in my legs. My insides feel like they're on fire, and there's no doubt about it – I'm slowing down.

'Kate, you have to stop.'

He's gaining on me. There's a voice in my head that reminds me we're in a public place and that he can't do anything to me. Yet I can't seem to reconcile my actions with that thought. I can't stop. I can't call for help. I can't face him. There's something about the way he's coming after me, something that makes me want to get away from him as quickly as possible.

But ... his voice.

Have I heard it before?

I take a sharp right, running into a small newsagent's that's tucked into the corner of the street. The door chimes as I barge it open with my shoulder. Warm air hits me in the face. I've never been in here before. It's not much – a gloomy, claustrophobic space with narrow aisles and a small counter at the back of the shop. Generic pop music crackles through the speakers. The old woman sitting behind the till looks up from her phone, and despite her poker face, I sense that my dramatic entrance has caught her by surprise.

'Evening,' she says in an unfamiliar accent. Then she's back to her phone.

I manage a single word.

'Hi.'

Okay. It's going to be alright. I'll walk the aisles for a few minutes and get my shit together. Catch my breath; wait for the weirdo to go somewhere else. I'll buy something, a cold drink. One of those fancy sports drinks with electrolytes in them, because I can feel the sweat dripping down my back.

I breathe in and out slowly. Glance at the window. Has he gone past yet?

I hear a whisper in my mind.

Was he even there?

My heart is thumping, and right now, I'm doing anything but getting my shit together. Standing in front of the fridge, I stare at my haggard reflection in the glass. The terror in my eyes is unmistakable.

Why is that man chasing me?

I open the fridge door and browse the selection of drinks like a normal person would. The cold air on my face is heaven. I want to climb inside, shut the door and never come out.

There's a sudden noise behind me.

The shop door chimes, and someone walks in. The sound of heavy breathing fills the cramped space.

'Evening,' the old woman says.

I see him in the glass. My pursuer, standing dead still apart from the heaving of his chest. There's a painful grimace on his face. His eyes dart left and right, like someone wary of ambush.

My body starts to shake.

'It's okay,' he says in a quiet voice, taking a step towards me. His hands are up. 'I'm not going to hurt you.'

Yet he's blocking the only exit.

I step to the left, spinning around to face him. Then I back into the nearest aisle, chocolate bars, crisps and chewing gum on both sides. He follows me. With each step we take, the aisle seems to narrow.

He throws a frantic look at the shopkeeper, but she's on her phone again. Paying no attention to us. Then he's back looking at me.

'I'm not going to hurt you,' he repeats. 'I just want to talk. Please believe me – you *want* to hear this.'

He inches closer. Eyes big and desperate.

I shake my head. 'Leave me alone, or I'll scream.'

'Please don't do that.'

He hurries forward, but his left leg buckles, and he's flung off-balance. His elbow clatters off a spinning rack of sweets. The rack wobbles, and several packets topple onto the floor. The woman at the counter looks up.

'Hey!' she calls out.

I hear an alarm-like bell ringing in my head. That's my signal to get the hell out of there.

I pedal backwards, take a right to the end of the aisle, then a sharp left, and from there it's a five-metre dash to the door. I don't even think about it. I run hard, grab the door handle and hear the chiming noise again. Then I'm outside. I hope I've got enough speed in my legs to carry me home.

'Come back!' he yells from inside the shop.

There's another noise. The sound of sirens. Coming this way.

'Please come back!' he yells, hobbling through the shop door behind me. I hear him gasp in pain as his leg betrays him. The shopkeeper is still calling from the counter too, demanding that we come back and pick up the fallen sweets.

The man stops dead on the pavement. And I see it. The look of horror on his face as he becomes aware of the blaring sirens.

Still, he calls to me, his voice heavy with defeat.

'You *have* to hear this.'

8

I come off the main street and run uphill along a winding pathway that leads to the gate of a local playground. The gate is right next to a primary school. The school itself, a barrack-like block with square windows, looks abandoned and makes for a creepy silhouette as daylight fades.

My legs are burning thanks to the uphill run.

Thank God, the playground is still busy, at least for this time of day. I guess this is where parents in the nearby houses go to wear out the kids for the rest of the evening. The playground is floodlit from all four corners, so it's bright. Thank God. The sound of children laughing and yelling is a reminder that this is a safe place. A fluffy dog barks. A boy yells for his mum to push him higher on the swing.

This is good. I'm okay here.

Still, that gnawing pain is back in my head. I'm not sure it ever went away.

I walk through the gate, glancing up at the blueish-purple sky. It looks like a giant bruise, and it's darkening too quickly for my liking. Soon the mums and dads will round up the kids and take them home. I don't want to be alone here. I don't want to be alone anywhere. It's still a ten-minute walk to get home if I go back the way I came.

Where is that man now? Did someone notice him chasing me? Did they call the police?

I sit on the bench, the sound of laughter fading into the background. I take a deep breath and several others to follow. I just need a minute.

What is going on around here?

I flinch as a rubber ball bounces in my direction. The pitter-patter of light footsteps as a blonde girl of about seven chases after the ball, paying no attention to the loner on the bench. My heart is still pounding. I clear my throat, and it's dry and prickly. I'd love some water right now.

What the hell just happened? Did I really get chased down the road by a complete stranger? Yet, a stranger who knew my name.

It doesn't make sense.

What did he want to tell me?

Something's not right here. I find my thoughts drifting back to the car crash on Saturday night. The crash that I supposedly dreamed. Nothing's been right since Saturday night. I feel like crap, but I'm willing to put that down to the booze.

What, then, about the crash?

So far, three people have tried to persuade me that there was no car crash. Tommy told me it was nothing more than two bottles of wine playing tricks on my mind while I was asleep. Tommy is my fiancé, for God's sake. Why would he lie to me?

He's not lying. They're all correct. They're all telling the truth. Tommy, Donna and Sarah.

Yet I can't swallow it.

I don't believe them. The car crash *did* happen. I know it happened because dreams don't feel the way that crash did. It's Monday now, and I still haven't shaken off the experience like I have every other dream in my life. The crash happened. I trust my instincts, and come to think of it, what about the look on Tommy's face when I told him about Sarah yesterday? That *strained* look on his face. He was holding something back, but instead of trusting my gut, I doubted myself.

I feel a rush of adrenaline. This is real.

But what is real?

What is *this*?

My mind lights up like a Christmas tree. At the same time, it feels like a giant weight has been lifted off my shoulders. This is good, but it's also terrifying. What happened outside my house on Saturday night? And why can't anyone else remember?

Not can't.

Won't.

I'm not ready to say it out loud because I know it sounds crazy, and it'll sound even crazier if I say it. Not that there's anyone to say it to. But I trust my gut. This is what's real. Someone wants to keep the crash quiet. Someone who has tremendous influence. That's how they did it – that's how the crash magically disappeared by Sunday morning. And there's a connection between the car crash and the man with the limp. I saw his eyes, saw the way that he was so desperate to speak to me in that shop. Desperate to speak to me on behalf of someone else, that'd be my guess. To get the message across.

And the message is?

Stay quiet.

They want to shut me up because I've been talking. Asking questions.

I feel a dizzying sense of elation as the pieces start to come together. It's like being drunk, but so much better, and for now, at least, my headache is gone. Another ball bounces past me as I sit on the bench. The sound of little feet running is there and gone. This is good. For the first time since Saturday night, I'm beginning to understand. It's scary as hell, but at the same time, like I say, it's a weight off my shoulders.

Somebody is out there silencing the locals – the ones who live on or around my street. Anyone within earshot of the crash.

Somebody wants the crash to disappear.

Someone powerful. But who? And why?

Questions, questions. I've got so many questions spilling out of me, and trying to focus on each one is like trying to catch sunlight in a net.

What about the third person in the car? Not the driver and not the girl with the skinhead-style hair. Number three. Who was that, and why didn't they come out like the other two?

Oh shit.

This is big. This is very big. I've already checked the internet several times, and there's no mention of the crash anywhere. There's nothing. Not a peep, and if it's not online, then you know someone is covering it up very well.

What sort of person can do that?

And where does that leave me? Because I *know* the crash happened. I also know that I'm not crazy, and I'm not dreaming either.

I close my eyes for a second, soaking up the sound of children playing. This is a safe place. I'm okay here.

There'd have to be a good reason for Tommy to lie to me like he did. Tommy loves me, so the obvious question is – were threats made? Has something sinister invaded our small-town life? This thing, this incident, it disappeared so fast. Like, overnight fast. They – whoever *they* are – must have been working all through the night and into Sunday morning to wipe out every trace of it. Did someone threaten Tommy when he left the house for rugby on Sunday morning? What about the other neighbours? Did everyone get a knock on the door in the early hours of Sunday morning?

And if so, who did the knocking?

I stare at the kids playing. The mums and dads. Could something like that really happen here?

What if Tommy did get a message, and he didn't pass it on to me?

Keep quiet. And tell your woman. Or we will.

It makes sense. The last thing that Tommy would want to do is scare me. If someone paid a visit on Sunday morning, he'd do everything in his power to keep it hidden from me. Yes, he's lying, but it's because he's protecting me. He wants me to think the crash was a dream because that's the safer option. As for Sarah and Donna, they have their own reasons for keeping quiet. Threats have been made, and for them, it didn't happen. They're protecting their own.

Yes, yes, yes!

I burst out laughing, and the blonde girl with the rubber ball gives me a weird look. The crazy woman on the bench. I smile at her, and she goes back to playing with her friends by the slide. Keep away from the crazy woman.

Except I'm not crazy. It sounds crazy, but I'm not crazy.

There's a silencing in this town.

Oh shit.

I knew the driver's face was familiar. Is he the son of someone famous? A high-ranking politician? Is there a royal connection? Maybe it's not the driver – maybe it's the girl? Most likely, it had something to do with the mystery person in the back seat. The person who didn't want to be seen by anyone.

This is big.

The man who chased me. He knows I've been asking questions. Maybe that information came from Sarah or Donna or both, but one thing's for sure – he wasn't trying to mug me tonight. Muggers don't follow their victims into public places and try to strike up a conversation.

They're trying to shut me up, and the guy with the limp wanted to make sure I got the message.

Keep quiet or else.

9

I don't tell Tommy about the man with the limp.

Don't get me wrong, I want to talk to him. I want to ask him – are you trying to protect me? I know it must be a burden to carry that around and that he's carrying it for the both of us. I want him to know that I understand and that I'd probably do the same if our roles were reversed. Easier to dismiss the crash as the dream of someone who had a little too much to drink. The alternative is too frightening.

He loves me. I get it.

We're both quiet at dinner. Afterwards, we spend some time in the living room, not really doing much. I sit on the armchair, pretending to read my book. Really, I'm just looking at the words. Tommy's flat on his back on the couch, watching an action movie with Bruce Willis and a lot of machine guns and helicopters.

Every now and then, I look over the top of my book at Tommy.

What's going on inside his head? Is he even watching the

film, or is he pretending like I'm pretending to read my book? I wish I could say what I'm thinking. I get the feeling that something's bothering him because he's so quiet. If I ask, he'll just say he's tired.

Does he know that I've been asking questions about the crash? He knows about Sarah, but is it possible that he also knows I asked Donna at work today? But even I don't really know my neighbours. Or the people I work with.

My eyes go back to the book.

Who was in the back seat of the Subaru? And why didn't they come out?

I close the book and set it down on the armrest. While Tommy watches (or pretends to watch) TV, I dig my phone out of my pocket and do another quick online search for anything about a car crash in our area. Not a thing. I spend the next ten minutes scrolling through an online conveyor belt of cute animal videos and people doing stupid pranks for the entertainment of others.

I stare at the living-room window, at the curtains tightly pulled. Even with the curtains drawn, I have the strangest feeling of being watched. I look at Tommy again, and he's still staring at the TV.

There's no way it was a dream, I think.

What sort of person can silence an entire neighbourhood? It's not just one person – it's bigger than that. Who is it? A gang boss? Jesus, I almost laugh out loud. What would the son or daughter of a gang boss be doing here in Boringville? This isn't exactly mafia country.

Now, I'm pretending to watch TV. Same as Tommy. But my mind is racing over the possibilities.

There are several options as far as I can tell. A major celebrity, a high-ranking politician or a member of the royal family (or someone closely associated with the royal family). Maybe they weren't directly involved but were involved by association. It was their son in the car, or their daughter. Now they're on clean-up duty.

Ouch.

I need some pain relief for this headache. But I don't want to take any more pills in front of Tommy.

I'm desperate to talk about this whole situation, but I know that Tommy will go into the same routine as last time. He'll do everything in his power to persuade me that the crash didn't happen. He'll tell me again it was a dream, and then he'll use Sarah and all the other neighbours against me. And I have no defence against those tactics, at least not right now. He'd rather pretend I'm a silly drunk than admit to the silencing.

I might have been drunk, but I'm not crazy.

Tommy sits up and ruffles his hair. He yawns and stretches his arms like he's trying to touch the ceiling. Then he looks over at me.

'I'm having a beer.' He gets up off the couch, his joints cracking. 'Want anything?'

I shrug. 'Like a drink?'

'One glass is fine.'

Does he want me to drink?

'No, I'm okay.'

Tommy walks towards the kitchen door, eyes still on the TV. 'Well, just the one for me, eh?'

'I'm going to bed,' I say, standing up. I speak a little too abruptly, and it sounds like a formal declaration. 'But I need some water. Can you get me a glass, and I'll take it upstairs?'

Tommy takes his eyes off the film. He's giving me that

look again. The one I saw yesterday when I spoke about the crash.

'Headache, still?'

I simply raise my eyebrows.

Tommy walks back over to the couch. To my surprise, he picks up the remote and turns off the movie. The living room is silent.

'I don't need a beer,' he says. 'I think I'll turn in too.'

We walk upstairs and go through the motions of getting ready for bed. Exhaustion gets the better of me, and I find it so hard to do the simple things. Wash my face. Brush my teeth. As I stand in front of the bathroom mirror, the toothbrush feels like a dumbbell in my hand.

I need the oblivion of sleep, but how am I supposed to sleep with everything that's going on?

I take a couple of headache pills while I'm in the bathroom. Then I climb into bed, and Tommy kisses me goodnight before turning out the light. I close my eyes and see the man with the limp emerging out of the darkness. Coming after me. Weaving his way through the slow-moving traffic.

Kate.

You have to hear this.

I hear a noise and open my eyes. Whatever it was, it's gone. Probably nothing more than the wind, and I push aside the protesting voice at the back of my mind that reminds me there is no wind outside. That voice isn't satisfied. It wants me to get up and check it out. It makes a good point. The night is dead still and—

Enough!

I've got work in the morning, and I really need to get to sleep, but it's hot, and the pills aren't working. Maybe I should've had that glass of wine, just to help me sleep. I toss and turn for a while. Kick the covers off my legs, but the air is too cold. I cover them up again. Too hot, too cold. Another ten minutes of tossing and turning, doing my best to ignore Tommy's ridiculous snoring.

Who was in the back of that car?

I'm pondering the options (celebrity/politician/royal) when my eyelids finally grow heavy. But just as I'm drifting off into much-needed sleep, I'm pulled back from the brink.

That noise again.

It's real, and it's coming from downstairs.

I lift my head off the pillow and stare at the gap around the bedroom door. Hoping it's the wind and knowing fine well that it isn't. It's something else – a quiet, rattling noise. I sit up, my back damp with cold sweat. Tommy keeps snoring while I stare at the door.

It's still there. Still happening, even as I long for it to stop. A persistent rattle that chills my blood.

'Tommy,' I whisper.

I can't take my eyes off the gap in the door. Can't blink. Don't dare to blink. I keep expecting to see the bedroom door slowly push open from the other side. To hear the hinges groan in the dark.

'Tommy.'

He doesn't stir.

10

'Tommy?'

I whisper because I don't want whoever's at the door to hear me.

'Tommy! Wake up.' More urgent now.

I shake him, and the bed groans, but Tommy doesn't budge. I give him a solid dig with my elbow, and it's like a toothpick attacking a mountain. Bloody rugby players.

'Tommy,' I say through clenched teeth. I hear the note of panic rising in my voice, but I fight to keep it down. 'Someone's trying to break into the house.'

Nothing. I consider picking up the glass of water on the bedside table and emptying it over Tommy's head. But he'd cry out and startle the intruder. That's not what I want. I *have* to see who's down there, and somehow, I can't explain why, the thought of not knowing is worse than the fear of the break-in itself.

I push the sheets off my legs. Get up and tiptoe as quietly as I can towards the door. But the floor creaks under my weight, and it's like a sound effect from a haunted house movie. Almost comical.

I stop for a second, then keep moving. Still on my tiptoes, approaching the top of the stairs. I ignore the millions of years of survival instinct that are telling me to do anything but approach that noise downstairs.

I have to know.

Is it him?

Now that I'm closer, things are a little clearer. The rattle isn't coming from the front door like I first thought. It's at the back door. Whoever it is, they're trying to get in through the back, which leads into the kitchen. Then what? They're going to walk through the kitchen, either into the living room or the hallway. Take the stairs. Move towards our bedroom.

It's him, I tell myself. *The man with the limp.*

I go downstairs, and in my mind's eye, I see him earlier that evening. Crossing the street, dragging his leg. Inside the shop. His reflection in the fridge door.

Kate.

He knows where I live. Of course he does. The crash happened right here on our doorstep, didn't it? He knows my name; he knows where I live and most likely where I work too. He didn't follow me from the playground because he didn't have to. He knows exactly where to find me. I'm in the same place as all the other people who've been silenced so far.

They, whoever *they* are, are watching us. They know I've been asking questions and that Tommy didn't pass on the warning like he was supposed to. I'm talking about something I'm not supposed to be talking about. I'm a problem, and now they're coming for me in my own house.

Is this a final warning? Or is it something else?

I'm downstairs. Opening the hallway cupboard as quietly as I can. We keep all sorts in there – medicine box, packaging, tape, and tools. I only discovered the toolbox in there the other day when I was looking for something else. Guess it's Tommy's thing. Right now, it's the claw hammer that I reach for, and I grip the steel handle so tight that I can feel my forearm shudder.

The rattling at the back door continues. And something else – a faint scratching that sounds like someone picking at the lock. I sense urgency from the intruder, and that isn't a comforting thought.

With the hammer in my fist, I force myself along the narrow hallway towards the kitchen. My legs feel like they've got quick-drying cement hardening inside them. Each step is more laboured than the previous one. I stop at the kitchen door.

It's partially pulled over, blocking my view of the back door.

What now?

I hesitate, but then some fierce instinct takes over. I kick the door fully open, rush into the kitchen, one hand scrambling for the light switch, the other holding the hammer back over my shoulder. At that moment, I'm ready for all-out war.

I look at the back door. There's a shape behind the glass. Looks to me like someone crouching over, dark clothes, maybe a black beanie on the head.

'Fuck,' I whisper.

I freeze. I have no idea what I'm doing, whether I'm about to charge that way or run the other way, back into the relative safety of the house.

Then it stops. No more rattling. The hunched shape at the door disappears, and I hear something else – the frantic *tip-tap* of footsteps travelling over the garden path. There's a distant thud, which tells me our potential intruder has vaulted over the gate and is most likely now on the road behind the house.

Then silence.

I stare at the glass for a minute, still expecting a ghoulish face to appear at the door or at the window. I'm terrified and at the same time oddly disappointed because this leaves me with more questions. I needed the big bad wolf at the door to answer my questions. Was it the guy with the limp? And if so, how did he get over the gate so nimbly? Or was it someone else?

My heart is thumping. My skin and clothes are soaked with sweat.

After a few deep breaths, I walk into the living room. I notice that I can still hear Tommy snoring from upstairs, oblivious. What a hero. I walk over to the window, and my hand shaking, I peel back the curtain a few inches. I don't know what I expect to see, but the street is dead except for a single moth that's enchanted by the pale glow of the streetlight beside our house.

I stare at Jack and Sarah's perfect fence.

'Fuck it,' I whisper.

I go back into the kitchen and pour myself a glass of wine. It's medicinal. I need something to help me sleep if I'm going to function like a normal human being tomorrow.

The glass trembles in my grip. I go to the back door and triple-check it's still locked. I stare at the handle and wonder if there are scratch marks on the other side, something that'll make Tommy believe me.

I lean my back against the kitchen counter. Still staring at the door. What would've happened if he'd got into the house, without me hearing him? Would I have woken up with a hand clamped over my mouth and nostrils? The sensation of suffocating. Would there have been a weapon pointing at my head or at Tommy's head? Something sharp, something blunt. And the hiss of a stranger in the dark, reminding us that nothing happened on Saturday night. Reminding me to stop asking so many questions.

Last chance.

My reflection in the window looks back at me. Wrinkled Mickey Mouse T-shirt, hair like a bird's nest and the realisation in my eyes that any intruder in his right mind would run a mile if they saw me.

I sit down at the table, sipping the wine. If Tommy comes downstairs now – well, it's not a good look. Most likely, it'd confirm his worst fears that I'm a raging alcoholic. *But there was an intruder at the back door, Tommy, honestly!*

I pour a second glass. No way I'm getting back to sleep tonight. A second glass of wine won't help, and I know it. I'll be hearing that rattling noise for the rest of the night. I consider calling the police, but what do I say? How do I tell them about a car crash that everyone else, including the officers who were called out that night, have been pressured into forgetting?

Who, I think, has the influence to put pressure on the police like that? This is big. This is *very* big. It can't just be any old celebrity sitting in the back seat of the Subaru, so it has to be something political or something that's connected to the royal family. Someone doing something stupid. Something that'll make someone important look bad.

I'm not crazy just because I believe there's a massive cover-up going on. They want to scare me into silence.

Well, I'm not ready to submit to them.

There's so much noise swirling around my head, and I want to make sense of it. I get up and grab a notepad off the top of the microwave. I look around for a pen and find one in the top drawer next to the cutlery tray. I scribble on the cover to make sure it's working, then return to the table.

Another sip of wine.

I start writing like a possessed person.

Who was sitting in the back of that car? (Black Subaru – reg??) How can I ask questions if everyone insists it didn't happen? People are scared. Fear is the only way to keep everyone quiet, including Tommy. Why is everyone pretending it didn't happen?

I drop the pen.

Well, Kate. You wanted some excitement in your life. Here it is.

I glance over my shoulder at the bottle of wine on the counter. One more glass, then I'll try to get some sleep.

11

It's me. I'm the one. I'm the intruder. I'm the one breaking into someone else's house in the middle of the night, picking the lock. I hear the rattle, and it's me. The scratching noise. It's me. I'm the one turning the door handle, wandering around in someone else's brightly lit kitchen.

What am I doing here?

I keep walking until I'm in someone else's living room. Sitting down, watching their TV. I'm laughing like a mad person, and there are other people in the house asking me what I'm doing there. They're really pissed off that I'm there, and why wouldn't they be? The children are screaming. I get up and run away. Somehow, I know my way to the front door. They give chase, and now we're on the road, and there's a car coming straight for me ...

'It's my fault!'

I wake up, my body soaked in sweat. The bedroom is in utter darkness, and the house is silent. Tommy makes a groaning noise, but I think he's still asleep. I hope he is. I lower my head onto the pillow, willing my heart to slow down.

What did I say when I woke up there? I can't remember, but there was an overwhelming feeling of ... *guilt.*

What the hell? Maybe the wine really is giving me fucked-up dreams. Two glasses, wasn't it? Three?

I really have to stop drinking.

12

The atmosphere at breakfast is cold. Tommy says he didn't sleep well either, but I assure him that he did because I was awake for half the night, listening to his snoring. I guess I must've slept a few hours. That in itself feels like a miracle, but the sleep did me little good. I feel like crap. And surprise, surprise, my headache is worse than ever.

After a quick shower, I take some more pills, and then we're both in the kitchen grabbing a bite to eat before work. This is our shared time; a cup of tea in hand, I'm eating toast like it's jam on cardboard.

I feel obliged to say something.

'Did you hear anything weird last night?' I ask.

Tommy leans back against the kitchen counter. His eyes are bleary as he chews listlessly on the toast. He's such a messy eater, it's a miracle he doesn't get crumbs all over his suit. 'Hmm?'

'I tried to wake you.'

'What for?'

'I thought I heard someone at the back door. Trying to break in.'

He slurps his tea, then puts the mug back down on the counter. *World's best lover.*

'What?'

'Someone tried to break into our house last night, Tommy.'

Finally, it looks like Tommy's joined the land of the living. He straightens up and stares right at me. 'Are you serious?'

'You think I'd joke about something like that?'

'And you tried to wake me?'

'Yep.'

He shrugs. 'Well, you couldn't have been trying very hard. It's not like I was in a coma, you know?'

I glare at him. 'You could have fooled me.'

Tommy breaks eye contact, and I see him glance at his watch. 'Nothing happened, though? It was probably just a—'

'Dream?'

'Kate—'

'That's right. Silly Kate and her vivid dreams.'

There's a bulge at the side of Tommy's neck. It's the big vein popping up. Another glance at his watch like he didn't check the time a minute ago.

'I don't know,' he says. 'It's possible, isn't it?'

'Possible, yes. But it's not what happened. Why are you so unwilling to believe me?'

Tommy sighs, and I can see he's desperate to look at his watch again. That or the clock on the wall. 'I suppose it could've been the wind. Plus, the door handle's been loose for a while. I've been meaning to fix it.'

'It *has* been loose, Tommy. On the *front* door. I'm talking about the back door. For fuck's sake – are you even listening to me?'

He puts his hands up to appease me. 'Yes.'

'Someone tried to break into our house last night. And you don't seem that bothered about it.'

He's looking at his shoes now.

'I didn't hear anything,' he says. 'Sorry.'

The silence that follows is brutal.

'Tommy.'

'What?'

'Is there something you want to tell me?'

He rolls his eyes like I'm being annoying for the sheer hell of it. Maybe I am, but as far as I'm concerned, this is important. 'Like what?'

'Anything.'

Another sigh from Tommy, and this one is followed by a dumb shrug of his hefty shoulders. 'Can you be a little more specific?'

He's trying to protect me. I know this is hard for him, and I'm trying not to be a bitch about it. So I soften my tone. 'Did anything unusual happen lately?'

'Apart from this conversation?'

It's no good. He's not going to admit it. They – whoever they are – have put the fear of God into Tommy and everyone else on the street.

I stare at the last slice of toast on my plate. I'm totally without appetite.

'Are you okay?' Tommy asks, putting his empty plate and mug in the dishwasher. He studies the load, weighing up whether to do a wash or not. He's doing everything he can to avoid looking at me. In the end, he decides against putting the machine on, then inches towards the door. Fidgeting with his watch strap. I know he's about to go upstairs, brush his teeth and get the hell out of Dodge.

'I'm fine,' I say.

'Just seems like you've been tired lately. A bit ... off. Are the headaches still bad?'

I nod.

'Maybe you should see a doctor. You could always stop in at that new practice on your way to work. Book an appointment. Just to check, you know?'

I don't say anything, and Tommy walks out of the kitchen, shoulders slumped. He plods upstairs to the bathroom.

I look up at the ceiling, listening to his heavy footsteps going back and forth. Then I follow him out of the kitchen, stopping at the foot of the staircase. I call up to him.

'Someone chased me yesterday.'

Those heavy feet quicken across the upper landing. Tommy appears at the top of the stairs, looking down at me. There's a puzzled frown on his face. A toothbrush hanging out of his mouth, which he removes.

'What?'

He grips the banister, and I see the white tips of his knuckles. Sharp as daggers.

'Someone chased you?'

I nod. 'And last night, someone – possibly the same person – tried to break into our house.'

I can almost hear his brain sizzling from here. His lips move, but his voice seems delayed, perhaps by shock. Finally, he speaks. 'What the ...? Why the hell didn't you tell me last night that someone chased you?'

'Never mind that. I'll ask you again. Is there anything you want to tell *me*?'

Looking like someone who just got slapped, Tommy releases his grip on the banister. Takes a backward step like he's about to retreat.

'What's with you this morning?'

I want to come out with it. I'm desperate to tell him that I've worked it out about the silencing and that he can talk to me. And then a thought occurs to me – is the house bugged? *Would* he talk about it even if I confronted him?

My body shivers as if the house just turned cold. My eyes dart back and forth along the walls and ceiling. Up, down. Up, down. Searching out some subtle imperfection. A sign of interference. I wouldn't be surprised if they'd bugged every house in the neighbourhood, come to think of it. Just to keep a close eye on things.

People chasing me. Trying to break into our house. Bugs, for God's sake. What have we got ourselves into here? Why did this crash have to happen on our street? Of all the streets in the world, why this one?

'Kate!'

Tommy's voice is like a bell ringing in my mind. Summoning me back to the present.

'What?'

'What's wrong with you?'

'Nothing's wrong with me,' I say. 'Listen, you'd better hurry, or you'll be late for work.'

He screws up his face like I'm talking backwards, then gives up and returns to the bathroom to finish brushing his teeth. I stay where I am, staring at the empty space at the top of the stairs where he just stood. What does Tommy even do anyway? I must've stopped paying attention at some point, and then it got too embarrassing to admit that I've got no interest whatsoever in the specifics. It's office work. Decent money. He wears a suit and does something related to marketing. But I can never keep up. Tommy changes jobs a lot.

I'm still there in the hallway when he comes back downstairs, his work bag draped over his shoulder.

'We'll talk later,' he says. He leans in for a kiss. 'See you tonight, eh?'

The kiss is lifeless. I watch him open the front door, and it's on the tip of my tongue to ask him – *who was in the back seat of that car?* But the door slams shut, and Tommy's gone. He probably doesn't know who was involved or the specifics behind the silencing. All he and the other neighbours could possibly know is that it was someone important. And all they have to do is forget it happened and get on with their lives.

Yeah, I know. It sounds crazy. But stranger things have happened.

I hear the chirp of the car unlocking. The engine growls, and Tommy's quick getaway is complete.

The house feels even colder now. Maybe he'll open up to me if we get out of the house, just in case someone is listening in on our conversations. But will he tell me even if we are somewhere else, somewhere seemingly safe? What's the state of our relationship? Are we drifting apart?

Apart?

We're not even married yet, for God's sake.

Here we go again. I walk back into the kitchen, dump my toast in the bin and summon the energy to get ready for work.

ONE HOUR LATER, I'm stacking shelves in Little Market. Standing on the stepladder, pulling down multipacks of toilet roll from the overstock and lining them up on the correct shelf below. It's easy work, and autopilot takes over. I barely even notice the excruciating Muzak anymore, but it's there.

I still have that feeling of being watched. There's nothing going on – not that I can see from the top step of the ladder. It's nice up here, away from everything else (except the Muzak). Looking over the shelves from aisle to aisle, scanning the shop floor as best I can. Staff, customers – no one acting out of the ordinary. No one taking too much of an interest in the Little Market grunt putting out the toilet paper. Still, these aren't low-level criminals we're talking about. These are the sort of people who can silence not just a small, insignificant neighbourhood but law enforcement too.

Would they really come into Little Market to intimidate me?

I have to know who was sitting in the back of that car on Saturday night. It's eating away at me, the not knowing, like a physical wound that's festering inside me. The identity of the back seat passenger – that's the key to solving this puzzle. I'm certain of it. It pisses me off just thinking about what I could've done better. Why didn't I go over and take a closer look on Saturday night? Peer through the window. Why can't I be more of a nosy neighbour? I would've seen a face, and that, at least, would be something to work with.

I could try talking to the people who did approach the car. Who tried to get the back seat passenger to come out. But they've been silenced, too. They *know*, but if I talk to them, I'll get the Jack and Sarah treatment. I'll get the Tommy treatment.

It was just a dream, Kate. Oh, poor Kate thinks it was all real.

It *was* real.

I face up the toilet paper on the top shelf, lining up the packets in a straight line. Looks good. I take pride in my work even if it's not important work.

But I'm miles away. Thinking about the giant puzzle I have to solve.

Were there illegal substances in the car? Guns? Did any of the neighbours capture the moment on camera – someone who perhaps didn't go outside but watched from a bedroom window? Even if the footage exists, they wouldn't show me. It all goes back to the same thing – everyone's terrified. Everyone's keeping quiet.

I stand paralysed on the top step. No longer lining up toilet paper.

Do you hear yourself?

There it is – the voice of doubt. Still trying to bring me back down to earth, still trying to tell me that the silencing is nothing but a figment of my imagination. That would be the easiest thing in the world – just give in. Admit that I'm bored or crazy or a silly drunk in search of purpose. Seeking out drama in my dull life. Maybe that's what these powerful people rely on – either we doubt ourselves, or others doubt us. Imagine if the neighbourhood grouped together and took this story to the press. Who'd believe us outside the usual conspiracy nuts?

I feel lightheaded. The drill in my brain momentarily stops, and something comes back to me, out of nowhere. A dream. It was last night's dream in fact, the one I had after two (three?) glasses of wine. The intruder in someone else's house. The chase. The intruder on the road, running in front of a car. White lights. Brakes screaming.

The weirdest thing. I felt guilty waking up this morning. It's the first thing I remember, and the weight of it was unbearable. Guilt and shame. But it was only a dream for—

'Kate?'

A twelve-pack of Andrex slips out of my grip and lands on the floor. It bounces at Donna's feet. I almost lose my balance and topple down the stepladder after it.

'Sorry,' I say. 'That didn't hit you, did it?'

'No, it's fine.'

I climb down the steps.

Donna watches my every move closely. I see concern on her face, intermingled with a polite and tight-lipped smile. 'Are you okay? I thought I heard you talking to someone up there.'

I pick up the Andrex packet, moving it aside to sort later. Then I straighten up. The normal, agonising service of the drill in my head is resumed. 'I wasn't on my phone, if that's what you were asking.'

'Of course not.'

She sounds defensive.

We both cling to our smiles. I haven't forgotten that the guy with the limp chased me yesterday *after* I'd spoken to Donna. Not Sarah, not Tommy. *Donna.* Coincidence? I get the feeling she hasn't come over to say hi. Which begs the question – is she checking on me for someone?

'You look a bit pale, Kate.'

I nod. 'Got a headache that won't quit.'

She nods like it's the answer she was expecting. 'Hmm. Why don't you go home and get some rest? It's quiet. We can manage without you for a day.'

The Muzak is slowly eating my brain.

'Are you sure?'

'Absolutely. I'll get James to finish up with the toilet paper. You go – grab your coat and get to bed.'

Wow, I must look worse than I feel. But sure, I'll take the day off. I thank her, then go upstairs to collect my bag and coat. This isn't good – my head is splitting, and I'm so tired. It's like the fatigue is deep in my bones. I'm terrified it's something serious, but how can I think about that when all this madness is going on around me? I want to hit the floor. I want a hug. I want someone on my side.

I see Donna on the shop floor as I walk towards the exit. She's talking to James, a student, who works part-time in Little Market. She waves, her smile too good to be true.

I wave back.

Who's going to chase me home today, Donna?

I walk through the sliding doors but not before one last glance over my shoulder. Donna's watching me, and I catch her in the act. She looks away, but it's too late. Ha! I hurry across the car park, a fierce breeze whipping at my cheeks. I need to get away from Little Market, but there's no warm, fuzzy feeling waiting for me when I reach the main street. I even speed up as I pass strange and familiar faces on the pavement. Some of them look at me a little too intently for my liking.

I'm not imagining it.

13

It's a tense walk home from Little Market. I'm waiting for the guy with the limp to show up and start hobbling after me. As I hurry along, my eyes dart back and forth in all directions. Anyone looking at me must think I'm a nervous wreck.

There's no sign of him. I have left work early today, so maybe I've caught him out.

I walk past the shitty old man's pub, and for the first time ever, I feel it calling to me. I look inside, and it's dead quiet. Doesn't even have to be a drink that I go in for. Just to catch my breath, I tell myself, but it's not a good idea, and I know it. Plus, I don't need a drink. I don't feel like I even *want* a drink. It's not like I'm shaking or I've got the sweats, and that's how I know I'm not the raging alcoholic that Tommy thinks I am.

I just need to go home and lie down. Catch up on some of that sleep I missed out on last night.

My heart pounds at the sound of footsteps behind me. Rushed, frantic footsteps. I freeze as a woman walks past, pulled at speed by an energetic Border collie on an extendable lead. The dog is itching to go faster. The woman breaks out into a jog to keep up.

'Oh God,' I say.

I can still hear the man with the limp. His voice, like he's whispering in my ear.

You have to hear this.

There's a part of me that wishes I'd listened to him. Just stopped running, stood my ground and listened to the warning that everyone else on the street received. That way I would've known for sure, and there'd have been no room for doubt. Easier said than done. I was being chased, and the instinct to run was strong.

I keep walking.

Nothing happens during the walk home. No one calls my name or staggers across the street, dodging traffic to reach me. Once I close the door, I stand with my back against the wall and feel the sweat dripping down my face. My uniform is soaked. It feels like I've been for a hundred-mile run in the Sahara, my headache shadowing me all the way.

I want to cry, but I've no water left for tears.

How long can I live like this?

I pour myself a big glass of water in the kitchen. Drink it, then pour and finish a second. I take a third into the living room along with some ibuprofen for the drill in my head. All I want to do is crash on the couch and close my eyes.

All I want is for things to ... *stop*.

Before lying down, I make sure the doors are locked. Front and back.

I collapse onto the couch, and my heart's still racing like a mad thing. There's a whooshing noise in my ears, and it's in perfect rhythm with my excited heartbeat. Deep breaths, in and out. Staring up at the ceiling. Fuck. I feel lost. I don't recognise the person I've become. I realise that at some point, I settled for something ... *shitty*. I fucking hate my life, and I have no memory of choosing it.

Where are these thoughts coming from? It's almost like someone else's voice is running around inside my head, and I can't restrain it.

Who was in the back seat of that car?

Everything will make sense if I can make sense of that crash.

This mass silencing – holy shit, is it real or not? Where are my friends and family in this shithole of a town? Why am I so isolated, and why does my headache get worse every time I try to fit the pieces together in a way that makes sense?

Oh, get a fucking grip, woman.

Is it me? Is this one of those rare moments of clarity where it feels like I'm looking at myself from the outside?

Who was in the back seat of that car?

No one.

Who was in the back seat ...?

Fucking no one.

I understand that years of boredom and dissatisfaction can have a profound effect on someone's life. But I'm only twenty-what-is-it-again? I'm young. But if I've been unhappy for this long, doesn't it make sense that I might be inclined to invent drama in my life? That's not what's happening with the crash. Is it? I remember everything about that night. It wasn't a dream, and I didn't invent it as a way out of my dull existence.

But I hear the voice in my head, and it's no longer so sure. My statements sound more like questions.

I drink more water. I could think a little more clearly if

only I could get rid of this headache. Maybe some wine? Just to help me sleep. Fortunately, my eyelids grow heavy without having to get up, and I don't fight the sensation pulling me towards sleep. It feels so good to sink into what I hope is the beginning of deep sleep.

All I want to do ... is ... sleep.

I WAKE up to the sound of footsteps directly outside the house. I have no idea how long I've been out for the count, but my head is a swirling fog of confusion. I glance at the window beside me, the curtains still pulled over. Then I hear it. The low-pitched groan that our gate makes when it's pushed open.

I sit up. There's a ton weight in my chest and head, and it's hard to breathe. Oh man, there's even drool on my chin. I wipe it off.

But I'm wide awake.

There were footsteps, but they have stopped. There's nothing now, and it's got me wondering – did I imagine them? Was it a dream, again?

I sit on the couch in silence, staring at the gap in the living-room door. Towards the hallway. Waiting.

The handle on the front door squeaks. Someone's trying to get inside.

I locked the doors.

Is it Tommy? No, it can't be Tommy. He's got a key, and even if he'd forgotten it or lost it, he'd knock. He'd call. He'd go to Little Market to get the spare because I'm not supposed to be home at this time of day.

The handle squeaks again.

It's him. It's the man who chased me. He's come back to

break in, but this time he's doing it in broad daylight. Who are these people?

The squeaky handle goes silent. I hear something else. The sound of a key turning in the lock.

I don't recognise my voice as I call out.

'Tommy? Is that you?'

There's no answer. It's not Tommy. I know it's not Tommy. I scramble for my phone – it's on the floor beside the couch. My hand shakes as I grab it. I look at the screen, and everything is strange – like I'm an alien who just picked up an iPhone. Then it comes back to me. I'm about to call the police when I hear someone pushing the front door open. It's enough to make me drop the phone.

There are footsteps inside the house.

'Get out!' I yell. 'Get the hell out!'

There's someone in the house, and they've come to shut me up.

'Who's there?' I call.

No answer. Just the loudest footsteps in the hallway. Big and heavy. Clumsy, almost. Exaggerated. And here they come, plodding in my direction, coming straight towards the living room.

My voice turns shrill with terror. 'What do you WAAAANT?'

The intruder enters the living room, and I emit a feeble gasping noise. There are no words for this. It's like I've been clubbed out of my senses.

She has a gorilla mask over her head. A gorilla mask. I say she because I see the curves under her black T-shirt. Slim waist, black jeans, Adidas trainers. And a fucking gorilla mask. A thick, rubbery mask that covers her head entirely. I'm too stunned to speak. I just stand beside the couch with my mouth hanging open.

Gorilla Girl waves at me. She proceeds to walk through the living room and disappears into the kitchen. I hear the fridge humming. Then she's rattling around in the pantry.

My tongue isn't working. 'W-w-what are ...?'

Why can't I speak?

Gorilla Girl marches back into the living room with an apple and a glass of water. She falls into the armchair, grabs the remote control off the armrest and turns on the TV. A news broadcast fills the room, and Gorilla Girl turns the volume up to excruciating. I wince. It feels like my head is about to explode.

'Who are you?' I shout over the TV. My voice is no match for the latest doom and gloom headlines being read out. 'What do you want?'

It's a dream. I even pinch myself on the wrist, my nail slicing into the skin. It hurts but I keep going. But I don't wake up, and Gorilla Girl doesn't disappear. She's still there on the chair. Watching TV. Watching me.

'W-w-what do you—?'

She takes off the mask, and sure enough, it's a blonde girl of about eighteen or nineteen. She's pretty, and her forehead glistens with sweat. A classic girl next door, and to my horror, she's grinning at me.

I clear my throat. 'Who ... are ... you?'

She bites into the apple. Her only reply to my question is a carefree shrug of the shoulders as if to say *that isn't important*. Then she takes another bite of the apple and tosses it onto the floor. It rolls past the coffee table towards the TV.

This doesn't feel right. This feels like falling.

'Please,' I say. 'Who are you? What are you doing?'

That's when the fog shifts and clarity hits.

Tommy was right. Sarah was right and so was Donna. There was no crash and no conspiracy to keep it quiet. This is you. It's all you, and you're skydiving into batshit crazy territory without a parachute.

I scream at her. 'Who are you?'

All I get back is a puzzled expression. She's looking at me in a way that makes me feel like I'm the intruder here. She grabs the remote off the chair and turns off the TV. The silence is deafening. Gorilla Girl stands up, tall with a straight back. Like she's been called to attention. Then, with the mask tucked under her arm, she runs for the door. I can't move. Can't breathe. All I can do is watch as she leaves the living room and disappears down the hallway. Her feet sound light now. Like a child's footsteps skipping as she bounces off the floor.

The front door slams.

I stand there in the living room. The house feels like a sick, twisted fairground ride that won't let me off. I look around. What is this place? Is it really ... *home*? The patterned wallpaper is blurry, the shapes spiralling in and out of focus. I stare at the discarded apple on the floor. The glass of water on the table beside the chair.

'No,' I say. 'No, no. NO!'

There's a violent rage stirring inside me. What I don't want to face is that I'm angry at myself. And now, even though I'm running towards the front door, down the driveway and onto the street, I know that I'm chasing a ghost. I want it to be intimidation. I want the car crash to have happened. I want the silencing to be real.

Stop blaming everyone else, says the voice in my head. *Stop blaming the world.*

There's something wrong with me. My internal wiring has snapped, and that's why everything has been so foggy recently. That and the drinking. The headaches are most likely stress headaches. Severe stress headaches. I don't want this life. I don't recognise this life, so here I am, making shit up to feel something other than numb. What exactly am I imagining here? A conspiracy where everyone in the neighbourhood has been silenced except me?

Oh shit, Kate. Look what you've become. You're chasing an intruder in a gorilla mask, an intruder who doesn't exist. The man with the limp was just some random weirdo, and so what, he knew my name. I walk around Little Market with a name tag pinned to my uniform. I was wearing my badge that night. And as for the break-in attempt? I guess Tommy was right. I was hearing things, and my imagination turned it into something bigger.

I have to talk to Tommy when he comes home tonight. I'm going to see a doctor. I'm going to ask for help, and I'll do whatever it takes to get better. I mean that.

There's some relief in that decision, I guess. I've taken the first step and admitted I've got a problem. That's the hardest part, isn't that what they say?

God, I hope Tommy stands by me. Who wants the burden of looking after someone like me?

Well, there's only one way to find out. I walk back down the middle of the road, feeling lighter than I have in a long time. Ready to let go of my delusions. Rock bottom is calm. It's peaceful. And the only way to go from here is up.

I'm about to swerve onto the pavement and walk back to my gate when I stop. There's something lying on the road. Something that catches my eye, in between my house and Jack and Sarah's.

I take a couple of steps to the right. Towards Jack and Sarah's perfect fence.

I squat down to get a better look. My breathing is still heavy after running out of the house and down the road.

Time stops. The object on the road sparkles as I lean in for a closer look. I almost faint when I realise what it is.

14

It's a diamond stud earring. Just like the one the driver was wearing on Saturday night when he crashed the car into Jack and Sarah's fence.

I saw it. I remember it. And that's it – that's the driver's earring lying on the road. He must have lost it in all the excitement.

Am I dreaming now?

I take it back – I take it all back. It's not me, it's them. I'm not crazy; everyone else is hiding something that *did* happen. My head's spinning. I don't quite know how I feel about this. But here it is – the evidence, a tiny sparkling dot locked in between my forefinger and thumb. It's so ... *real*. The driver was here. The crash happened. No more bouncing back and forth between madness and conspiracy. There was a car crash on Saturday night, right here on our street. And someone's trying to cover it up.

'It happened,' I say out loud, making it real.

My attention turns to Jack and Sarah's perfect fence. And

beyond that, to their nice, trimmed lawn, their potted plants and their front door. And I remember what she said to me on Sunday morning when I brought up the crash. The look on her face. I remember the way she made me feel.

'You lying bitch.'

15

I hammer my fist on their front door. It sounds like I've got a battering ram in my grip. As I wait at the foot of the steps that lead up to the door, my body ripples with anger. Especially so when I glance over my shoulder and see their perfect fucking fence.

I knock again, in no mood to be kept waiting by these liars. There's a beat of silence. Then I hear muffled voices from inside the house. I knock again and again and again. The message is clear.

I know you're in there.

Footsteps approach.

The hurried sound of a key turning in the lock. The door groans open a few inches, and Sarah's head pokes through the gap. Her eyes are wide with apprehension – she looks like she's expecting the Grim Reaper.

I stare at her.

'Kate, are you okay?'

It takes every ounce of control I've got not to punch her in the face. *Don't come across as the psycho here.* Still, my voice cracks. I'm full of anger that can't be contained, and for now at least, it's in my voice.

'Tell me the truth.'

Sarah's eyebrows arch. The gap in the door widens a little, and she takes a step forward, a step that might be considered a threat.

'Excuse me?'

I hold my hand up. 'Stop it, Sarah. How dare you? How dare you stand there and act like there's something wrong with me?'

'Kate, what on earth are you talking—?'

'You know why I'm here.'

'I can assure you I don't.'

'The crash. I'm talking about the car crash that happened right here on Saturday night. The one you said *didn't* happen.'

Her shoulders drop, and her thin face takes on a pitiful expression, like a wounded bird. I want to hit her, but that would make me look like the crazy one, and after finding the driver's earring on the road, I now know I'm not the crazy one.

'Oh Kate,' she says. 'I thought we'd dealt with this.'

'Don't lie to me again. Don't you fucking dare.'

'Kate—'

'Shut up.' And then I lean forward, lowering my voice to a whisper. 'I know they're forcing you to stay quiet. You don't have to pretend with me.'

I see the blankness in her eyes. It's like staring into the void.

'Is there a bug?' I whisper. 'Can they hear us?'

She gives me a sorrowful smile. 'Where's Tommy, sweetheart? Is he still at work? I'd like to give him a call if I can.'

'Look at this,' I say.

I hold up the diamond earring still wedged in between my thumb and forefinger. Sarah stares at it like it's an indecipherable code.

'What's that?'

'Saturday night. The driver wore an earring just like this. Guess someone must have missed it during the clean-up. Well, it's understandable. It's small. And it was dark that night, wasn't it?'

Sarah narrows the gap in the door again and peers at me with those pinched eyes of hers. Although she's clinging to a demented half-smile, I don't think we're far from her slamming the door in my face.

'Kate, please don't take this the wrong way. But are you ... have you been drinking this afternoon?'

'What?'

'It's not your fault. It's a disease.'

I nod. 'I'm supposed to shut up, aren't I? That's what they want. It's what you want. Everyone is just supposed to pretend like it didn't happen.'

Sarah sighs. 'Kate, this isn't healthy.'

'They cleaned it up, didn't they? Cleaned it up and covered it up. Your fence was repaired, and everything else was sorted, but they missed this earring.'

Sarah looks at me. 'I'll call Tommy.'

'Just admit it.'

She sounds flustered. 'Admit what?'

'The truth.'

She inches forward again. Her face pushing into the gap. 'The truth? The truth is I think you need help, Kate. I think you're very sick.'

I lash out at that, kicking the door with the flat of my

shoe. There's an angry thump as the door goes in, and I feel a gust of heat escape the house. Sarah staggers backwards. She gasps as I rush onto the welcome mat, grab her arms and pull her outside. She feels so thin, like she's made out of paper.

I maintain a strong grip as we stand on the top step. Now we're face to face. So close that our noses almost touch.

Sarah's eyes bulge with terror. 'Jack!' she calls.

'There *was* a car crash,' I insist. 'Who told you to be quiet? Who threatened you?'

Her eyes narrow. 'Jack!' she shouts. 'JACK!'

'I *have* to know, Sarah.'

Jack's voice is a blur as he storms down the hallway like a mad bull. 'What the hell is going on here?'

I let go of Sarah, backing off down the stone steps and onto the garden path. Without taking my eyes off the house, I retreat to the gate.

They're standing at the door. Watching me.

'You're lying,' I declare. Then I make a sweeping move of my arm towards the other houses on the street. 'You're all lying.'

Jack is out of breath after his short sprint. He throws a protective arm around his wife's shoulders, pulling her back into the safety of the house. They look like they're retreating from an angry bear.

'Stay away from us, Kate,' he says.

The door slams shut. I hear their voices from inside and even grasp snippets of the conversation. One word I don't miss is *crazy*. And there are others:

Doctor.
Drink.
Drugs.

I look at the earring sitting on the palm of my hand. Slowly, I curl my fingers and close a fist around it.

'Everyone here is lying.'

I look around. Staring at the houses on this lifeless street. Staring at the road, recalling the vivid memory of the black Subaru hitting the fence.

Fuck it.

I can't stay here, and there's no way I can go back into the house. I need time to think.

And I need a drink.

Double fuck it.

16

It comes out of nowhere. I'm about to set off for the main street when there's an explosion of pain in my head.

This isn't a regular headache. It's the worst pain imaginable. So painful that I can't even scream or cry out for help. My head feels like an inflatable ball with too much air coming in. We're past the point of no return, and the air is still coming in. There's no room for it. My skull feels like it's about to burst.

I double over, convinced I'm about to throw up, pass out or drop dead. I don't know how long the whole episode lasts – it's maybe less than ten seconds – but when I'm doubled over, dropping to my knees, that's when I see it.

I see *her*.

It's one of those rare moments of clarity where, despite the pain, I feel certain of myself. Of who I am. It's frightening, but it's real – I know *this* is real. I see the girl in my mind and know that I know her from somewhere. The one running out of the house and in front of the car. I feel like she's calling to me.

    Her name is Z—

    And then it's gone. Just like that, the pain cools, and my mind clouds over again. I'm on my knees in the middle of the road. I stand up quickly, not sure if my legs will hold me. I still have that feeling of being watched, but I can't see anyone at the windows looking back at me.

    What's going on? Nothing has been right since Saturday night. Nothing.

    Holy shit.

    I need that drink.

17

I hurry towards the town centre, grateful for the streetlights that line the route. It feels safe to walk in the warm orange glow; it feels like nothing can touch me there. But the people on the street bother me. There are so many of them – an endless conveyor belt of blank faces marching in both directions, seemingly unaware of the horror that's unfolding in this town. Unaware of dark forces. Of the silencing.

I reach the old man's pub, the Red Lion. It's a shithole. But, as usual, it looks quiet, and that's good enough for me.

I walk in, my heart still racing from the encounter with Sarah and the incident afterwards where it felt like my head was going to crack open. Right now, I feel great. Physically at least. I have no idea if it's the adrenaline giving me these extreme highs and lows. There's so much I don't understand, and, boy, does that feel like the understatement of the century.

Some quiet time. A break. That's what I need.

The pub is warm, maybe a little too warm. The wall is

covered with colourful sports pennants, football pennants mostly, and Guinness-themed mirrors that look like they belong in an antique store. Wooden tables are scattered across the floor, cracked and blemished. Crappy chairs. The faint smell of cleaning chemicals lingers. There's an old dartboard in the corner and a blackboard for keeping score. The chalk scribblings on the blackboard are faded, dusty.

A silver-haired man stands behind the bar. He's short and wiry, a slight hunch to his back. He's watching an old box TV fixed to the wall. Looks like a football game from the Middle East with a commentator shrieking in Arabic whenever anything exciting happens.

'Help you, love?' he asks, turning my way.

I order a white wine, down it, then buy two more. I take my drinks two and three to a booth near the door. The TV continues to blare. Seems like it's impossible to drown out the excited football commentator.

The second glass of wine goes down better than the first. My headache subsides although I'm still groggy. Sleepy. Once again, I recall the moment outside Jack and Sarah's house – it was sheer agony, but it was like the fog had momentarily lifted.

What triggered it? Will it happen again?

And who was the girl I saw there?

I don't know what the truth is, but I know something strange is happening in our boring little town. There's no more 'did or didn't it happen' for me. I found the earring, and that tells me that someone wants this thing brushed under the table. That makes me a problem because, unlike the neighbours and unlike Tommy, I didn't receive, or heed, the message to shut up.

The police have been silenced. What about the media? I

suddenly realise that I could make an anonymous phone call and tell them everything.

But equally suddenly, I realise they'd think I'm mad.

A car crash that disappeared? A man with a limp and a girl in a gorilla mask trying to intimidate you? We'll, umm ... let you know.

Click. Call over.

I feel a hot, prickly sensation on the back of my neck. I glance over my shoulder, and the bartender is watching me. Caught in the act, he looks quickly at the TV. The corner of his eye twitches.

I sip the wine.

What do I do? What's my next move once I leave the pub? The only thing that seems logical is having it out with Tommy. Face to face when he gets back from work. I'll show him the earring and see what he says. If anyone is going to break the silence, it's him. It's Tommy. It's not enough to protect me from the silencing. I need to hear someone tell the truth. I need it more than I can ever say.

I'm about to finish the final glass of wine and leave when the door swings open. There's a gust of cold air, and a young man in his early twenties walks in. He has a knitted beanie on his head. He's skinny, dressed in double denim and white Reeboks. He looks my way for a split second, then approaches the bar and orders a pint of lager. The bartender's expression isn't welcoming, but he pours the drink and takes the young man's money.

He brings his pint of lager to the table opposite my booth. A table that's in between me and the door. Is that weird? A pub full of empty seats and he chooses the table closest to me. Maybe I'm overthinking again.

He takes off the beanie and drops it on the table. Ruffles

his dirty brown hair, takes a sip of lager and looks at me again.

This time there's a jolt of electricity inside me. I know that face. I'm not sure *how*, but I know it.

Now he isn't looking at me – he's *staring*. His eyes light up, and I get the sense that he's trying to communicate without speaking.

Holy shit.

It's the driver of the car. He's shaved off the beard, but I swear that's him. That's the guy who fishtailed the Subaru up and down my street on Saturday night and then steered it into Jack and Sarah's fence. It's him! I recognise that face. Those narrow, angular features. It's him. I'm not imagining this.

He's sitting at the table next to me. Trying to catch my eye.

What does he want?

Why did he follow me into the pub?

His eyes are shimmering. I feel the same desperate energy that I saw in the guy with the limp. Is this all part of the same intimidation routine?

I stand up, and he flinches, a look of dumb surprise on his face. I know that face, and there's something else too. Something that's just out of reach. He's the driver, yes, but there's something more.

'Everything alright?' the bartender asks.

'Fine,' I reply.

I should talk to him. I want to talk to him. But the driver's face is flushed, and he stands up, too, still with that intense longing in his eyes. Then he retreats to the door, pulls it open and shakes his head. He disappears, and the door swings to a close.

The bartender coughs into the back of his hand. Then he points at the door. 'Was that guy bothering you?'

'No,' I say.

'You sure?'

I nod, then slide back into the booth. With my body trembling, I finish the glass of wine and find myself longing for another. I look at the door, wondering if he'll come back. But the only thing that comes back is my headache.

18

My body feels sluggish as I walk back home to confront Tommy. But my mind is a rollercoaster.

Maybe I do have a drinking problem, and maybe there is some other health issue at play that needs addressing sooner rather than later. The headaches. The brain fog. They're not good and could mean something bad, but whatever they might mean, it doesn't change one simple fact. The car crash happened. It wasn't a dream or the drunken imaginings of some bored suburbanite. It happened.

And everyone else is lying.

Tommy should be home by now, wondering where I am. I haven't checked my phone to see if he's sent a text or called and left a voice message. Doesn't matter. I'm going home, and we're going to have it out, one way or another. But it has to be face to face. I have to look him in the eyes to do this.

I have a bad dose of butterflies in my stomach.

It's almost dark by the time I turn the corner onto our street. The days feel shorter and shorter these days. Midday might as well be midnight. I'm not sure how much time has passed since Donna sent me home, since the nap on the couch, since Gorilla Girl, the confrontation with Sarah, and the silent encounter with the Subaru driver in the pub.

It's been a testing day.

A brief glance across the road. I'm sure Jack and Sarah's curtains just twitched.

It's hard to believe that a massive conspiracy can happen right here on my doorstep. This entire neighbourhood was silenced except me, and when I started asking questions, that's when the intimidation tactics started. The guy with the limp, the attempted break-in, Gorilla Girl and now the guy in a beanie following me into a pub. They want to frighten me. And if that doesn't work, they're happy to let me think I'm insane.

I'm so sick of this shit.

I open the gate and walk up the path. Tommy's car is in the driveway, and there's honestly still a part of me that hoped he was out. But there's no hiding from this. The front door is unlocked. I open it and step into the hallway. The TV is blaring in the living room – sounds like a weather report and not a very promising one at that. I hear the rattle of pots and pans in the kitchen. Something's bubbling on the stove.

That's right. It's Tommy's turn to make dinner. He's probably hoping for a quiet night.

I walk into the living room. Make my way towards the kitchen. I think about turning off the TV, but there's something comforting about its endless drone in the background.

Here we go. Let's see if Tommy still wants to play let's pretend.

I call out to signal my arrival.

'Tommy?'

His voice is muffled over the noise in the kitchen.

'In here, honey.'

There are two doors into the kitchen. One from the hallway and one from inside the living room. I decide to go back and enter through the hallway door. I'm not sure why I do that except that it's closer to the front door, and maybe I still want to make a run for it rather than have this confrontation.

I stop at the door. Wrestle with the voice in my head that tells me to run. One last deep breath, then I push the door open and walk into the kitchen. The heat smothers me – it's like walking face-first into a furnace.

'Tommy, we need to t—'

I stop.

I scream.

It's not Tommy. There's a stranger in the house, and he's on his knees beside the kitchen cupboard, pulling out a frying pan. There are various utensils, food packets and jars scattered around the room. A beer can open on the counter. The stranger straightens up when he sees me, the frying pan in his hand. He's wearing a red and white checked apron. *My apron.*

He lowers the pan onto the counter.

'Hi, honey,' he says. 'How was your day?'

His smile fizzles out when he sees the look on my face. There's a brief glance around the room, as if searching for a dead body on the floor.

'What's wrong?'

He walks towards me, arms open as if coming in for a hug. Maybe it's the terrified look on my face, but something makes him stop. Holy shit. The way he's looking at me right now. Like I'm the one who isn't supposed to be there.

I wrestle with the knots in my tongue. 'Who ... the hell ... are you?'

He looks at me like I've lost my marbles.

'Kate? What's wrong?'

Something snaps inside me. I almost hear the inner string breaking, and I march forward, close to picking that frying pan up off the counter and whacking him across the head with it.

'Enough of the bullshit. Who are you? What are you doing in my house?'

He blinks hard. 'Honey, what do you mean? It's me. It's Tommy.'

He's serious.

'What the fuck are you talking—?'

'Kate, what's happening here?'

I look at him.

This is *not* Tommy. My eyes aren't suddenly deceiving me, for God's sake. This is *not* Tommy. My Tommy's a giant rugby player. He's built like a brick shithouse, over six feet tall, all muscle and broad shoulders for days. His face is covered in a permanent coat of dark stubble. His voice is deep.

This man is short. He's shorter than me, and I'm a lot shorter than Tommy. His strawberry blond hair is combed in a neat side-parting, and he's got a well-trimmed goatee that does nothing to hide his boyish features. His tight-fitting pink shirt and tan trousers are wrinkle-free. His skin glows reddish pink. He's *too* clean. Too smooth. He's more like a mannequin than a man.

His voice is gentle. It's like he's talking to an anxious child who's convinced there's a monster under her bed.

He approaches me. His delicate hands up in the air.

'Kate, you're okay. Listen to me – you're okay.'
'Stay where you are,' I growl.
He does.
'Who sent you?' I ask. Hot tears are streaming down my face. 'Are you the next one who's supposed to intimidate me? Make me feel like I'm a raving lunatic?'
'What are you talking about?'
'All this to hide a car crash, right?'
His face wrinkles up. 'What?'
'Someone in that car was connected, right? High connections, and no matter what, it has to be kept quiet. Doesn't matter if we ruin lives in the process – just keep the crash quiet by any means possible.'
There's this dumb, wounded look on the man's face. Like I slapped him.
'Kate, why are you doing this?'
'You're not Tommy.'
He makes a loud whistling noise.
'If I'm not Tommy,' he says, 'then how do I know about the pear-shaped birthmark on your right thigh?'
He points to a framed photo on the wall.
'That's us in Menorca five years ago. Look, will you? Please look at the photograph.'
My head turns slowly. I almost pass out. I don't remember the holiday that well, but sure enough, it's me and this man in the photo. On a beach in Menorca. Smiling and a little sunburned.
I put out a hand, as if to block all sight of it.
'We have lots more photos,' he says in a gentle voice. 'We even have a few collections put together from our favourite trips. Which one would you like to see first? Berlin? Sydney?'
He puts a hand over his heart, as if to convey sincerity.

'Honey, please. You've been so weird lately. I think ... I think something's wrong.'

A tear spills down his cheek.

'I'm scared, Kate. I just want to look after you.'

He inches forward.

'We're going to get you the help you need, I promise.'

I look again at the photo on the wall. And I try to remember something of that holiday, but it's like looking at someone else. It's *me*. That's me in the photograph.

'Kate,' he whispers, 'I know you haven't been happy lately, and I have to take some responsibility for that. Heck, I guess we both do. We're living our lives on automatic pilot, and ... the drinking ... we let it get out of hand.'

There's a hurt expression on his face.

'Maybe you *want* me to be someone else? Is that it? Someone you find more attractive. Someone who fits better with the life you once imagined for yourself.'

I shake my head. 'This is bullshit.'

He reaches for me again. 'I just want to talk.'

'Don't touch me!'

I turn and run out of the kitchen. Sprinting down the hallway, my skin burning like it's on fire. I pull the front door open and run out so fast I almost trip over my feet. Down the steps. Onto the path. I look straight ahead.

A dour evening gloom has settled over the street. The temperature is plummeting.

I stare at the other houses. At the windows. And I see their faces watching me.

'Kate!'

He calls after me from inside the house. I freeze on the path, his voice like cold fingernails clawing at my ears.

'Kate! Come back. I love yooooou!'

19

It's dark, but the street is well lit. I hurry but don't run towards the gate, unlatch it and step onto the pavement.

'Oh shit.'

The neighbours are coming out. There are doors opening everywhere. I hear their hushed voices and their feet on paths and gravel driveways.

Another sudden explosion of pain doubles me over. I clench my fists and feel my body shudder. There's another brief moment where I'm convinced that my head is about to blow up. It feels like my brain is swelling up. Like I'm having some kind of aneurysm.

'Fuck!'

And then it clears, and for a moment, I feel elated. I can't explain it. It's like there's a wall inside my head. And there's something on the other side of that wall, something trying to get through.

I close my eyes and see her.

The girl.

'Zara,' I say. That's it. She's called Zara.

Oh God, I need time to make sense of this. It's close – I feel like I'm close to something, within touching distance, but I don't have time to sit down and clear my head. I straighten up and wipe the sweat from my face. I look across the street and see Jack and Sarah standing at their front door. Two silhouettes huddled close together. Watching me. There are plenty of other neighbours standing in their doorways. Some have ventured onto the pavement. There are a couple on the road.

'What do you want?' I yell.

There's no answer.

Is this the latest act of intimidation, or am I trapped inside a madhouse here?

'Honey, please stay where you are!'

I hear Tommy – *not Tommy* – step outside. He's on the path, shuffling after me with a strange, penguin walk that makes me cold all over. He couldn't be any less like my Tommy.

'Kate! I'm coming.'

I slam the gate shut and hold my hands out as if ready to push back a tank.

'GET AWAY FROM ME!'

He's still talking in that wet, gentle voice. High-pitched and trembling. 'You need help, honey. And that's okay. Look at me – it's Tommy. It's *your* Tommy. We're going to get married, and we'll—'

I scream again. 'Get away from me.'

I'm running. Turning my legs over like a sprinter. I don't know where I'm going, but I'm never going back there. That place isn't home. It's a place of madness.

'I love you, honey!'

Fake Tommy is still chasing me. Running like an awkward bird, his clipped steps narrowing the gap between us.

'Come back!'

I hear Sarah's voice from across the street. 'Kate! Please stop. We just want to help you.'

Help *me*? Of course, I'm the crazy one. How could I forget? Even now, they're sticking with the lie. At this point, the best option for them is to discredit me. They'd put me in the asylum if they had their way.

I need time to interpret what's going on in my head. That sharp, explosive pain is terrifying, but I feel like it's blowing crappy thoughts out of the way, like dry leaves off the pavement. It sure as hell is getting rid of the fog. I see her more clearly now. The girl. Zara. I can't remember who she is, but I know she's important. That, somehow, she's connected to all this.

I'm no runner, and even a short sprint is causing me to fold over in exhaustion. My limbs feel flaccid and hollow, and all the while, Fake Tommy's gaining on me. His silly, terrifying run is faster than mine.

'Get away from me!' I yell.

Don't Jack and Sarah see it? What about the other neighbours? It's not Tommy running after me – don't they see it?

There's a screeching noise behind me. The howl of brakes as a car makes a sharp turn onto our street. Then I hear the roar of an engine. The growl of acceleration. Still just about running, I glance over my shoulder. Blinding headlights race down the middle of the road. The car speeds past the houses, past Fake Tommy, and there's another piercing shriek as it jerks to a sudden stop about ten metres in front of me. The passenger door is flung open from the inside. I stop running. Stare dead ahead.

'Get in.'

I know that voice.

I hurry towards the car, peer inside, and sure enough, I see the driver. His clean-shaven face. Knitted beanie.

'Get in,' he repeats.

I shake my head.

'You have to trust me,' he says, twisting around in his seat to look through the rear window. Then he looks back at me. 'I'm not one of them. Listen, I know what's happening – what's *really* happening around here. It's not what you think.'

'Tell me.'

He shakes his head. 'I will. Get in the car and—'

He stops, his eyes wide with panic. We both hear it.

The sound of sirens.

The driver's face is chalk white. For a second, he looks lost, and then he snaps out of it and turns back to me.

'Get in, or stay here and deal with this shit by yourself.'

'Kate!' Fake Tommy screams. He's waving his arms wildly to grab my attention. 'Stay away from that man. He's dangerous.'

I look at the driver. At the same time, I hear the sirens growing louder. Sounds like a whole fleet of cops coming after us. I am *not* insane.

'Do you know someone called Zara?' I ask. 'Does that name mean anything to you?'

The driver looks at me, his eyes filling with sadness.

'Yes. It's a long story.'

I nod.

The decision is made.

I get in the car and slam the door shut behind me.

20

We take off at high speed. I lock in the seatbelt and see blue and red lights flashing in the side mirror. The blare of sirens is ferocious. A platoon of police cars emerges through a gathering mist, forming a convoy behind us.

The driver glances in the rear-view and hammers his fist on the wheel. 'Oh shit.'

'You crashed the car on Saturday night,' I say. 'Didn't you? You crashed it into that fence back there.'

'I don't know if this is the best time to talk about that.'

I shake my head. 'Am I losing my mind?'

He keeps his eyes on the road. 'No. Don't ever think that. It's *them*.'

He looks in the mirror again, grimacing at the flashing lights and the screaming sirens. The gap in between them and us holds steady for now.

'I'm dead,' he says. 'If they get their hands on me ...'

I stare through the windscreen. We're on the main street. This is the route I walk to work, but the town centre is eerily quiet. It's dead. I can't see any people – not a single soul out and about, and that's not right at this time of day. No cars, no lights from the shop windows. It's like everything's shut down.

'Tell me what's going on,' I say.

The driver skips a red light. I hear him breathing hard.

'You don't recognise me at all, do you?'

'You're the driver. I saw you on Saturday night when you crashed the car through my neighbour's fence. That *did* happen, didn't it?'

He nods.

I shudder with relief. Just hearing someone else say it hits hard, but this isn't the time to break down. I'll cry later. Get angry later.

'You're not safe here,' he says.

'Tell me about it. Why is everyone lying? Why are there people chasing me, freaking me out? Why is there a stranger in my house telling me he's my fiancé?'

The driver talks as fast as he drives. 'I need to get you somewhere safe first. We gotta shake these cops off.'

'Where are we going?'

'I don't know. I don't even know if there is a way out of this bullshit place. At least not by road.'

I wince at the pain around my temples.

'You okay?' he asks.

'Nope.'

'Headaches?'

'All the time.'

'That figures,' he says. 'God knows what they're pumping into you night after night.'

I take my fingers off my head. 'What?'

He floors the accelerator, and I jerk backward in the seat.

We're opening up a decent gap between us and the chasing police cars.

'Drugs,' he says. 'They're giving you a specific, high-dose cocktail of drugs. That combined with hypnotic suggestion is designed to make you forget—'

The driver yells.

'Oh shit!'

We blitz past a tight junction as a third police car appears out of nowhere. Lights flashing. Now the sirens are blaring as it joins the army of pursuit vehicles. The driver takes a sharp right, and we skid into the turn. I cry out, but it seems like he's in control – at least I hope he is. I don't want to die in a car crash and especially not before I get the answers I want.

Drugs? Hypnosis?

Yet it sounds familiar.

'Things are becoming clearer,' I say. 'My head doesn't feel so heavy.'

The driver nods. 'That's because your re-dose is overdue. Right now, someone's shitting bricks because you're about to remember who you are.'

We pick up speed again. At any moment, I expect to see a wall of police cars blocking the road ahead. But there's only empty space. The town abandoned. I think we're further out on this road than I've ever been, and I have no idea where it leads. Right now, I'll take it.

'Alex and me,' the driver says. 'We conned our way in by pretending to be extras and actors.'

He glances at me.

'I'm David. I drive. I do stunts. Don't you remember me? We've known each other for years.'

The more I force it, the harder it is to remember. 'Your face is familiar. But ... who's Alex?'

'Alex is the guy who followed you into the shop. The guy with the limp. He was trying to tell you that this – all this – is a lie. But they got him. Haven't seen him since. Haven't heard a peep.'

'I feel sick,' I say.

'I can't shake them off,' David says, looking in the mirror. He floors it again, and we race through another set of traffic lights, and to my horror, I'm starting to see the same old scenery whizzing past outside. The same shops, landmarks and street names. We've done a loop. It's like we're trapped inside an urban labyrinth.

The sea of red and blue lights is still on our tail. I think it's five police cars in total, but it could be more.

'Is there no way out?' I ask.

The driver shakes his head. 'This isn't a town. It's a prison.'

'A prison?'

'Not the regular type. But it's as good as—'

Another swarm of cars charges in from the left. Fresh sirens join the orchestra, which feels like it's building to a terrible crescendo. The lead car from this second pack comes at us like a four-wheeled berserker. For a second, I think it's going to slam right into us in some kind of diabolical kamikaze manoeuvre. But it skids sharply to the right and, along with a second car, stops dead. That's a two-vehicle roadblock in front of us. Meanwhile, the first pack is catching up from behind.

We're trapped.

David screams, 'Fuck!'

He's starting to reverse when the lead car from the first

pack rear-ends us. We're both thrown forward, but the seatbelts hold us in place. I gasp. Feels like I've been punched in the stomach. More cars move in, encircling us like a pack of hungry predators.

The driver grimaces. He looks at me. 'Are you okay?'

I nod, but I'm a long way from okay.

'Listen,' he says, unlocking his seatbelt and twisting his body towards me. The movement makes him grimace again. 'This is very important. You—'

Footsteps rush towards the car. The driver's door opens, someone locks an arm around his neck and pulls him outside. His eyes bulge. He makes a choking noise. He puts up a frantic struggle, but once outside, he's quickly overwhelmed and disappears under a sea of navy uniforms. I hear muffled cries of despair.

'Leave him alone!' I yell.

The passenger door opens.

'C'mon,' says a gruff voice. 'You. Out now.'

Strong hands pull me out, and a wall of overpowering torches hits my face. I try to blink it off. *Blink*. I see the grim expressions on their faces. *Blink*. Dead-eyed men, staring at me. Then it happens. The ferocious grip on my arm is released. He lets go just for a second, and the voice of instinct is an instantaneous scream that pushes all other thoughts aside.

Run.

It seems hopeless, yet I do it. I run, perhaps sensing it's my only chance at escaping this, whatever *this* is. I run from the maddening torchlight. Into the night. I hear angry voices behind me. I hear the driver calling after me. His frightened voice escaping through the net of bodies holding him down.

'Go! Go! Go! Your name is H—'

I don't catch the last part. Now I'm running through a gap in between two shops – a newsagent and a jeweller.

The driver makes a squawking noise, and I don't hear his voice again.

I run down a dark alley. It seems to go on for ever. Then the buildings that surrounded me on either side of the alley disappear, and now there's only darkness in front of me. I don't know where I am. I don't know where I'm going. I could trip and fall at any second, but the alternative of slowing down is much worse.

I can't scream for help. There's no one to help me.

I hear the policemen coming, and it sounds like a stampede in my ear. A stampede that's catching up with me.

'Run!' I yell to myself.

After I run in a straight line for what feels like for ever, the alley ends with a chain-link fence. There's no time to hesitate. I vault over it. Land on a narrow path, still on my feet. I keep running, but where am I? I see a path leading uphill. One cloaked in darkness. I have no idea what's up there, but I have to go that way. I run, holding my hands out in front of me so I don't run face first into a tree. I'm blowing hard on the uphill, my legs filling with lead. Holy shit, I can't hold this pace. Much to my relief, the path flattens out. It also narrows, and the last of the stooping trees that lean over it disappear.

My hand brushes against one of the trees.

The branches feel like … cardboard?

I'm slowing down. It's not just all the running. I'm wary of a sizzling electric light up ahead – it's the first real light I've seen in ages. After the chain-link fence behind the shops, I wondered if I was running into some sort of woodland area because of all the trees hanging over the path. But were they real trees? It was too dark to make out much of anything, and I was running for my life.

The light beckons me forward.

I walk into a vast, open space. It's some kind of warehouse, and it's located at the back of the steep path leading out of the woods. The fake woods with their cardboard trees. There are crates stacked on top of one another at the back wall, as many as fifteen or twenty high. Wooden pallets with paint cans on top. A forklift truck parked in the corner. I can smell fresh sawdust, and when I look up, the night sky has given way to the distinct outline of a gable roof. It looks like an empty warehouse, but I didn't run through any doors.

I was outside; now I'm inside.

I *was* outside, wasn't I?

Your name is H—

My headache is gone. I don't know if the hard running did something to my body, but now that I'm still, I realise there's no pain. The mist begins to clear, and I see the cracks in this town. Maybe the drugs are wearing off and, like the driver said, I'm overdue another round of chemicals and hypnotic suggestion.

I don't even flinch when I hear them running up the path. Not even when I hear them call out to me. When they grab me, throw me to the ground and cuff my wrists.

Are they even real police?

Doesn't matter. It's too late. There's nothing they can do now.

I remember everything.

PART II
JIMMY

21

Jimmy can see his nervous breath leaving his body. Every time he exhales.

Why is the bathroom so cold? All the money this massive network has and they can't even install basic heating in the bathroom? Then again, he's always felt the cold, ever since he was a little boy. His dad thought he was a bit soft. Of course, the old man never said as much (his mum would have gone ballistic), but Jimmy could see it in his eyes. That look of disappointment when Jimmy kicked a football or tried his hand at karate. *Soft. Too sensitive.* That's what those beady little eyes were saying.

Still, the old man mellowed over the years, and besides, that's a thought for another day. If ever he decides to go see a shrink.

Now Jimmy stands next to the hand dryer. Staring at his reflection in the full-length bathroom mirror. *Oh God*, he thinks. *What have I done?*

What am I doing here?

He leans against the sink and takes the phone out of his

pocket. Calls Allie. He told her he'd call before he goes in there. Another glance in the mirror as he presses the phone tight to his ear.

A click.

'Hey you,' Allie says.

The sound of his wife's voice is heaven in his ears.

'Hey!'

'You'll be fine,' Allie says. 'Stop worrying, will you?'

'I didn't say anything.'

'You didn't have to. I can hear it in your voice.'

'Really?'

'Stop worrying, Jimmy. They hired you for a reason, didn't they?'

'Hmmm.'

As he talks, he looks over his outfit for the hundredth time that morning. Smart, pale blue shirt and charcoal trousers. Not a crease in sight (Allie did the ironing). Hush Puppies on his feet. The clothes are okay, but the worst thing was that Allie insisted he get his long hair cut. Jimmy can't stand it. He looks like the sort of guy who works in a bank. And to make matters worse, the short haircut has revealed the beginnings of a slight receding of his hair at the temples. He's only twenty-four, and it looks like he's going bald.

'Did you eat something this morning?' Allie asks.

Right on cue, Jimmy's stomach rumbles. All he could manage was a cup of tea for breakfast, and he couldn't even finish that. His appetite has deserted him. It's this job. Ever since moving into the studio, he's been living off snacks.

'Jimmy?'

'What?'

'Did you eat breakfast?'

'Yeah, I'm stuffed.'

'Where are you calling from?'

'Bathroom.'

She laughs. 'Last minute pit-stop, eh?'

Jimmy tries to smile, and when he looks in the mirror, it's like his mouth has forgotten what to do. The shape it makes is horrifying. 'Yeah.'

'When do you go in?'

'I should probably go in now. I just came in here to ... oh man, I'm nervous, Allie. I'm really nervous about this thing. I keep thinking it's a mistake, you know? Taking this job. Being a part of this. Is this really ... *me*?'

A beat of silence.

'Want to talk to Tina?'

This time Jimmy smiles for real. Just the thought of his four-year-old daughter and everything is instantly brighter.

'Go for it.'

'She's downstairs. Give me a second.'

'Sure.'

Jimmy waits while Allie fetches Tina from the living room. He uses this time to practise his diaphragmatic breathing, which, according to the Google-sourced article he read, helps to trigger the body's relaxation response. To turn off fight-or-flight.

He was freezing cold a minute ago. Now he's hot. It feels like he's standing on hot lava, and he wonders if the floor is heated after all.

The control room. That's where he has to go next. No more hiding from it.

There's a crackle down the line. Distant giggling.

He hears Allie whisper, 'Say hi to Daddy.'

Nothing.

'Tina!' Jimmy says, putting his lips closer to the phone. 'Hi, how are you?'

There's a long pause and more whispering between mother and daughter that Jimmy can't quite make out. He hears Allie's voice next. 'Doesn't seem to be in the talking mood today. Too busy on her tablet.'

'What game is she playing?'

'Have a guess.'

Jimmy could never remember the names of all the games that Tina liked. She liked a *lot* of games, and she had a lot on her tablet. Today it was probably one of those fashion or makeup-themed games sponsored by the big influencers. Those games were huge. Jimmy wasn't too keen because Tina was only four, and sometimes it felt like there was someone older living in his daughter's head. She loved pretending to be a YouTube presenter in front of the mirror. Giving fashion tips to her imaginary audience. Makeup tips. It was cute, but Jimmy and Allie knew they had to keep an eye on it.

'Too many to guess,' he says.

'I thought you'd say that.'

He takes a deep breath. 'Hey, I'd better get in there. Can't hide in the bathroom for ever.'

'That's the spirit,' Allie says. 'Good luck, and remember this – we love you, and you're going to be great.'

Jimmy wants one last hug from his wife before going into the control room and sitting with the two big dogs. 'Thanks. Hey, one last thing.'

'What?'

'I've been laying off the internet, but I wanted to ask about the protests. Are they still—'

Her voice is firm. 'Jimmy, don't even think about that, okay?'

'Just tell me this. Is it still a big deal?'

He senses her hesitation.

'Yes.'

Jimmy knows she'd never lie to him. And she doesn't this time. He glances down at his fingers, the nails chewed to the quick. He hasn't been a nail-biter since he was five.

'I'll talk to you later,' he says. 'Love you.'

'Love you.'

He ends the call and decides on one last visit to the cubicle. Might be a while before he gets another chance. Afterwards, Jimmy washes his hands and sets off to the control room, where he'll spend most of his working day. The long corridor is dark and silent.

He shouldn't have asked Allie about the protests. That was a mistake. He's got a job to do no matter what's happening on the outside.

'Sensitivity consultant,' he whispers.

That's his job title. The one Allie can't stop laughing at, even though it's a growing role within the media and entertainment industries.

His phone vibrates in his pocket. He takes it out and sees a message.

> You got this xxx

Jimmy sends back a love heart emoji. Then he stares at those three words. It's a timely reminder from Allie to focus on the task at hand despite his reservations about the Project. He's there out of necessity and because he has a young family to support. Simply put, this is what he has to do right now. He and Allie were childhood sweethearts, and to say that parenthood caught them by surprise is the understatement of the century.

Jimmy had never been so scared in all his life as he was the day she told him they were expecting. He never planned on being a dad at twenty. There *were* plans, but all that changed, and he knuckled down at college, studying media and communications, alongside working several part-time jobs on the side. Some of those jobs, such as waiting tables in an airport restaurant, had nothing to do with the entertainment industry, but Jimmy did land some gigs studying scripts, and to his surprise, he had a knack for probing dialogue, searching out anything that might cause 'unnecessary offence' to vulnerable or overly sensitive viewers. The term sensitivity consultant emerged, and Jimmy's pretty sure that he was one of the first in the country to specialise in that sort of thing. He wasn't just good at identifying problematic issues, but also at finding solutions.

Sometimes, though, it sucked. Jimmy was well aware that he'd censored some exciting and innovative material simply because of the risk of hurting someone's feelings. He didn't like it, but he needed the money. And in this emerging role with few competitors, it was easy to get his name passed around.

That's how he ended up here at the Project.

This was different. This wasn't a fictitious drama with actors reading from a script that could easily be altered. The Project excited half the nation, but it fiercely pissed off the other half. There was no middle ground here. Jimmy wasn't sure how to be a sensitivity consultant in this context. He'd be sitting in a dark control room for hours every day with two of the most powerful players in the industry. Making sure that nobody went too far. At least, that's what he was supposed to do.

Which begs the question. What's 'too far' look like in a venture like this? And if something did occur and Jimmy had to intervene, would the big guns listen to a nobody who'd officially graduated less than five months ago?

This was too big. Too controversial. And, for once, if someone said the eyes of the world were watching, it wouldn't be an exaggeration.

Jimmy walks the corridor, feeling like it's narrowing with his every step. He glances at rows of framed pictures on the walls. Stills taken from the network's standout TV shows – chat shows, game shows and soap operas mostly. There are portraits of well-known celebrities from the past six decades, all associated with the network. Some faces are missing, those celebs later exposed as paedophiles and perverts. Wherever the wall of shame is, that's where those people belong.

The old-school entertainers look down at him. Jimmy can sense their disappointment. He can even hear their voices in his head.

Going to ruin all our fun now, aren't you? Sensitivity consultant, ha!

He reaches the padded door that leads into the control room. Even though it's not the sort of door you can knock, Jimmy knocks, then enters.

'Morning,' he says.

Helen Hassani and Joel Masterton are sitting behind a wide desk that reminds Jimmy of one of those fancy mixing desks in a recording studio. The sort that music producers are always sitting behind and that always pop up on those making-of-this-classic-album documentaries. Lots of dials and blinking lights. More buttons, switches and sliders than he can count. There's also plenty of space for laptops and, at either side, a phone-charging station.

The control room is small to the point of claustrophobic. There's a low roof that would be classified as dangerous to basketball players. A whiff of fruity perfume makes Jimmy's nostrils twitch, and he regrets the fact that he has to close the door. The room is dominated by three gigantic screens – a master screen in the centre with two smaller (but still big), alternate angle TVs on either side. The screens are hung in front of the desk.

'Good morning,' Helen says.

Joel gives him a nod. Then turns back to the screens.

They're both wearing headsets, tapping away at their laptops. Jimmy has only met them briefly before – when he first came in for a hush-hush interview that he wasn't allowed to tell even Allie about. He did anyway. But it was an assistant who conducted the interview that morning, and in the end, he had little direct contact with Helen and Joel.

Now he's stuck in a room with them. The big dogs.

He wonders if they're going to say anything else. Give him some instructions perhaps?

They keep working with their backs facing him. That quick hello from Helen and Joel's unimpressed look were all he's going to get.

It's okay, Jimmy reminds himself, walking towards the two-seater couch at the back of the room. *It's close to show-time, and they're stressed. Everyone involved with the entire network is stressed, and the protests aren't helping.*

He wonders how bad it is out there.

The two-seater couch at the back of the room is Jimmy's desk. There's no actual desk – it's just the couch. He sits down and unzips his rucksack to pull out the laptop. The squeaky zip is loud enough to make Helen look over her shoulder.

'Sorry,' he says.

If there's one person Jimmy doesn't want to piss off, it's Helen Hassani. She's the creator of the Project. God in a dress, as one of the security guards downstairs called her. Jimmy doesn't know how old she is – in her late forties or early fifties most likely. She's in tremendous physical shape, standing six feet tall, and that's without the heels. This morning she's dressed in a tight-fitting business suit, and as she preps for launch, she has the face of a stern Hindu goddess.

Joel is an American in his mid-fifties. He's a cliché in some regards – overweight, loud and a gaping arsehole of a human being. But there's no doubt he's good at what he does. He's got an impeccable track record when it comes to producing and directing some of the most celebrated and innovative shows in both the US and the UK. Before working in TV, he was involved in rock concert promotion and music videos. The man knows his way around the entertainment industry. He also drinks coffee like it's going out of style.

Jimmy isn't surprised he's been put at the back of the room. He glances right and left, wondering if there's any tea- or coffee-making facilities in the room. Nope. Not even a jug of water. He should have brought something up from the cafeteria to keep him hydrated. Then again, best not to drink too much fluid on the first day. He'll be up and down to pee, and that's only going to piss off the big dogs.

He listens while Helen and Joel communicate with the heads of other departments. These heads are scattered around both the studio and the set itself. There's so much to coordinate that Jimmy feels dizzy just thinking about it. He's been down there. It's a brilliant set – there's no denying the authenticity of what they've created. It's a *real* town. And to think they built it so fast.

Serious money was pumped into this thing. Helen's sister, a famous politician, undoubtedly pulled some strings. And she had good reason to, but Jimmy's not about to bring that up with Helen.

The tension is unbearable as the lights on the ceiling dim.

'And here we go,' Helen says to Joel. Then, into the mouthpiece of her headset, 'Good luck, everyone. Let's make this work.'

'This is television history,' Joel says. He takes a giant swig of coffee from his flask.

Jimmy sits upright on the little couch. After all that time in the bathroom, he needs to go again, but there's no chance, so he's just going to have to hold it. He leans forward. What would a good sensitivity consultant do right now?

He keeps quiet. He pays attention.

As final orders are given to department heads, Jimmy thinks about Allie and Tina. This is good for them. It's a huge opportunity, albeit a terrifying one.

Remember that, he reminds himself. *Remember that when you start thinking about the protests.*

Helen and Joel sit perfectly still at the desk. No more talking. No typing instructions on laptops, phones or talking to the other departments.

You belong here, Jimmy tells himself.

The ceiling lights dim further. Then the big screens light up in unison, and a white shimmering light fills the control room. Someone counts down the numbers.

Three. Two. One.

The centre screen cuts from a shimmering white square to what looks like an ordinary living room in an ordinary house. Jimmy swallows hard. He knows it's anything but ordinary.

He's watching a young woman. She's fast asleep on the couch. There isn't much light except from the TV, which is playing a science-fiction horror movie at low volume. Some kind of *Alien* rip-off by the looks of it.

Jimmy's palms are greased with sweat. This is it. They're on network TV. They're livestreaming on the internet.

The Project happened. It's happening.

'Okay,' Joel says, talking into the headset mic. 'She's bound to wake up in a minute or two. Let's see if this drugs and hypnosis combo works when it matters most.'

Helen talks quietly into the mic.

'Calling the comms department. Get word to the actor playing Tommy upstairs. Make sure he approaches within at least ten minutes of her waking up. No more than that. He must say her name several times over. He must call her Kate and start reinforcing the programme from the get-go. Is that understood?'

22

No one in the control room has said anything for ten minutes.

Jimmy's watching her on the centre screen. 'Kate'. At the beginning, she was completely out of it, and no wonder given the heavy doses of God knows what she's on. It's not just one drug – it's a super cocktail of memory suppressants. And that's before factoring in the hypnotic suggestion. What must it be like in her head right now? What's it like waking up and believing that you're someone else? Living someone else's life, so far removed from your own.

But she's sitting up now. She looks okay. Tired and pale but okay, like the cobwebs are starting to clear.

Jimmy watches the way she rubs circles on her forehead with her fingers. He does the same thing when his head's splitting.

The power of suggestion. She'll believe it all. The clinical trials were extensive and went according to plan. None of the subjects involved in the first- or second-phase trials reported any lasting side effects from the cocktail. Jimmy, along with many others, has his doubts and wonders if all the data was released with the published report. He knows the guinea pigs were paid very well.

He sits back, resting his head on the couch. There's a hum from the ceiling vents, and he welcomes the gust of cool air that blows onto his face. He watches her on the centre screen. Kate is sitting on her couch, looking at the sci-fi horror movie, and he can see that she's trying to make sense of it. Why it's on. Whether or not she was watching it.

He shakes his head.

This is going to be tough, he thinks. *And it's only day one.*

Jimmy notices the wine bottle that's been left on the table. It's a nice touch – that'll explain the initial grogginess and forgetfulness. It also reinforces the possibility of Kate's drinking problem.

'Is everything set?' Joel asks into the mic. Someone responds, and he gives Helen the thumbs-up. 'Car crash prep is complete. We're good to go.'

Helen clears her throat. Her next message is addressed to the stunt co-ordinator, who's somewhere on the set.

'Tell the driver to start his approach.'

23

Jimmy watches the Subaru as it fishtails at speed along the road.

The chaos is inauthentic. Completely manufactured. What they're watching is a carefully choreographed stunt that's been rehearsed to death. The car accelerates and brakes on command. It races towards Kate's gate the way it did in rehearsal. Again, on command, it turns late and slams into the neighbours' gate instead.

'Wow,' Joel says, applauding the big screen. 'Good work, driver. That guy was awesome, huh?'

Nobody else says anything. They're all watching the centre screen, the focus back on Kate inside the house. She heard the crash. Of course she did. Now she's standing at the living-room window, peering through the curtains.

'Well, she's up on her feet,' Helen says. 'That's a good sign.'

Joel nods. 'Oh yeah. Some of the people in the lab tests weren't too steady on their feet after they woke up. Some of them couldn't even stand.'

Helen gives Joel a little sideways look. Jimmy's not sure, but he thinks it's a silent message to shut that kind of conversation down. Especially with a sensitivity consultant sitting at the back of the room.

'Let's make it a little colder when she goes outside,' Helen says into the mic. 'The lower temperatures might revive her more.'

Joel watches Kate, still standing at the window. 'What if she doesn't go out? She might be too fuzzy. Might be content to just stand there at the window, especially if all the other neighbours are out.'

'We'll get Tommy to suggest it if she doesn't. He'll *insist*.'

Joel starts typing on his laptop. 'Better start getting the neighbours out.'

'Not all at once,' Helen says. 'Don't make it look too ... *forced*.'

'Roger that.'

Jimmy's watching the smaller screens now. These offer a variety of street angles taken from the cameras in the streetlights. He leans forward on the couch. He thinks he should say something. Anything to let the big dogs know he's paying attention.

He points at the left-hand screen.

'Is that smoke coming from the back of the car?' he asks. 'You think the passengers are okay in there?'

'They're fine,' Helen says in a blunt voice. She doesn't even look at him, and before Jimmy can react, she's talking into the headset mic again. 'Sam, what are the early viewing figures like?'

Silence in the control room. Helen sits back in the chair, listening to someone rattle off numbers in her ear. She shakes her head. 'Not single totals, please. I want combined. TV and livestream.'

Jimmy leans to the left. He wants to see her face when she hears the numbers. He's not sure what to expect. Excitement? Disappointment? If it's going well, the protests will intensify. If it's a flop, the protests will ... *intensify*?

'That's excellent,' Helen says, her expression static throughout the conversation. Although Jimmy might have seen a split-second sparkle in her eyes. He's not sure. 'Thanks, Sam. Keep me updated every two or three hours.'

Jimmy feels a gnawing discomfort rising inside him, and he can't quite pin it down. He took the job, didn't he? He's here. He's going to have to deal with it. There's action on the centre screen as the street fills up with neighbours. Front doors open. Lights flicker on. The neighbours – the actors playing neighbours – are emerging with well-rehearsed concern on their faces.

'Good news?' Joel asks Helen.

There's a soft knock on the door.

'Come in,' Helen says.

The padded door opens, and a young woman in a cream-coloured apron walks in pushing a trolley of tea and coffee items. There are snacks and biscuits on the lower shelves. Her smile is nervous.

'Tea or coffee?' she asks in a tiny voice.

Helen shakes her head but at least smiles and looks at the woman. Joel waves her away without so much as a glance. What does he need coffee for when he's got a house-sized flask sitting on the desk?

The woman looks at Jimmy.

'Maybe later,' he says, smiling at her. 'Thank you.'

She seems to appreciate that. With a smile in Jimmy's

direction, she reverses her trolley through the doorway. Jimmy gets up to help her, and when she's in the corridor, he closes the padded door. He turns around, and the fruity perfume at the desk catches his attention again.

He sits back down, glaring at the back of Joel's head.

'So, was it good news?' Joel asks for a second time.

Helen manages a stiff thumbs-up, and somehow this casual gesture seems out of place coming from her. 'We're already in the millions. *Hundreds* of millions.'

Joel smiles. 'Can't say I'm surprised.'

Jimmy waits for one of the big dogs to mention the protests. Didn't Sam provide any updates there, or was it all viewing numbers?

'Okay,' Helen says, fully focused on the screens again. 'Where are we now?'

She answers the question herself.

'Kate and Tommy are outside on the street with all the other neighbours. She'll be back in the house soon. All relevant departments, do you hear what I'm saying? Pay close attention to Kate – let's see what sort of state she's in after walking around for a bit, not to mention the mental stimulation of the crash. Does she look awake? Does she look tired? If she goes to bed, we need the team ready to go in there and give her a top-up. Higher dose next time. Builds tolerance. Let's keep this train moving. We're on air, and hundreds of millions of people are watching.'

24

Kate sleeps for ten hours that night, and she receives her higher dose. Except it's not really night, at least not in the real world. They can make it any time of day they want in there. They control everything – the light, the temperature and the weather. When Jimmy walked around the fictional set after getting the job, he was stunned at how they were able to make indoors feel like outdoors. The air was just right. And looking up at the sky, you'd never know it was a projection. The clouds floated. Birds sang, whistled and flew like this world was the real deal.

Jimmy manages about four hours' sleep after his first shift. The studio is home right now, as it is for the vast majority of people working on the Project. No luxury accommodation here. The rooms are small and sparsely decorated. Bed, bathroom and bare walls. No windows and a sickly yellow light dripping out of the ceiling bulb. There's also a constant hum that Jimmy can't place, but it feels like it's in the walls. The distant rattle of machinery. They aren't the sort of rooms that anyone wants to stay in for too long. Not if they value their sanity.

He makes a brief call to Allie before he falls asleep.

'Everyone's talking about it,' she says. 'Like, literally everyone. It's on the news. There are formal debates about the ethics of it. It's everywhere.'

Jimmy knows his wife. She wouldn't say that if it weren't true.

'What about the protests?'

'They're not talking about them in there?'

'Not in the control room. I think they're happy to pretend like it isn't happening.'

'Yeah, well, it's happening.'

'Same intensity or—'

'Bigger. Sorry, I know you don't want me to lie about it.'

'No.'

Her voice is soothing in his ear. 'You're not responsible, sweetheart. You're just ... you're just a guy doing your job.'

'Gotta go,' he says. 'Better grab some sleep before shift number two.'

'Love you.'

'Love you too. Give Tina a kiss from me. I'll call you soon.'

Jimmy signs off and turns out the light. He lies on his single bed in the dark, and it's like lying on a brick. That maddening hum is never gone for long, but that's not the worst of it. He's certain he can hear the protests outside, but that's impossible. The studio gates are far away from this building.

He could check his phone. See what's happening, but he decides against it.

After a restless night, he walks back into the control

room. There's a brief nod from Helen and nothing from Joel, who seems like the kind of guy who'd prefer that sensitivity consultants didn't exist. There are several SCs besides Jimmy involved in the Project. Jimmy wonders if Joel had a bad experience with one of them. Or maybe he doesn't like Jimmy's vibe.

The feeling is mutual.

The big dogs were still at their desks when Jimmy signed off yesterday. He wonders if they got much sleep.

Jimmy sits down and unzips his laptop. He opens up a Word document with his notes and sits quietly, trying to catch up. Nothing much since the crash except sleep, drugs and a reinforcement of the hypnosis strategy.

The poor woman's head must be like mashed potato.

He sighs, feeling more like an ornament than an employee. Kate is sluggish on-screen. Not surprising considering she's been dosed again, a higher dose too. Tests were done, sure, but Jimmy knows fine well they're still in experimental territory here. Messing with someone's mind, quite possibly causing permanent damage. Not cool.

She gets up, walks downstairs and makes breakfast. Tea and toast. Or at least she begins to make breakfast before she gets distracted. She's staring across the street.

Joel giggles.

'Oh boy. Here we go.'

Jimmy doesn't think giggling at the subject's discomfort is appropriate. Not much he can do, but he does make a note. Anything to put a black mark against Joel's name.

Will anyone care, though?

Kate abandons breakfast. She goes outside and stands in the middle of the road. Street cams catch her dumbfounded expression from various angles. Hands on hips, shaking her head. All trace of the crash she witnessed is gone. The debris is gone. And, most notable of all, the mangled fence is perfect.

It's like nothing happened.

Jimmy takes his eyes off the screen. It's not an easy watch, and although he knew it wouldn't be, it's harder than he anticipated. He notices a tiny fly as it floats past him, and wonders how it got in the control room. Back to the screen. Back to that poor woman's confusion. He wants Kate to snap out of it. He wants the Project to fail, but it's the best payday of his young working life, and being part of such a high-profile event will open doors down the road. No doubt about it. So what if he's an ornament and the two chief architects are completely ignoring him? He could choose to sit at the back of the room, play games on his laptop and watch the money roll into his bank account.

Helen and Joel would most likely prefer it that way.

'Huge spike in the livestream audience,' Joel says, his voice raspy as he browses the updated stats on his laptop. Jimmy wonders if the producer had a late night. There's a staff bar on the fifth floor for socialising, not that anyone in the higher-ups is going to ask Jimmy (or any of the sensitivity consultants) along for a drink anytime soon.

'*Huge* spike,' Joel repeats.

Jimmy sips from a cup of green tea he made for himself in the staff kitchen. He lowers the cup onto a coaster on the floor, watching Kate as she walks over to the neighbours' fence. A fence that should be wrecked after the car crash.

'You gotta laugh,' Joel says. His headset is off. This is a private exchange between him and Helen. 'Right?'

Helen doesn't take her eyes off the big screen. 'It's not a comedy.'

'Of course not,' Joel says. But the smirk remains on his face. He knows what television gold looks like, and he's got it right here.

Jimmy thinks he should say something. But he's distracted when Helen starts talking to someone else in another department. She's prepping for the neighbour to come out and initiate a conversation with Kate.

'Everything set?' Helen asks into the mic.

A pause.

'Good. A nice, relaxed walk to the end of the garden. All she's doing is putting a rubbish bag in the bin outside. It's just another Sunday morning. Let's see if Kate starts asking questions. If not, Sarah can strike up a conversation. About the weather. About anything that isn't the crash.'

Helen watches Kate for a few seconds before issuing final instructions.

'Sarah will need to improvise depending on what Kate says to her. But the essence of her response remains the same. Deny. Deny. Deny.'

25

Joel walks back into the control room after a long visit to the bathroom. As one hand pushes the heavy door shut, the other tugs at the zip on his fly as if to make sure he closed *that* door properly.

'Hot damn. I needed that.'

Jimmy watches as the big producer goes back to the desk. He sits down with an epic sigh, and the floor shudders under his weight. Jimmy thinks he can smell something drifting to the back of the room, and he wants to believe it's funky-smelling soap.

'Hope you washed your hands,' Helen says, watching Joel pick up his phone off the table.

'Always.'

Jimmy has his doubts.

It's Monday in Kate's world. Nothing much is happening on-screen. Kate's at work in Little Market, and despite some apprehension in the control room, she put on her uniform that morning as if she'd done it a thousand times before.

Same thing with walking to work – navigating the route from the house to the main street and through the sliding doors of the supermarket. Saying hello to long-time colleagues she'd never met before. Going upstairs to the staff room. To the bathroom and then back down to the shop floor to work. Knowing and living out the routine that was pre-programmed in her mind.

It's incredible, Jimmy thinks. *And awful.*

Jimmy watches as she goes through the motions of Kate's life. The actors masquerading as Little Market employees keep her busy. They reinforce too, using 'Kate' over and over again in conversations to the point where it sounds odd. But little things like that help, according to the science people. Just in case the chemically induced brain fog lapses and true memories start spilling through.

Jimmy wonders what it feels like inside her head. Does it feel like a dream? A dream of being someone else? It must be so weird. Lifelong truths buried alive under drugs and force-fed lies. She's suffering from headaches, that much is obvious. On top of that, she's having to deal with people denying the car crash.

A sudden sweat breaks out, and Jimmy unbuttons his shirt at the top to let some air in. The control room is too warm today. He looks at the screen. At Kate. She's not the victim; that's what they say. She was put here for a reason. For a good reason.

He can't fixate on any of that. He has to remember his *why*.

Allie. Tina.

Career advancement.

He flaps his shirt, trying to conjure up a breeze.

Joel leans a little towards Helen. It looks like he wants to have a private conversation, yet there's no attempt to lower his voice. 'Hey, I got a call when I was sitting on the john.'

Helen doesn't look surprised. She *does* lower her voice, but Jimmy, with a little effort, still catches it. 'And?'

Joel makes a strange whistling noise that makes him sound like a kettle. 'They're getting excited.'

'They've seen the stats.'

'The numbers *are* good,' Joel says.

'I know what they want. But it's still too early to even think about *that*.'

'Is it though?'

'Yes.'

Joel points at the big screen. He's grinning from ear to ear as he watches Kate stacking shelves in Little Market.

'This thing could've crashed and burned before take-off. The drugs could've failed. Maybe the hypnotic suggestion. Maybe none of it takes, and she remembers from the get-go. But look at it, Helen. We've got something magical here. It's flying high, beyond our wildest expectations.'

He gives a little round of applause.

'Congratulations, Helen,' he continues. 'You just created the greatest television show on earth. You know people used to praise my early shows in the States and call them revolutionary. Bullcrap. *This* is truly revolutionary. All the shit you had to go through to get this thing done. And here we are. And just ... look at it.'

He shows his approval with a chef's kiss.

Helen glances at the producer. There's not a flicker of emotion on her face. 'This is more than a television show.'

'Right,' Joel says. 'I didn't mean anything ... you know?'

The room falls silent except for the hum of the ceiling fan.

Jimmy sits back, watching Kate. There's a heaviness to the way she moves from aisle to aisle. She looks sad and broken, but only because they've got her believing it. Jimmy feels the sluggishness in her arms as she lifts packets of sliced bread off the trolley and slides them onto the shelves. She stops for a second, her vacant eyes scanning the surroundings. Jimmy wonders if she remembers. If something of her true self is trying to break through the fiction.

She goes back to stacking shelves again.

Jimmy squirms in response to a growing tightness in his stomach. Again, he flaps at his collar to cool down, and he wonders if the ceiling fan is working properly. It's not the toast or banana he ate in the cafeteria that's making him uncomfortable. He can't stop thinking about Tina. There's a nagging thought that he should text Allie and tell her that they need to limit Tina's tablet time. Can't be good for a child, that's what Jimmy's mum says, and maybe she's right. She's *definitely* right. Tina needs to go outside more. She definitely needs to go outside more and go easy on the influencer games.

But that's more of a face-to-face conversation with Allie. And there's going to be a lot of protesting on Tina's part.

Still, it has to be done.

'So,' Joel says to Helen. 'What do you think?'

Helen's response is immediate. 'I'm still in charge. That's what I think. They shouldn't be calling you to try to influence me.'

Joel lowers his voice again. 'Well, you know how the network views things, right? They're in charge, not us. I mean, they're paying the bills here. Right?'

'What are you saying?'

'They've seen the numbers and, well, it doesn't feel like they're asking anymore, you know?'

Helen sighs. 'It's not a good look. Considering there are still ... objections.'

Objections, Jimmy thinks. *Is that what she calls the protests?*

'What else did they say?' Helen asks.

Joel takes a heroic slug of coffee and wipes the back of his hand over his chin. He lowers the flask onto the desk. 'Just what you'd expect to hear. This was always on the cards if the show took off. Well, it took off, and they've got major brands contacting them left, right and centre. And the money they're ready to throw at us – it's disgusting.'

Jimmy nods. Now he knows what they're talking about, and it only confirms a rumour that's been floating around the studio since the start.

Ads.

Joel sighs. 'They make a valid point, you know?'

'What point is that?' Helen asks.

'That justice doesn't have to exclude profit.'

There's a subtle shake of the head from Helen. Jimmy can't see her face, but he imagines that she's wincing. Or maybe he's projecting his own feelings about Joel and his marketing pitch.

'You know why we're doing this,' Helen says, 'don't you?'

Joel hesitates, like he's searching for the right thing to say. He clears his throat, and Jimmy is sure he can smell the man's coffee breath from across the room.

'Of course I do. And I understand it's more than just a television show for you and your family. It's more than a show for me too, but this is a very unique situation. It's *unprecedented*. There's no previous template to work from.'

Helen says nothing.

Joel keeps working at it. 'It's inevitable,' he says. 'It was always inevitable, and I think, deep down, we both knew it. Brands advertise where eyeballs are. And right now, all the eyeballs are on our show. *Your* show.'

'The people who're against us,' Helen says. 'How do you think they'll react to ... *ads?*'

Joel is quick to respond. 'It won't be pretty at the beginning. But we keep it subtle. Soft introduction. Minimal intrusion only, and the network has already said that if we do this, they'll make the usual philanthropic noises, you know? Five per cent donation of ad revenue to the appropriate charities. All that stuff looks great on paper.'

Jimmy is dying to ask, *What about the other ninety-five per cent?*

He's convinced they've forgotten he's in the room with them. Or, at best, they think he can't hear them because they're lowering their voices. Still, he keeps quiet. He doesn't want to throw them off.

'The Project is a very expensive setup,' Joel says. 'There's also that to consider.'

'We have direct government funding.'

'Sure,' Joel says. 'But a little financial cushion is good for the Project. Keeps our options open, don't you think? And it's good for the longevity of what we're doing here. I mean, who knows how far we can go if this thing succeeds? Television, law enforcement, justice – we're pioneering something truly revolutionary here.'

There's that word again, Jimmy thinks. *Revolutionary.*

Helen and Joel continue to go back and forth on the merits of advertising. Meanwhile, Kate drops a can of tinned beans that she was about to shelf in Little Market. She stares at it for a while as it rolls away down the aisle. She plods after it, stiff and zombie-like. Bends over to pick it up. When she straightens up, Kate rubs her temples. She winces. Then looks around with that glazed expression. Like she isn't really there.

That's too much for Jimmy. He gets up and leaves the room, not caring if they notice or not.

26

'What the hell ... did you see that?' Joel jumps to his feet faster than a man his size should be capable of. He's pointing at the centre screen.

'Did you see that?' he yells. 'That son of a bitch across the road is signalling her. He's ... he's *talking* to her, for God's sake!'

They all saw it. Jimmy sure as hell saw it. Kate's walking home from Little Market, and there's a man across the street, trying to get her attention. Jimmy's no lip-reader, but even he can see that he's calling her by name. Not her real name but the name she thinks is real. He walks with a limp, and he's shadowing her every move. Looks like he's waiting for a break in traffic.

Helen stands up, bending forward for a closer look at the screen. 'This is not part of the schedule.'

Joel grabs the headset off the desk. Puts it on. 'Damn straight it's not!'

He yells into the mic, 'This is an emergency call to ALL

departments. Suspected sympathiser inside the town and across the street from Kate right now. Brown hair, long coat, pronounced limp. You see him trying to get her attention? This is a problem. Talk to me.'

Helen remains a statue, staring at the screen. 'If he gets within earshot ... if he says the wrong thing ...'

'Emergency intervention,' Joel barks into the mic. 'We need an emergency intervention now. NOW! Send the police. Lights flashing. Sirens blaring. Let's scare the shit out of this guy, whoever the hell he is.'

Helen's fingers curl into tight fists. She keeps them balled at her sides.

'If he says her name—'

Joel doubles over like he's going to be sick on the desk. 'It's toast.'

Jimmy's the only one in the room still sitting down. He watches the big dogs as they panic. No wonder Joel's feeling sick with all that proposed ad money at stake. Which is strange. Joel Masterton is already a multimillionaire and one of the most successful television producers in recent history. How much money does he need?

Jimmy is aware of the excited fluttering in his stomach. There's no denying his reaction to this unexpected incident. He's rooting for the man with the limp, and it should feel like a betrayal of his employers and of his position. But it doesn't. It feels natural. But he knows the guy with the limp is up against powerful forces, and if something is going to happen, it has to happen now.

'Run, for God's sake!' Joel yells at the screen. He's got his hands clasped over his head. 'Run, you stupid bitch.'

Ordinarily, Jimmy would've taken note of that last word, and he still might do later if he remembers. Build that shit list against Joel. Why the hell not? But there's too much happening right now, and a chase has broken out on the main street. The 'suspected sympathiser' has weaved his way through traffic, and now he's on the pavement on the other side, hobbling after Kate. There's a manic look on his face. No wonder she's running.

'Who the fuck is that guy?' Joel asks. 'Where are those goddamn cops? I wanna hear those sirens now!'

They watch as Kate runs into a corner shop. The man with the limp isn't far behind, but they can't be sure if he saw her go in or not.

'Do we have a camera in there?' Joel says into the mic. 'Talk to me, you motherfuckers. Do we have a camera in that store?'

He gets the answer, and it looks like he's been punched in the ribs.

'Negative.'

'No camera?' Helen asks.

'I said negative.'

To their horror, the man with the limp follows Kate into the shop. They have no footage of what's happening. No audio. It's anyone's guess as to what's going on, and Jimmy's trying to think of something useful to say when he hears the first of the screaming sirens in the studio speakers. It's getting louder by the second. Sounds like the town is on fire.

'Hurry up,' Helen says. When she looks at Joel, Jimmy sees a taut vein sticking out on her neck. 'We need them there now.'

Jimmy wants to calm things down, but that feels impossible in the heat of the moment. He wonders what the police officers will do to the man with the limp when they get hold of him. Who's in charge of making that decision? Jimmy doesn't even know if the police officers are real law enforcement. Are they just actors like everyone else? Or do they have any actual power?

Helen and Joel stare at the shop exterior. The footage is taken from one of the many street cams up and down the main street. It's like authentic CCTV footage but with far superior picture quality.

'What the hell is happening in there?' Joel asks.

Helen has a hand clamped over her mouth. It looks like she might pass out at any second. Slowly, she sits down. Her eyes never leave the screen.

'They've been in there too long. This isn't—'

'Look,' Joel gasps. 'She's out.'

Kate races through the door. She's back on the pavement and straight onto the road, cutting out in front of traffic that stops and slows too easily for her. No one toots their horn. No one yells or calls her names.

She keeps running.

The man with the limp comes out just as the first police car pulls up. He's yelling after Kate and paying no attention to the police. The car doors are flung open. Two officers (or actors) in uniform run out, swarm the man and forcibly drag him towards the car. He's still yelling over the sirens. Still yelling when he's cuffed. But whatever the message is, it's lost in the racket.

27

'This doesn't feel right,' Jimmy says.

It just happens. He finally speaks up, and he's not sure why or what triggered this sudden desire to make his voice heard. That's what Jimmy tells himself, but in reality he knows exactly why he did it.

It's Tina. Again.

About an hour ago, Allie sent him a photo of Tina sitting on the living-room floor, playing with her tablet. Lost in that world. Today, it's games. Tomorrow, social media and then what?

Allie wrote a message alongside the photo – *Tina misses you a lot. She even cried last night because you weren't there.*

The message caught Jimmy off guard, and he had to go for a five-minute bathroom break. He didn't cry or anything like that, but he sat there on the toilet, feeling like his heart had been ripped out. God, it was awful being away from them like this.

He sent a love heart back to Allie and Tina, then tucked the phone into his pocket.

Jimmy poured some cold water on his face. Then he went back to the control room, sat on the couch and felt lightheaded. He was ready to move on, but there was something nagging away at him, and as much as he tried to ignore it, it wouldn't leave him alone. How many kids around the world were losing themselves in games and social media and influencer stuff just like Tina? It was happening whether people liked it or not. Sure, it wasn't perfect. But it was happening, and there had to be a better way of—

C'mon, man, he urges himself. *Get it together.*

He looks at the centre screen.

A few hours have passed since the man with the limp was taken away in the back of a police car. Jimmy doesn't know what happened to him. It won't be pretty considering the guy was on the brink of derailing everything – the show, the incoming ad revenue and whatever else the Project was bringing home for those invested in its success. The shit certainly hit the fan after that near miss. Frantic calls were made. There was a lot of shouting. Not surprisingly, the higher-ups in the network have fast-forwarded the introduction of advertising. Tests have already begun on the livestream (skippable and non-skippable ads), and soon old-school ad breaks will be introduced into the network broadcast.

No announcements will be made. It's happening, and it remains to be seen how the public will respond.

Jimmy's not sure how much more he can take of this. What if it were Tina up there? What if *this* becomes a thing and fifteen or twenty years from now, it's Tina up there? Thinking she's someone else while the world watches and laughs and absorbs pop-up ads for toothpaste as they flash in the sidebar?

Joel's talking to Helen about the livestream 'pause' ads when Jimmy speaks out. He's telling her that if you pause the livestream, a static ad appears on the screen. *Not intrusive at all*, Joel says like it's a noble thing he's doing. As soon as you hit play again, the ad is gone. Hardly interferes with the viewing experience at all.

That's when Jimmy says his piece.

'This doesn't feel right.'

The big dogs both look at him like a china figurine on the mantelpiece just said something. A cold fire burns in Helen's eyes.

'What do you mean?'

Jimmy's got their attention. But now he's got it, he's not so sure he wants it. 'I don't know. It feels personal. It's ... it's ...'

'Spit it out, kid,' Joel says, looking amused at Jimmy's discomfort. 'What good is a sensitivity consultant who can't talk? Or is that insensitive of me? I'm not sure what I'm allowed to make fun of these days.'

He laughs at his own crass joke.

'How long before they charge to watch this?' Jimmy asks. 'How long before there's a subscription fee or it becomes a pay-per-view model or something like that?'

Joel's amused expression is gone. It's like someone flipped a switch. 'Huh?'

Jimmy thinks about Tina, and it's her face that distracts him from the slow, heavy churning in his guts. Feels like he's about to throw up. He's blushing too, but the dim light in the control room conceals the redness of his face. At least he hopes so.

'You guaranteed no fees. No ads.'

His voice is reedy and weak. Surely they can't take him seriously.

'Charge?' Helen says. 'You think we're going to charge a fee?'

'Yes.'

Joel cuts in. 'Listen, kid. You don't need to get your knickers in a knot. We've got government and corporate sponsorship. No need to charge a fee, not that it's any of your business, *Sensitivity Consultant*.'

The producer gives Helen a look as if to say, *why is this guy even in the same room as us?*

'Spit it out,' Helen says. 'Whatever you're saying, I'm sure there's someone else out there saying it too.'

The control room has never felt so small to Jimmy. It feels like they're having this conversation in a phone box.

'I don't get putting ads on the platform,' he said. '*This* platform. What it's supposed to represent.'

Joel manages a smile. He's already halfway turned back to the wall of screens. 'No offence, son, but that's not your concern.'

'Well, actually—'

Helen's hand goes up, cutting Jimmy off.

'I respect your curiosity but remember why you're here. One, it ticks the right boxes. Two, your job is to notice the little things that we of an older generation might miss.'

'I don't think young or old will approve of ads,' Jimmy says.

Joel grunts what sounds like a swear word under his breath. Then he spins around to face the couch, coffee flask in hand. 'Advertising and revenue have nothing to do with your job description.'

Helen looks at Joel. 'Pull up the comments on the livestream.'

Joel sighs. He grabs his mouse, clicks on the livestream and browses the chat and comments. 'People are pissed.'

Helen nods while still looking at Jimmy. 'But are the numbers down?'

'Well, there are a lot of people threatening to stop watching,' Joel says, still browsing the comments. 'Guess they've noticed the ads.'

'What about the numbers?'

'Still going up.'

'That's what I thought.'

Helen gives Jimmy a stern look. Then she pulls out a sheet of A4 paper from a folder in her laptop case, holding it aloft, but from where Jimmy's sitting, he can't see much. A bar chart? A wall of text underneath, perhaps.

'I got this report about half an hour ago,' Helen says. 'Global numbers – *global* numbers, that is – have risen consistently since we launched. Meanwhile, protests are fizzling out both online and in person. I don't like it any more than you do, but ads are an important part of broadcasting reality. They're inevitable.'

'In other words,' Joel says, 'relax. Okay, kid? We have a finance department to worry about funding. You just worry about how we can avoid offending fourteen-year-old girls with too much time on their hands.'

Jimmy keeps his focus on Helen. 'Considering why you created the Project,' he says, 'I honestly can't believe you're good with ads. Don't you think they ... *cheapen* it?'

There's a flash of cold fury in her eyes.

'No.'

That's all she says. Both Helen and Joel are done with the conversation and back facing the three screens. That's it. They've swatted back Jimmy's rebellion with ease. It went out with a whimper only to confirm what Jimmy knew all along – that he is no match for these people.

They watch the screens in silence.

It's night-time in Kate's world. They watch as she jumps out of bed and tiptoes downstairs in search of a burglar. On one of the smaller screens, Jimmy watches an actor at the back door of the house, scratching at the lock. It goes on. Nothing much happens, but Joel is clearly having a great time, and Jimmy can't imagine the man more entertained if he were in the cinema with a giant bucket of popcorn soaking up his all-time favourite movie.

'This is phenomenal,' Joel says.

Helen shows little emotion throughout Kate's potential-intruder ordeal. For the most part, she checks the stats.

JIMMY DOESN'T SLEEP much that night. Sleeplessness is fast becoming a habit, and he's doing his best to get by on less than four hours. When he walks into the control room the next day, Joel and Helen are at their posts. Not for the first time, he wonders if these people ever sleep.

No greetings are exchanged this time. They don't even look at him. Jimmy's pretty sure it's got everything to do with him speaking out against the ads. Sod it. He's not there to make friends.

He sits down and unzips his laptop. Before paying any attention to what's happening in Kate's world, he replies to a text from Allie. General chit-chat. Another picture of Tina and, thank God, she's not playing with her tablet this time. She's at the table eating breakfast – probably thinking about playing with her tablet after kindergarten.

Jimmy puts his phone on do not disturb. Then he

watches Kate on the centre screen. She's in the supermarket, but then she comes home early that day, looking even more exhausted than Jimmy feels. It must be the drugs, he thinks. They're upping the doses. Giving her too much.

He looks at his notes. Mostly a collection of black marks against Joel and two pages of bullet points touching on the ethics of advertising in this particular context.

The drugs.

Is this something he can use against them?

Probably not. The Project depends on Kate literally being out of her mind. And to do that, they have to big-time dose her.

After going home early, Kate takes a nap on the couch. But Jimmy knows her peace and quiet won't last. The Project has something else planned for her today even though she's exhausted.

He didn't expect this coming in. To have so much sympathy for this woman.

Jimmy puts his laptop to one side. He sits forward on the couch and clears his throat loud enough for the others to have no choice but to notice.

'Can we at least give her time to catch her breath? Let her sleep a little?'

There's a long silence. Joel doesn't even look at Jimmy, but he gives a nonchalant shrug.

'Okay,' Helen says, much to Jimmy's surprise. 'Let's give her twenty minutes uninterrupted. Send word to the street team. No cars. No loud *noises*. Keep the extras quiet if they're working the site right now.'

'Thank you,' Jimmy says.

Helen acknowledges him with a curt nod. Jimmy wonders if she respects him more now because he challenged her about the ads. Or is she doing just enough to keep the sensitivity consultant quiet?

Whatever. At least Kate will get some much-needed sleep.

Joel makes the call. Then he gives Helen the thumbs-up. 'Done.'

Twenty minutes, Jimmy thinks. *I should have said thirty.*

'Camera seven, please,' Helen says, talking into the mic. 'Let's make that the focus for the next segment. It gives the best view of the living room, and we get a clear view of the door leading into the hallway. That's where she'll be coming from.'

'Prepping for Uninvited Guest,' Joel says.

The big dogs tap away on their laptops. They send texts and converse with other departments on their headsets.

'I thought she was getting a rest,' Jimmy says.

Helen glances at the digital clock on the wall. 'Her twenty minutes will be up by the time her visitor arrives.'

'We've got an audience to entertain,' Joel says. 'They're not tuning in to watch her take a nap.'

He laughs.

'Then again, there's plenty of people who'd do just that.'

Jimmy watches Kate sleeping on the couch. She looks as peaceful as he's ever seen her since the Project launched. No one's dosing her with anything. He looks closer. Wonders if she's dreaming as Kate or—

Fuck.

He closes the ads that keep popping up on his laptop livestream. Others pop up right away. What was it Joel said? Not intrusive at all?

'Wakey-wakey, everyone,' Joel says, securing his headset. 'Here comes the uninvited guest.'

Helen turns a dial on the desk, dimming the control-room lights. A street cam follows the blonde girl in the gorilla costume as she walks towards Kate's house. The head is tucked under her arm. She stops at the gate and looks back over her shoulder. There's a wave in that direction, as if acknowledging a signal. She puts the gorilla head on. Gives a thumbs-up to whoever gave her the signal.

Jimmy opens up a brand-new Word document. In bold letters, he types:

THIS IS WRONG. THIS IS NOT JUSTICE.

'Is the front door unlocked?' Helen asks.

Joel nods. 'Check.'

'Alright,' Helen says. 'Three-two-one—'

She pauses the count for a moment, and Jimmy's surprised to see her glancing over her shoulder at him. He realises he's slouching and sits up straight. All the while, trying to hold her piercing gaze.

'Don't feel sorry for her,' Helen says in a soft voice. And then she points at Kate on the centre screen. 'Remember who she is. Most importantly, remember what she did.'

28

The Uninvited Guest prank went according to plan. Until it didn't.

The first part was excruciating for Jimmy. He had to sit there at the back of the room, listening to Joel laugh throughout the poor woman's ordeal. It was surreal to watch. Kate was stunned as Gorilla Girl marched into the house, the living room, the kitchen and then back into the living room, where she sat on the armchair, turned on the TV and began to eat an apple. It looked spontaneous, but like the car crash, it was a routine that had been rehearsed to death. There was nothing spontaneous about it.

Jimmy wondered if the stunt would have any impact on Kate's memory. Was there any chance she would see something familiar and remember?

It didn't happen. Not that Jimmy could see. Gorilla Girl did her thing, but after she ran out, Kate went after her.

That was when things started going wrong.

Now, the control room is simmering with tension. Joel sure as hell isn't laughing anymore, and that silence is music to Jimmy's ears. Helen, Joel and Jimmy sit watching the big screen, and Jimmy imagines it's the same across all the departments. Horrified expressions. The realisation that heads are going to roll for one simple mistake that might just have ruined everything. That might have killed the Project.

Kate has found an earring on the road. At first, no one knew why it mattered. It was just a little diamond stud – unusual to find it on the road, but so what? Although there wasn't meant to be any litter or debris lying around on the pavement or road after the crash. But big deal. Right? Then someone in another department called, informing Helen about the driver on Saturday night. Told her he'd been wearing an earring just like the one in Kate's hand. Several people had noticed it.

Looks like Kate noticed too.

After the call, Helen slams a fist on the desk, and Jimmy feels the walls of the control room shudder. She sits there in silence for a second. Even Joel is wary of talking.

Helen lets out a slow whispering hiss that forms a word. 'Fuck.'

It's the first time Jimmy's heard the creator swear. But Helen's a smart woman. She knows what Kate's discovery could mean for the Project. For everything she's worked so hard to build.

'That fucking driver,' Joel yells, gesturing to the screen. 'It must have been all that jumping around he was doing. Stupid freaking asshole lost his earring.'

Now, Kate's marching over to Jack and Sarah's house. She knocks the door and almost gets into a fight with the actress playing her neighbour.

'Oh shit,' Joel says, his hands clamped to his head. There's a waxy, yellowy tinge seeping into his California suntan. 'This is teetering on the edge of chaos. What do we do? What *can* we do?'

He looks at Helen.

'Shut up, Joel,' she hisses. 'I'm trying to concentrate.'

Kate's confrontation with the neighbour lasts several minutes. Hidden mics capture most of the conversation, but the audio isn't required to know what's going on. Kate holds up the diamond earring. It's almost a straight-up fight after that, then the husband shows up, and Kate backs off.

'She knows they're lying,' Jimmy says, but he might as well be speaking to himself.

Street cams follow Kate's every move. Instead of going back home, she hurries towards the end of the street, looking back at Jack and Sarah's house. Looking up and down the street. Shaking her head.

'She needs to go home,' Joel says. 'She needs to go home, chill the fuck out and go to bed so we can dose the shit out of her. Maybe she'll forget the earring, who knows?'

Jimmy feels a weird flutter of excitement in his stomach. Still, he marks that phrase down – *dose the shit out of her.*

Thanks, Joel, he thinks.

But maybe he won't need a shit list to ruin Joel. If Kate remembers—

Helen stands up with enough force to topple her chair. There's a loud clattering noise that interrupts Jimmy's thought process. Helen leans over the desk, grabs the headset mic and speaks in a shrill tone.

'Who missed that diamond earring on the road during the clean-up? I want that bastard's head. And the driver's too. My God. We made a car crash disappear, but we couldn't manage to pick up one little earring? Look where that leaves us now. She knows – she knows the crash happened.'

29

Jimmy leans back on the couch and stretches his legs out. He's tired. He misses his wife and daughter more than words can say. But still, this is the best he's felt since walking into the studio.

All that power, control and self-importance brought down by a sparkly earring.

It's beautiful.

Since Kate's discovery, he's gone to the bathroom to check his phone. He wants to catch up on outside news. The protests – what's happening with the protests? But to Jimmy's surprise, the staff Wi-Fi is down. And when he turns off the Wi-Fi tracker, he can't get a signal.

He stares at his phone.

Are they blocking us?

He wonders if it's got something to do with the protests. What else could it be? Jimmy doubts they're fizzling out like Helen said; more likely, they're getting bigger. More intense, especially with the discovery of the earring. She's so close to figuring out the lie. The network doesn't want people working on the Project to see the latest developments and freak out. There are probably other doubters like Jimmy on the inside. And how much or how little would it take for them to switch sides?

How close are they? Jimmy wonders. *Did I really hear them the other night down at the gate?*

Back in the control room, Joel sits at the desk, watching Kate as she walks into town.

'We gotta get her home,' he says. 'Get her sleeping. Get the drugs inside her. It'll all be fine after that.'

'We can't force her back to the house,' Helen says. 'It's not even that late. Let's just see what happens.'

'Why don't we make it later?' Joel asks. 'We can do whatever we want. We're God here, remember?'

Helen nods. She talks into the mic. 'Darken the sky. But keep it subtle. And start bringing the commuters out on foot, bicycles, cars and public transport. Let's make it feel like home time in there. With any luck, she's just cooling off after the argument with the neighbour.'

'I thought she was going to beat the shit out of that actress,' Joel says. He's unscrewing the lid of his coffee flask. 'Or get the shit beaten out of her. Either way, not cool.'

'The actors are insured,' Helen says. 'Right now, our main concern is securing the Project. Making that earring discovery disappear. I hope the hypnotists are paying attention to this. We're going to need them to—'

Joel cuts her off. 'Shit.'

'What is it?'

He's looking at his laptop. His face is haggard and older when he's stressed. 'You're not going to like it.'

Helen's voice is flat. 'Why doesn't that surprise me?' She sighs. 'Tell me anyway.'

'They want her to find out.'

'What?'

'The majority of viewers want Kate to find out she's not Kate. They want her to rumble the whole thing. There's a poll in the comments, and eighty-nine per cent are in favour of Kate figuring out the puzzle.'

Jimmy watches Helen's right hand as it balls into a tight fist.

'For God's sake,' she says. 'The Project isn't a fucking game show. There's not a cash prize for finding out the truth. She's in here because ... have they forgotten what she did? Have they forgotten what she *did*?'

Joel takes a slug of coffee from his industrial-sized steel flask.

'I don't know.'

Helen turns back to the big screen. Jimmy hears her voice tremble from the back of the room. 'She's not a hero. She's a ... killer.'

30

They watch as Kate goes inside the pub. There are pinhole cameras installed in the vast majority of buildings in her fictional town. Anywhere with the potential for social gathering was high on the list, but some (including the corner shop where Kate had the encounter with the limping guy) were left out, most likely for financial reasons as the overall costs of the Project skyrocketed. Those places had to make do with street cams on the exterior.

But Helen, Joel and Jimmy can see her now.

She orders a glass of wine. Blitzes through it, then orders two more and takes them to a table near the door. The pinhole zooms in, and Jimmy notices the dazed expression on her face, intermingled with confusion. And why wouldn't she be confused? Everyone in town is lying to her.

Another customer comes in. A young man in his early twenties. He buys a drink at the bar, then looks around for a seat.

Helen's fierce gaze is all over it. 'I don't like this. Why is he sitting so close to her? The pub is empty. There are seats everywhere.'

'Something bothering you?' Joel asks.

'Yes. Something is bothering me. *Look*.'

Joel takes in the bird's-eye view of the seating area, as well as the front door. 'What are we looking at here?'

Helen's attention is divided between her laptop and the big screen. Her eyes are strained, and it looks to Jimmy like she's trying to look *through* both screens. 'That man – is he trying to signal her?'

'What?'

'You heard what I said. He keeps looking over at her.'

Joel takes a moment. 'I don't see it.'

'I saw something,' Helen says. 'I'm sure of it. It was a look – a gesture. Can we get an ID on that man?'

'We can send someone in after she leaves.'

'Shit. We need an instant identification process. We can't afford to have any more sympathisers in there. They're posing as actors, getting hired and coming in to warn her.'

'I still don't see it,' Joel says.

She points at the centre screen. 'Why did he choose *that* seat? Two people in close proximity in an otherwise empty pub. Look at the way he's facing her. Are you trying to tell me that's not awkward in any other situation with two strangers? Unless—'

'Unless what?'

'Unless he's not a stranger.'

Jimmy types notes into a separate Word document.

Something IS familiar about the guy in the pub. Doesn't feel like a coincidence he showed up. Or that he sat there like that. Helen's not wrong. Who is he?

Joel gasps. 'She's up,' he says, pointing at the screen. 'Oh shit, he's up too.'

It all happens so fast. They're on their feet, and words are exchanged between the bartender and Kate. The young guy, perhaps spooked by something, takes off. He makes for the door and leaves his drink without putting the slightest dent in it. Kate doesn't stay in the pub for much longer. Soon she's back on the pavement, walking under the streetlights. Heading for home, or at least somewhere in that direction.

'I don't like it,' Helen says. 'What if he's another sympathiser? Do we have eyes on him?'

'Negative,' Joel says.

'Not good enough. Find him and get him off my set.'

The tension is palpable inside the control room. Jimmy knows that all this technology, as cutting edge and as probing as it is, can't put Helen inside Kate's head. They can see where she is, but they don't know if cracks are forming in her mind, specifically in the Kate narrative she's been drugged into believing. Such an insignificant thing, a diamond stud on the road. And what a disaster it's been for their intricate prison. She knows the car crash happened, and she knows the neighbours and Tommy have been lying to her. Now they're counting on getting her back to the house so they can drug her again.

'Looks like she's going home,' Helen says.

'Yeah,' Joel says. 'Which means we've got a problem.'

'What now?'

'Are we still on for the next one?'

'Hmmm?'

'Partner swap,' Joel says. 'It's scheduled for her going home this evening. The audience know it's coming too.'

'We should cancel.'

Joel sighs. 'I don't think that's a good idea. Might negatively impact momentum, you know? The numbers are consistently going up.'

Helen winces. 'Shit.'

'There's a lot of excitement in the comments. Again, momentum. I think we need to go ahead with it and keep those numbers rolling in. Partner swap – it's a good one.'

'She has to sleep at some point,' Helen says, looking at another sheet of stats. 'No matter how she reacts to Partner Swap, she has to sleep, and wherever that is, we'll be ready to go in and at the very least double dose her. Make her forget about that earring.'

Jimmy's phone vibrates in his pocket. He must've forgotten to put do not disturb back on. He takes it out and looks at a picture of Tina wrapped up in a blanket on the couch. Tablet in hand. There's probably a cartoon playing on TV too. He smiles and feels sick inside.

Double dose. Double dose.

He's about to ask questions about the safety of double dosing when Joel cuts him off.

'She's almost home,' the producer says into the mic. 'Look sharp, people. Everyone on set, get ready for this.'

Jimmy looks up from his phone as Kate walks along the street. She looks over her shoulder like someone who thinks they're being followed. Once, she even stops as if waiting for someone to emerge from the thickening gloom that hangs over that prop of a street.

A final glance across the street towards Jack and Sarah's house. Then she opens the gate and walks to the front door.

Helen and Joel are busy giving and receiving instructions via the headset. To Jimmy's horror, he realises they *are* prepping the next stunt. Or rather, it's been prepped, and they're simply finalising the last few details with relevant department heads and those on the set. The psychological trauma that Kate is going through doesn't warrant a mention. Their only concern is making sure they get through the next prank and then dosing that diamond earring out of her mind.

He has to say something. Not just because it's his job, but he's terrified they're causing lifelong damage to the woman. Is that what they want? Is that the revenge that Helen's been chasing all along?

Jimmy gets to his feet. 'I-I don't think you should go ahead with this one. Too dangerous. She's already in a fragile state and—'

Joel's hand makes a frantic waving gesture. 'Shut up, kid.'

'It's too dangerous.'

'Shut up!'

'As sensitivity consultant, I'm—'

Helen gives Jimmy a look that makes it feel like there's ice water coursing through his veins. He sits down. He's only there to tick the boxes.

Kate opens the front door and steps inside.

'Operation Partner Swap,' Joel says with a wry grin. 'Here we go.'

He looks at Helen and smiles.

'I think she's already forgotten about the earring. Maybe it was the wine, you know?'

Jimmy can't watch. He feels dirty just being there. No one's talking about rehabilitation or justice anymore, and by God, he was so gullible to think at one point that those things were relevant. That they were really on the table. The two big dogs haven't spoken about much excepts stats and audience expectations and ads.

And those fucking ads are everywhere. He can hear them popping up on the livestream on his laptop.

Pop-pop-pop.

Follow all the updates on our socials ... subscribe for email updates ... pop-pop-pop.

Jimmy looks at the photo of Tina on his phone. He doesn't want to watch the Project anymore. He hears the shock and excitement as Kate walks into the kitchen and finds Fake Tommy making dinner. He winces at Joel's wild shriek of laughter as Fake Tommy works the room and tries to persuade Kate that he's the real Tommy.

'Man, that guy's a good actor,' Joel says. '*I* almost believe he's Tommy.'

There's a lot of shouting before Kate bolts. Through the door, onto the street, and Jimmy hears Joel ordering Fake Tommy to chase after her. *Pursuit. Pursuit! We want action!* He wants the neighbours to go outside too. All of them.

'Fuck yeah!' Joel yells, getting to his feet. He fist-pumps the air and then stops dead. His face turns white.

'No.'

'What's that car doing there?' Helen asks.

Something in the way she says it makes Jimmy look up from his phone. He zones in on the centre screen. Sees headlights on the dark road. Two balls of light, ballooning in size as a car races from the top end of the street to the middle, where all the action is taking place. It sounds like a drag race is underway in suburbia. The Tommy actor is running after Kate, calling out to her. All the neighbours are outside or at their windows, watching events unfold.

Joel screams into the mic, 'Unknown vehicle approaching. Emergency intervention required, now, now, NOW!'

'How many sympathisers are in the Project?' Helen asks,

a look of disbelief etched on her face. 'Is this another one! How many? This shouldn't be possible. We should've vetted every single one of these actors and extras.'

Joel's voice shrinks to a whisper. 'It's hard to check every single person's background. We didn't think—'

'Well, we should've.'

Both Helen and Joel bark orders into their mics, but it's too late to stop this happening. The car pulls in ahead of Kate, and the passenger door opens.

Jimmy's up on his feet. He watches with a clenched fist, willing Kate to get in the car. Maybe he shouldn't feel this good about what's happening down there on the set, but he does. There's a chance for her if this nightmare fails. There's a chance for all the people who'll follow in her footsteps.

31

The chase is on. The control room speakers are a wild cacophony of revving engines, shrill brakes and sirens blaring.

Helen, Joel and Jimmy are up on their feet, watching five or six police vehicles in pursuit of the car with Kate inside.

'Call them off,' Jimmy says, rushing forward. For the first time since the Project launched, he's standing level with Helen and Joel at the desk. Joel tries to block Jimmy's advance with an outstretched arm. Jimmy swats it away.

'Call them off,' he repeats, his heart thumping. 'They're going too fast.'

The emergency order has been given for all the actors to stay indoors. Building lights have been switched off, but it's not a complete blackout. Streetlights along the main street remain switched on for safety's sake. But when there are no blue and red flashing lights and screaming sirens, the town is a silent, ghostly place. The illusion of everyday life has ceased for now.

'Somebody's going to get hurt,' Jimmy says. 'Maybe even killed.'

Helen nods. 'This *is* too dangerous. The chase wasn't supposed to go on this long. It was supposed to be over in seconds.'

'The world loves a good car chase,' Joel says. He points at the big screen. 'Whatever else this is, it's great content. Check out those numbers.'

Jimmy takes a step back from the desk and pulls his phone out of his pocket. He wants to see the public reaction to this. But when he tries to go online, the connection is still blocked.

He looks at Helen and Joel.

'If people are loving this so much,' he says, 'why is the network blocking the internet in here?'

Joel looks at Jimmy like he's the inside of an unflushed toilet. 'What the hell are you talking about now?'

'I'm not an idiot.'

'The numbers, kid. It's all right there in the numbers.'

'No, it's not,' Jimmy yells. He's shocked at the ferocity of his own voice. Didn't know he had it in him. 'All those people who were against this. They didn't just go away. And you think they're going to like *this*? You're putting her life at risk and the life of everyone else in that chase.'

Joel groans. 'Fucking sensitivity consultants.'

'Six cars,' Helen says, seemingly ignoring the conversation taking place beside her. 'There are six cars, and the chase is *still* going on. There isn't enough town for a chase to last this l—'

Helen stops so suddenly that Jimmy thinks she's about to drop dead on the floor. He watches as she's fed information into her earpiece. Her skin is pale and lifeless as she absorbs the incoming information. Helen sits down and stands up again. It's an odd moment, like she doesn't know what to do with herself. Finally, she speaks.

'Are you serious?'

Helen stays on the line even when the car chase comes to an end. Even when Joel is shouting with excitement as a big police officer drags the driver outside. Sure enough, it's the man from the pub.

'Got you, motherfucker,' Joel says, rubbing his hands together. He hasn't noticed Helen's distress or that she's slowly lowering herself onto her chair and off again. 'Let that be a lesson to all those douchebag sympathisers.'

He touches his earpiece. Yells into the mic.

'Taser the bastard. That's right, you heard me. Shut him up and make sure everyone watching sees it up close.'

'You can't do that,' Jimmy says.

Too late. The Taser darts puncture the driver's skin, and he shakes and shimmies on the ground, his body paralysed. The cops swarm him. He's lost under the pile-up of bodies.

'What are they doing?' Jimmy yells.

Joel pretends to shoot a gun at the screen. 'Trespassers will be prosecuted. That's what happ ... oh shit.'

Kate wriggles free from the big actor who was restraining her. Jimmy sees the shock on her face as she realises her freedom and weighs up what to do with it in the blink of an eye. She runs off the main street, disappearing down a back alley in between shops where there are no cameras. The actors playing cops chase after her.

'Who are these clowns we hired?' Joel says. His arm is cocked back, and it looks like he's about to throw his coffee flask at the big screen. 'Don't they know how to restrain someone?'

The actors/cops are out of visual range.

'Helen,' Joel says, 'we've lost visuals on Kate. We can't let her get too far or she might find—'

When she doesn't respond, he looks at the show's creator.

'Helen?'

Helen's sitting down, palms resting on the desk. Looks like she's holding on for dear life. Her voice is distant, so much so that it sounds like it's coming from another room. 'That's the least of our problems.'

Joel screws his face up. 'The least of our problems. What are you talking about?'

'It's over.'

'Over?'

'The Project is over.'

Joel swallows hard. 'The protestors?'

Helen's watching the empty street where the car chase came to an end. The lights on top of the police cars are still flashing blue and red. Her eyes are dull. The scene in front of her might as well be a Sunday afternoon movie playing in the background.

'They're inside the building.'

Joel turns as white as a sheet. 'W-w-what?'

'They're inside the building,' Helen repeats.

Jimmy can almost hear the wheels in Joel's head turning.

'Okay,' the producer says. 'Okay. So a few of them got inside – no big deal. Nobody panic. We've got security. We've got police protection. Round them up, throw them in a cell and—'

'Not a few,' Helen says.

'Huh?'

'Thousands.'

Joel tries to say something, but the words are trapped in his throat. He makes a weird choking noise, then falls heavily back into his seat.

'I-I want to go home.'

'They got past the walls,' Helen says, talking into the mic. 'Past the guards. Any second now, they'll be inside.'

She looks at the screen.

'If they catch her, they'd better lock her in a room somewhere. I don't want these bastards parading her around like some kind of prize.'

Jimmy's the last one of the three still up on his feet. But he's not about to fall onto the couch and wait for the mob to take hold of him. Without a word, he starts packing his bag. Throws the laptop in. His coat. Then he zips up the bag and opens the padded door, wondering if they'll say something. They don't. They're like two statues behind the desk, not moving. Watching the wall of screens. Seemingly waiting for the end.

Jimmy runs out into the corridor and slams the door shut behind him. He listens. He can't hear anything, at least not yet. Once again, he pulls out his phone, and thank God, there's a signal this time. He notices five missed calls and several texts from Allie.

'Oh God.'

He looks at his feet. It feels like the floor is shaking underneath him. And a deep, dark rumbling from inside the studio. Distant voices begin to spill through the silence. Angry voices. This thing is happening fast.

He calls Allie.

Her voice is frantic. 'Jimmy – what's going on? Are you okay?'

'I'm okay. I'm getting out of here.'

Allie is crying. 'I'm watching it on TV. Jimmy – it's a riot. I don't know if it was planned or not, but everything just ... everything just turned in an instant. They stormed the gates, and now they're storming the building. You *have* to get out of there.'

He nods, listening to the growing chaos. Feeling it under his feet. From somewhere nearby, a woman screams.

'Can I talk to Tina?' Jimmy asks.

'But—'

'Please, Allie. Just ... just let me talk to my daughter.'

PART III
HAYLEY

32

Message received through the Contact Form on Mickey Morgan's official website.
Time: 12.01 a.m.

Hi Mickey!

It's me again. Hayley Davies.

I wrote to you before and sent a few DMs via your socials. Guess you didn't see them? I know you're super busy, and you must get a ton of stuff coming in on a daily basis, but I thought I'd try again.

Wow! Congrats on your success. It's AMAZING. Your YouTube videos are getting better all the time. I like the informal chats, the ask-me-anythings, but the big ones (the pranks and setups) are next frigging level, man. LOVE IT! I've sent a few Insta-DMs with some suggestions if you're interested/looking for ideas, so I won't take ages telling you again. But it's a good breakdown, and I think I have an eye for this sort of thing. Look for messages by @HaylsDV in your inbox.

Anyway, I love what you do. The world would be a much sunnier place if we could laugh at ourselves more. Corny but true.

Any advice for someone trying to break through?

I've been trying to get my channel going, but I can't get viewers to stick around, lol! That's if they turn up in the first place, which they don't. I don't know if pranks are my thing (I'm not as brave as you!), but I'm trying to do something. Find my brand. How do you do it? Is it just a case of hanging around long enough until something sticks?

Lol, I sound desperate, right?

Hope you don't mind me messaging again. There's no one else for me to talk to about this. Things aren't great at home, but I told you about that in the first DM, and I won't bore you again.

I think I can become an influencer. Any advice? (I know I've asked already, lol!) I'd appreciate it. Just a couple of words of encouragement would do.

Your NUMBER ONE fan,

Hayley Davies.

33

*S*he stares into the camera, her milky pale skin lit up in a narrow shaft of sunlight beaming in from the left. Her dull, brown hair falls past her shoulders onto a maroon sweater covered in cat hairs. She smiles and straightens up as if signalled by a clapperboard in her mind. Her back is against the wall, her eyes wrestling with the camera's gaze.
A nervous giggle. A deep breath.
She's ready.

HAYLEY: Hello, everyone! Welcome back to Hayley's Channel. If you don't know who ... umm ... what I mean is, for anyone who doesn't know me, my name is Hayley Davies. I'm sixteen years old, and today I'm making ... umm ... I think this is my third comeback to YouTube.
Another spurt of nervous laughter.
HAYLEY: Okay, well, let's talk about my second comeback. I guess that last video wasn't such a smash hit with you

guys. I think my cat is cute, and just for the record, Cecil *does* talk like an old man. And ... umm ... he does some other funny things too. Just not when I point a camera at him.

Ha!

Doesn't matter. Umm, that was then and this is now, and I'm back, I guess. Third time lucky.

Hayley stops. She glances off-camera, as if hearing a noise from somewhere else in the house.

She waits.

HAYLEY: Must've been Mum dropping something.

Her smile returns.

HAYLEY: What was I saying again? Oh yeah, message received loud and clear. No cat videos. Movie reviews weren't a hit in phase one either, so I suppose that's out too. The cooking vids – were they that bad? Yeah, I guess it helps if you can actually cook.

A mobile rings. Hayley picks her phone off the stand (without ending the livestream), and as she swings it around, we get a brief glance of her sparse bedroom. There's a full-length mirror on the wardrobe door. Faded white walls and a carpet with loose threads and other signs of cat damage. There's a single bed tucked in at one side of the room, and a poster of Mickey Morgan is the only sign of decoration.

She answers the phone.

HAYLEY: Hi, David. Let me put you on loudspeaker.

She does this before returning the phone to its stand.

HAYLEY: If you've watched any of my previous videos, then you'll probably know who David is. We go to school together. He's kind of annoying and follows me around everywhere.

David's voice is loud and distorted.

DAVID: C'mon, Hayls. Tell it like it is – we're best buds! We've known each other since we were toddlers.

HAYLEY: Whatever. Are you my one viewer?

DAVID: I felt sorry for you.

HAYLEY: Thanks.

DAVID: Don't feel bad. Hey, it sounds like you're a little rusty in front of the camera.

HAYLEY: Umm, there's no need to say that while I'm still filming. Idiot.

DAVID: But no one else is watching.

HAYLEY: There you go again.

DAVID: I've told you before, Hayls. This influencer/YouTuber thing is a long game. Mickey's numbers weren't always what they are now.

HAYLEY: He's flying right now. His last video is already on three million hits. Uploaded, wait for it, five hours ago. *Three million!*

DAVID: You love him, don't you?

HAYLEY: David, go away.

Another noise from downstairs. She stares at the door.

DAVID: You alright?

No answer.

DAVID: Earth calling Hayley Davies.

HAYLEY: What is it?

DAVID: I said, is everything okay?

HAYLEY: Yep. Mum's just been a bit clumsy recently. I'd better go down soon, make sure she hasn't fallen over again.

DAVID: Fallen over? Is that what she tells you?

HAYLEY: David, I'm live on YouTube.

DAVID: Sorry.

HAYLEY: I'd better go check. Bye.

DAVID: I'll call you later.

Hayley waves at her friend, then looks directly at the camera. Counting the stats in the sidebar.

HAYLEY: One viewer. Oh well – thanks for watching Hayley's Channel, David.

Clip ends.

34

SMS exchange between Hayley and David.
10.11 p.m.

DAVID: *Hey mate. Soz if I said anything stupid on your video this afternoon. Didn't mean it.*

HAYLEY: *S'alright. I'm stupid for trying again.*
DAVID: *Not if it's what you want.*

HAYLEY: *I don't know what I want.*

DAVID: *I just emailed you something.*

HAYLEY: *Okay. Give me a second. WTF?*

DAVID: *Mickey's signing his autobiography at Waterstones next month. Tickets going fast so I snapped a couple up. Call it an early birthday present. We can get the train.*

HAYLEY: *Thanks. You're a pal.*

35

The next video is titled – MUKBANG #1

Hayley and David have taken over the spare room in David's parents' house. *The bed and furniture have been moved to the opposite side of the room, out of shot. They're sitting on the wooden floor with a gigantic bowl of spaghetti in front of them. Next to that, a bottle of Pepsi and two glasses filled to the brim. There are lots of side dishes scattered across the floor, salad, garlic bread and much more.*

Both Hayley and David chew listlessly, poking their forks into the endless sea of spaghetti they've piled onto their plates. Twirling it around. Staring at the camera. Hayley leans over frequently, checking numbers on the livestream.

DAVID: No one's watching.

Hayley shushes him. She checks the stats for the hundredth time. Searching for comments and engagement on this, her first proper video since the relaunch.

DAVID: We're eating ourselves to death for nothing.
HAYLEY: It's a mukbang. They're popular.
David looks down at his plate in defeat. He runs a hand over his closely cropped hair and groans. His cheeks are glowing.
DAVID: I can't do this.
HAYLEY: What do you mean? This was your suggestion.
DAVID: I regret it.
HAYLEY: This is what you do in a mukbang, David – you stuff your face and talk to the audience.
DAVID: There's no audience, Hayls.
HAYLEY: You're such a wimp.
DAVID: Let me ask you a question in front of your massive *audience*. Are you willing to puke for this?
Hayley ignores him and turns her attention back to the phone on the stand. She winces as she checks the numbers again. Afterwards, she throws her fork down.
David points at the camera.
DAVID: Not even one?
A long pause. Hayley is still looking at the phone, her eyes dull with disappointment.
HAYLEY: No.
DAVID: Umm, should we turn it off now?
Hayley's still got that blank look in her eyes. She wraps spaghetti around the fork and forms a tight bundle, but then she lets the fork drop onto the plate.
DAVID: It's okay, Hayls. We can do other videos.
She gives a fed-up shrug of her shoulders.
HAYLEY: Mickey's just passed two hundred million subscribers.
DAVID: So what? You need to stop competing with the likes of Mickey Morgan. He's been doing this for ages, and

he didn't start off with two hundred million or whatever subscribers. But—

David hesitates.

HAYLEY: But what?

DAVID: Well, you want people to watch, but ... you're too nice. I know you like the guy and all, but let's be honest – Mickey Morgan is an obnoxious prick, and that's why he's on top of his game. It's too competitive on YouTube. Nice people will never be seen. We don't look at nice – we look at stupid, controversial and loud.

HAYLEY: I don't want to be obnoxious.

DAVID: Then don't do it. I don't want you to be obnoxious either – that's not who you are. I'm just saying it has to be exciting. Listen, we've got options. I can always get a car from my brother's friend who sells second-hand and does rentals. Not to boast or nothing, but I'm getting pretty good behind the wheel.

HAYLEY: Cars?

DAVID: Cars get you from A to B. From a boring place to an exciting place. We can travel. Find cool places to go and—

HAYLEY: Why don't you start your own channel, then?

DAVID: Because I don't want to be a YouTube star.

HAYLEY: That's right. You want to be a stuntman.

David points to the camera.

DAVID: Umm, is this conversation going out live?

HAYLEY: Don't worry. Still zero viewers.

They sit in silence, surrounded by spaghetti and neglected salad. Now and then, fizzing and popping sounds escape from the Pepsi in their glasses.

Hayley stares dead-eyed at the camera. Her jaw goes from side to side as she chews on the same forkful of tired spaghetti she's been working on for ages.

She reaches for the camera.
HAYLEY: Where are you all?

36

A cold evening in the busy city centre

Hayley's footage begins as she and David walk off the train, and she keeps filming as they make their way through the barriers and into the crowded station. Past the shops. Downstairs and outside, the city full of lights and people. Immediately, they're welcomed by the sound of a gruff-voiced busker singing 'Wonderwall'. The music drifts over late-night shoppers like a melodic breeze.

David drops a coin into the man's guitar case.

It's a short walk to the bookstore, where, on the second floor, a large crowd has gathered to see controversial YouTube sensation Mickey Morgan. Mickey is twenty-five years old, tall and bleached-blond handsome. Most of the time he dresses like a nineties rapper – XXL basketball jersey, gold chain, Timberland boots and backwards cap.

Mickey's autobiography, THE CONTENT KING, is a number one bestseller, and he's currently touring the UK and

Europe to promote the book, making appearances on TV, podcasts and radio.

Hayley and David take their seats. Hayley insisted they arrive early in the hope of grabbing two seats in the front row. They just make it before the last two are snapped up.

At seven o'clock, Mickey walks out to a massive cheer. He proceeds to read an excerpt from his book before sitting down with local journalist Sally Finn for a conversation and Q&A.

SALLY: Mickey, I have to ask – what do you say to your critics? Specifically, I'm talking to the people who refer to you as a menace to society? They say your stunts are cruel, dangerous and nothing more than childish attention-seeking.

There's a quiet oohing noise from the crowd.

MICKEY: My stunts are cruel? Anything in particular?

SALLY: Well, let's look at one of your most notorious stunts, for example. Dog-Grab. You went to three different parks in Chicago, looked for dog-walkers and, after approaching them in a friendly manner, snatched the lead out of their hands and ran off with their dog. Filming the whole time, of course. The owners were terrified. Isn't that cruel?

MICKEY: I didn't really *take* their dogs. I *borrowed* them for about a hundred metres max, and the video evidence backs that up. It's a shot of adrenaline. Nothing more. Know what I'm saying?

SALLY: Some might say it's a hundred metres too much.

Mickey leans back, stroking the blond fluff on his chin.

MICKEY: I believe that good art is disruptive. Good art *has* to be disruptive and more so in this day and age. As a species, we're asleep at the wheel, know what I'm saying? Society is asleep. What I do is jolt people out of their sleep and remind them that they're still alive. The human spirit wasn't meant to be stagnant and stale like it is now.

His face takes on a thoughtful expression. There's more fluff stroking.

MICKEY: Disruption is progress. I think that, in time, people will acknowledge that I'm performing a service, but that's how it goes – progression is rarely recognised in its own lifetime. They don't build statues of people like me until long after we're dead and buried. That's a pity. I'd kind of like to see that statue.

Laughter. A short round of applause.

SALLY: Right. Well, one thing's for sure – you *are* the content king. The number one influencer on YouTube. Let's have look at your journey on the big screen behind us.

The audience watches a montage of Mickey's career from humble beginnings as a clumsy teenager making amateur videos to superstar status. Hayley films everything from her front-row seat, soaking up the adoration that Mickey gets from the crowd. The cheers as they play a highlight reel of his best pranks. As they show the tearful video he made three years ago, thanking the audience for their support as mainstream media outlets slammed him for his pranks. Hayley takes it all in. Her eyes locked on the images – quick cuts of his recent and most daring pranks. She can't ever imagine being that brave or having the sort of high-quality production elements of a Mickey Morgan video.

She'll never be recognised on this level. She's just a stupid girl making stupid videos that no one is interested in. The gap between her and Mickey is night and day.

After the interview is over, Mickey takes his place at a table, signing books. He's flanked by security as he talks to fans and scribbles his signature over and over again. Hayley points the camera at a LONG line of people clutching their books for him to sign.

They join the queue and wait. David takes the camera when it's Hayley's turn. He films her, and her face is bright red as Mickey stands up and gives her a hug. She smiles and even cries a little. They take photos, and then Mickey sits down to sign her book.

David films the exchange between them.

HAYLEY: Umm, I have a YouTube channel myself.
Mickey doesn't look up as he signs her book.
MICKEY: Cool.
HAYLEY: I've got some pretty good ideas. You know, if you ever need an assistant ... umm ... I'm ...
MICKEY: Thanks. Got so many now.
His PA, a tall woman clutching a clipboard to her chest, intervenes.
PA: Let's keep it moving. We've got a car outside, and there are still a lot of books to sign. Sorry, sweetheart.
David captures the look on Hayley's face as she's brushed aside by Mickey's security. She walks on. Looking down at the floor.
Then she stops. Looks over at Mickey, who's already signing the next person's book.
HAYLEY (*calling back to the table*): I wrote to you long before you were famous. Why didn't you ever write back?
David hurries over. He pulls her arm, wanting to get her out of there.
DAVID: Let's go, Hayls.
HAYLEY: Why didn't you reply to my emails?

David manages to drag her to the top of the stairs before security do it themselves. Hayley sounds like she's hyperventilating. She stares at the book in her hands, her body shaking from head to toe.

DAVID: It's a book signing, Hayls. He can't spend ten minutes chatting to every single person.

Hayley is unable to speak.

Clip ends.

37

Message received through the Contact Form on Mickey Morgan's official website.
Time: 10.19 p.m.

To Mickey,

Fuck you.

This is the last email I'll ever send you. What a disappointment you were in person tonight. Boring and, to be honest, ugly! No wonder you use so many filters in your vids, jeez. And your clothes – HA! What the hell was I thinking?

UNSUBSCRIBED!

You're going to cry when I'm bigger than you will EVER be.

Frame this email, you ungrateful dick. What? You think I'm a stalker? You wish. You don't know me, and you never will. You lost a fan today.

So that's what it takes to make it? Be a dick. Fine, I'm in to get bigger and better than you. I can do so much better than your cheap, unimaginative dognapping. Especially if it means knocking you off your perch.

All you had to do was take me seriously.

Hayley Davies (remember the name!)

P.S. Binned your book. We all know someone else wrote it because you can't spell, let alone string a sentence together. DICK!

38

One year later

This is a perfect place. This is her safe place. Birdsong explodes from the sky. Hazy sunlight shimmers through narrow gaps in between the trees to create a shimmering and otherworldly backdrop. Lush green foliage for miles and no sign of a walking track or hint of other people.

The camera takes in the surroundings slowly, as if in awe. Then it turns to reveal Hayley sitting in a small clearing with the tall forest grass behind her. She's still, but the grass sways like a chorus of dancers.

Her long brown hair is gone; now it's cut short and dyed blonde. The style, she likes to tell people, is 'punkish'. She's wearing makeup and a white singlet. No more sweaters, even on a cool autumnal day.

HAYLEY: Hi there. This feels a little weird, but welcome back, yet again, to Hayley's Channel. Coming to you live from this beautiful forest that's located about two miles from my house. I come here a lot – this is my quiet place. I'd go mad without it.

Okay, where to begin?

It's been a while, hasn't it? Haven't uploaded anything new in over a year and a half. Time flies – I'm almost eighteen now.

She laughs, but it doesn't last. Then comes a long sigh.

Okay, where will I start? My parents split up five months ago. I live with Mum in the same house as before, and to be honest, I don't even know where Dad is since he moved out. It sucks, but truthfully, it's better that way because it was unbearable at home. And it has been ever since …

I don't know. Did I ever tell you about my sister?

Nah, I don't want a pity party.

Another long sigh.

My sister, Natasha, died in a car crash. This was a little over two years ago. She got hit by a drunk driver – an off-duty detective, as it happens. Oh man, it was so sudden. I mean, it was just so sudden. It's not like someone being ill and you've got time to prepare, you know? I remember the four of us sitting at the breakfast table that morning – and I still dream about that sometimes. It was such a … *normal* … morning. And I hate that word, normal. But that's what it was – there was no sign that that particular day was going to be any different.

And then … BAM! Natasha was going to college, and this detective hit her near the train station. I don't even remember saying bye to her that day. I don't think I even looked up as she walked out of the kitchen with her bag over her shoulder.

Just another day.

Normal.

Like I say, I don't want a pity party. Shit happens, but Mum and Dad never got over it. I think – I *know* – their marriage died with her. And a part of them died with her. Me too, I suppose. Everything went downhill after that. Blame. Resentment. Like a disease had taken over our family. The rot set in, and all their grief had to go somewhere. There was a lot of fighting, and sometimes it was physical.

The writing was on the wall. They were always going to split up, but, man, it took such a long time to get around to it. They never shouted at me. Never hit me or anything like that. I was just there, surrounded by it.

That detective never even went to jail.

Anyway, moving on. I'm actually feeling really good about the future. I haven't rushed into anything regards the channel. I took some time out. Been thinking whether or not there's even going to be a channel.

There is.

But no more half-baked efforts. My vision is clear.

And I'm ready to be brave.

39

Hayley and David are in a Toyota rental belonging to an associate of David's brother. Cruising through the city centre on a sunny afternoon. Hip-hop explodes out of the speakers, the bass buzzing and distorting and shaking their bones.

Hayley films through her phone, which is fixed to a mount on the dashboard. David keeps the car at a steady pace, dark sunglasses on, one arm resting on the open window. Employee access to the rental cars is a perk for David, a part-time employee at the sales/rental yard, who mostly washes the cars and performs general maintenance duties.

Hayley sits in the passenger seat. Red singlet on, her lean arms toned thanks to a regular home gym routine. Bottle tan. Lipstick. Glittery eye shadow.

She gives David a warning to let him know they're going live.

The countdown.

Three-two-one ...

. . .

HAYLEY: What's up? How is everyone doing out there? THIS IS IT – this is the official launch video that I promised you all. Live and unscripted because live is BETTER! Woohoo! Let me introduce myself to anyone who doesn't know me. My name *was* Hayley Davies, but from now on the world shall know me as Hayley T. Prank.

She points a thumb at David.

HAYLEY: This guy right here is my loyal driver, David. Sometimes he's a loyal friend too.

DAVID *(flashes the peace sign)*: Hi.

HAYLEY: Alright, listen up. It took me a long time to get here. But I know what you guys want now, and let me assure you, Hayley Davies is no more. You DON'T want cooking vids or movie reviews or mukbangs or cats. You want daring. You want risky. And I'm going to give you that.

Hayley leans closer to the camera. She has something written in black marker pen on the palm of her hand, and she holds it up.

NICE DOESN'T WORK!

HAYLEY: You live, you learn. Let's get on with the first prank, shall we?

DAVID: Perfect timing. We're here.

David steers the Toyota towards the side of the road. Hayley grabs her phone off the mount, steps outside and attaches it to a selfie stick. She's standing outside a row of shops on a busy city centre street. The monotonous hum of traffic is constant in the background. There are pedestrians, cyclists and electric scooters.

Hayley and David exchange thumbs-up signals. David rejoins the flow of traffic and drives the Toyota around the corner, and Hayley turns her attention back to the camera.

HAYLEY: Let me ask you a question. Have you ever …

Pause. A sheepish look around.

HAYLEY: Well, let me put it another way. Have you seen

those stories on the news about a certain MEGA sports brand and their sweatshops in East Asia? Have you ever wondered what you could do to protest? This company promised things were going to improve for its slaves, I mean employees, and these latest news reports show that nothing has changed. They charge a fortune for clothes, yet are barely paying their workers, many of them children, a decent wage.

She steps closer to the shop entrance. A retail store for the sports brand in question.

HAYLEY: My question, standing right outside one of their superstores, is – how easy is it to steal a baseball cap from that rack near the door? And is it a legit form of protest?

Answers in the comments below.

Hayley reaches up and takes her phone off the selfie stick. She folds the stick up and lowers the phone to her side, still filming. Then she walks through the sliding doors. The footage is jerky, and the footage is looking up from her waist.

HAYLEY (*whispering*): Okay – hats, hats, hats.

She walks past the security guard. A tall man with dark brown skin and a beer belly.

HAYLEY: Hi.

SECURITY GUARD: Hello.

She hums to herself as she walks up and down the aisle with the running shoes and running accessories. Then she turns around and retraces her steps, coming to a stop beside the display of baseball caps at the entrance. Hayley lifts a few. Tries them on in front of the small rectangle of mirror on the display.

HAYLEY (*still whispering*): How about this one?

She looks down at the camera, her eyes filled with doubt.

HAYLEY: Actually, folks, I don't know if I can—

She takes a deep breath.
HAYLEY: Fuck you, Mickey.
She holds the hat aloft. Turns around, waving it in the air like it's a flag.
HAYLEY: PAY YOUR WORKERS A FAIR WAGE. THIS IS FOR THE STARVING PEOPLE IN VIETNAM.
Hayley walks to the doors with the hat in her hand.
HAYLEY: Oh shit, oh shit, oh shit!
SECURITY GUARD: Excuse me. Miss?
Hayley explodes into a sprint before they can lock the doors against her. The camera shakes as she runs through the doors and takes a sharp left. She can hear the security guard running after her. She runs around the corner. The Toyota is parked at the side, hazard lights flashing. Fake registration plates on the rental. That's something David's brother and his friend know nothing about.
The passenger door opens. Hayley jumps in the car.
DAVID: Toss it!
Hayley throws the hat out the open window. She can see the security guard slowing to a stop beside the discarded hat. He was never going to last long, and he seems to have given up the chase. Most likely, he memorised the plates. It won't get him anywhere.
HAYLEY (*leaning her head out the passenger window*): Viet-NAM! Viet-NAM!
She's staring at the phone. Heart racing. Hands shaking as she struggles to reattach it to the dash mount.
DAVID: You know, you might want to think about wearing a disguise if you're going to do something like that again.
HAYLEY (*thumb pointing back towards the shop*): I'm not a thief. It's not like I kept the stupid hat. I was making a stand against the death throes of late-stage capitalism.

DAVID: Oh boy.

David follows the signs that lead out of the city centre. Soon they're back on the motorway, heading north.

DAVID: I said I'd have the car back no later than four.

Hayley sits forward, staring at the phone. Mumbling under her breath.

HAYLEY: Good art is disruption.

DAVID: What?

HAYLEY: Nothing.

She's silent for about a minute, her eyes never leaving the phone. Then she points at the screen and screams with excitement.

HAYLEY: Oh my God!

DAVID: What now?

HAYLEY: David, twenty-three people! I've got twenty-three people watching me!

40

Hayley is sitting on the couch with her mum. Mrs Alice Davies's head is resting on Hayley's shoulder. She's fast asleep, snoring softly. She's only in her late forties, but her face belongs to someone as much as twenty years older. Her skin is dull and grey. Heavily wrinkled. Her stringy hair is damp after Hayley successfully encouraged her mother to have a rare shower.

Behind them, barely visible on the window ledge, is a framed picture of the whole family – Mum, Dad, Natasha and Hayley – taken when the girls were twelve and ten respectively. The photo shows the family on a hike in the Lake District, a former holiday favourite. Everyone is smiling.

Hayley looks at the camera. She whispers so as not to wake her mum.

HAYLEY: This is a private vlog entry.

She looks at her mum again. Making sure she's definitely asleep.

HAYLEY: It's been two days since the hat prank. Oh, I don't know what I'm doing. I wasn't expecting ... *this*. I wasn't expecting to feel so sick and nervous about what I did. I thought it would be okay.

She lets out a sigh.

HAYLEY: Mum's not well. She's been coughing a lot more than usual, and while I don't think it's anything serious, it's got me thinking. What if something happens to me? Who's going to look after her? Every time I hear someone outside, footsteps on the path or a car speeding up the road, I'm sure it's the police.

Still, I have to hold my nerve. I'm not just doing this for me. I'm doing it for Mum too. This is our best chance of turning our lives around.

Hayley pulls the collar of her mother's dressing gown together to keep the cold air out.

HAYLEY: She wasn't always like this. Mum used to have more energy than all of us put together. I remember what Granny told me years ago – that Mum was a hyperactive child – a *berserker*, she called her – and that Granny and Granddad had to watch her like a hawk twenty-four seven. Said she took at least five years off both their lives with her antics.

Mum grew up and loved to travel. She went to Russia and all these other places, but the big dream was always to go to Australia. I don't know why. It's something she used to talk about all the time. Australia, Australia, Australia. We had boomerangs on the wall. Framed pictures of the Northern Territory, of red skies and rock-strewn deserts. It looked so frigging hot.

She loved it, though. I don't know why she never got around to going there. Life, I suppose. Us kids.

I can get her there. If my channel gets big enough and I attract enough hits, I'll be rich. I just have to be smart about it, and I have to keep my nerve. People want excitement. They want stupid things. Clever things. Funny things. The only thing they don't want is to be bored.

I have to keep going.

CUT.

The private vlog continues with Hayley and David sitting at the kitchen table. Hayley is looking through a bag of wigs, hats, sunglasses and other items of disguise.

DAVID (*points at camera*): Do you have to film everything?

HAYLEY: It's good to document things. Don't worry – not everything's going on YouTube. It's a private vlog thing.

DAVID: I'm sure it'll go public when you're rich and shameless.

Hayley ignores that last bit. She lifts a curly black wig off the table. Pulls a face.

HAYLEY: This is hideous.

DAVID: You have to be careful what you're uploading. I mean, in terms of actually breaking the law versus simply pissing people off.

HAYLEY: No more stealing from shops.

DAVID: That's a relief.

HAYLEY: Still, I can't guarantee there's never going to be any legal stuff to deal with. Mickey Morgan has had three major court cases since he got big. But, in the end, people don't bother to sue or prosecute or whatever. Action like that just gives the influencers more notoriety. Makes them even bigger.

DAVID: Yeah. So the hat-grab was a hit, eh?

HAYLEY: One hundred and eleven new subscribers in just under forty-eight hours.

DAVID: Well done.

HAYLEY: Yeah, but now the pressure is on.

DAVID: How?

HAYLEY: Because they're all waiting for the next thing. And I *seriously* have to deliver.

CUT.

Inside David's car.

They're driving on a quiet, winding stretch of road surrounded by trees and distant hills. Hayley's fixed the camera to the mount and is now filming a segment to be included in the next video.

HAYLEY: Welcome back, bitches! This is Hayley T. Prank coming at y'all with another prank to keep you laughing all day long. Please smash that like button and hit subscribe so you never miss a thing.

She flashes a peace sign.

HAYLEY: Okay, I'm here with David the driver. Say hi, David the driver.

DAVID: Hi.

Hayley looks at him. Then she pauses the recording.

HAYLEY: Hey, can you be a bit more enthusiastic?

David sighs.

HAYLEY: What's wrong?

DAVID: Are you sure you wanna do this, Hayls?

HAYLEY: Do what?

DAVID: Go down this road and become this obnoxious person you aren't. It can still be a one and done, Hayls.

HAYLEY: Obnoxious?

DAVID: *Bitches?* Since when did you start calling people bitches? I must have missed that part where you grew up in a ghetto.

HAYLEY: You want me to go back to cooking videos?

DAVID: I—

HAYLEY: Seriously, what's your problem?

DAVID: Does your mum know what you're doing?

HAYLEY: For real?

DAVID: Yeah, for real, *bitch*. Hayls, she's barely holding it together, but she's still your mum. And if something happens to you—

HAYLEY: I know.

There's a pause in the conversation. Hayley leans her head against the passenger-side window. She stares out at hundreds of fallen leaves shimmering in the sunlight. Brown and gold, they line the edge of the road beside a stretch of lush woodland. Hayley looks at a world of bright colours going by too fast. Then she takes her head off the window and turns back to David.

HAYLEY: Mum doesn't know or care that I'm making videos. She goes to work. Sleepwalks through her shift at the supermarket, then comes home and sits in front of the TV. I can barely get her to eat sometimes. She's living a half-life, and now she's got this cough going on. Wish me luck trying to get her to a doctor.

DAVID: I'm sorry. Can't your dad help?

HAYLEY: I've got more chance of getting Mum to a doctor than finding that waste of space.

DAVID: Oh man.

HAYLEY: Listen, this Hayley T. Prank thing isn't just an attention grab. Sure, I'm a needy brat, and I crave attention. I admit it.

DAVID: That's more than most.

HAYLEY: It's a good income. What I mean is, it's a good income if I can make it work. Potentially even a *great* income. Mum won't have to work a day in her life ever again, and that means she can concentrate on doing things that she likes. She can start living again. Hey, Mum, here's that ticket to Australia you've always dreamed about. First class all the way. A hot sun, blue skies and golden beaches. Go get it. Have you any idea how much I would love to do that for her?

Her eyes shine with excitement as she talks.

DAVID: Is that what she wants? To go to Australia?

HAYLEY: I think she wants to die.

DAVID: Oh shit, Hayls.

HAYLEY: No, it's okay. I can bring her back.

DAVID: By becoming another influencer?

HAYLEY: By becoming *the* influencer. You need to pay attention to what I'm saying, David. I'm not interested in mediocrity. It's go big or go home. People are already bored of Mickey Morgan – have you seen his numbers lately? There's definitely a downward trend happening. And no wonder. He's safe, doing podcasts and making public appearances at mainstream media events. He doesn't take risks anymore, and now there's a gap in the market for edgy pranksters. That's where I come in.

David nods.

DAVID: I noticed the singlet. Are you lifting weights now?

HAYLEY: I have to tone up my arms. It's all about catching the eye, you know? Putting the right shot in my thumbnails with the right headline.

DAVID: You mean clickbait?

HAYLEY: Since when did you become fifty years old? Are you on board for this or not?

DAVID: Me?

HAYLEY: I don't have a driver's licence.

DAVID: I know. And by the way, Hayls, that was a big risk I took being your getaway driver the other day. These aren't my cars. I can take a rental out for a few hours, but these are not my cars. Switching plates for a one-off prank, I can live with that. But what else are you expecting me to do?

There's a long silence in the car.

HAYLEY: David, I have zero prospects. Just back me up on this one, will you? Please?

David doesn't answer, so Hayley starts recording again. She immediately brightens up for the camera. Straightens her posture.

HAYLEY: Here I am with David the driver. Say hi, won't you, David?

David grins, showing all his teeth, and he waves enthusiastically.

DAVID: Hi!

HAYLEY: Hey, David, guess where we're going today?

DAVID: Where are we going today, Hayley?

HAYLEY: We're going to the beach.

DAVID (*feigns surprise*): Oooh! But wait a minute. The nearest beach is thirty miles away. Isn't it?

HAYLEY: Actually, there's one a little closer than that. Twelve miles from our current location, to be exact.

David drops the act. The look of surprise on his face is real.

DAVID: No way. Oh no, please tell me you're not talking about—

HAYLEY: Yep. Told you it'd be a surprise.

DAVID: Red Sands Beach? But that's a ... it's a ...

Hayley talks to the camera.

HAYLEY: That's right, folks. Today we're travelling south to Red Sands Beach. It's kind of a local legend around these parts, but it's a real spot on the west coast. A tiny little beach. Very nice. And since it's a lovely day here and the sun is out, we're going to see some interesting things. At least, we will if what they say about Red Sands Beach is true.

41

Red Sands Beach
12.31 p.m.

The camera jerks back and forth in Hayley's grip as she and David make a run for it. The footage is dizzying, but Hayley doesn't stop filming. They run over the flat, reddish sand away from the water's edge and onto the lumpy sand. The latter is much more challenging on their legs. They have to work to generate speed and keep their balance. Their calves will be burning.

They run towards the rope that runs along the edge of the beach. Behind the rope there's a grassy incline that leads back to the car park. They climb through the long grass, gasping for breath.

Angry voices yell from behind.

HAYLEY (*to camera*): Well, just in case you were wondering

– it's true what they say about Red Sands Beach. It *is* a nudist beach and—

DAVID: Stop filming!

HAYLEY (*ignoring David*): And we only had to wait half an hour before the first of today's nudists showed up. Eight of them. Ancient, like in their sixties.

The shouting gets louder.

THE NUDISTS: Give us our bloody clothes back!

David and Hayley pick up the pace, ascending the grass and approaching the car park. Both carry a bundle of clothing in one hand.

DAVID: Stop filming, Hayls. They're gaining on us.

HAYLEY (*still to camera*): What do you guys think? Are they gaining on us? Let me know in the comments.

DAVID: Stop it!

The camera swings back, just for a second. We get a glimpse of the greenish-blue sea and waves breaking on the beach. Something moves into shot, blocking the sea. Pink, blob-like figures, naked from head to toe, running awkwardly towards the camera. Expressions of rage and disgust. Shaking fists in the air.

THE NUDISTS: Get back here!

Hayley points the camera to the garments in her hand. Shirts, trousers, underwear and towels. It's an impressive haul for one hand.

David almost topples over on the lumpy sand.

DAVID: Fuck!

HAYLEY: Get to the car.

DAVID: I'm dropping this stuff.

HAYLEY: No, not yet.

The camera turns back to the nudists. They're still in pursuit. Eight people in total, climbing up the lumpy sand. Two of the runners in particular are fast and determined. They're closing the gap on the clothes thieves.

DAVID: Shit!

HAYLEY: Run!

They leave the grassy incline. Veer left onto a winding path that leads into the car park. David parked close and for good reason. They leap in the car, throwing the clothes in the back. The two speedy nudists are almost at the car park, and their eyes bulge with panic – as if realising for the first time that the thieves are intent on keeping their clothes and towels.

David fires up the engine while Hayley mounts the camera. They back out of the parking spot, and the tyres shriek. David floors it while the nudists yell obscenities.

About a half mile up the road, Hayley rolls down the window and throws the clothes and towels outside. Then she rolls up the window.

HAYLEY: Go!

David laughs with nerves and relief.

HAYLEY: You were so scared.

DAVID: I wasn't *that* scared.

HAYLEY: Really?

DAVID: Okay, I was terrified.

HAYLEY (*to camera*): How'd you like that? That's only a taste of what's to come on this channel. So hit that bell icon, bitches, and get notified every time Hayley T. Prank – that's me – uploads a new video. You don't want to miss a thing. It's going to be a wild ride.

42

Message received through the Contact Form on Hayley T. Prank's official website.
Time: 2.39 p.m.

Dear Hayley,

This is the worst opening line ever but ...
I AM YOUR NUMBER ONE FAN!!

LOL, but WOW!

Your channel has grown into something special over the past year. By the way, I'm not just jumping on the bandwagon because you're getting big numbers now. I was there from the beginning – from the legendary hat-grab video. You weren't as polished then as you are now. It's so inspiring.

And of course you were right to steal the hat! That slaves in Japan thing. That was important, and fuck the corporations. LOVED the recent Break-In prank too. Sneaking into people's back gardens in the middle of the night, turning their door handles and freaking them out. That was SO funny! I could go on and on about the pranks, but there's a word limit, LOL!

Your channel is getting big and deservedly so.

Sorry about your mum dying. That sucks so bad.

My parents aren't divorced like yours, but they work all the time and might as well be. Mum's in politics. Dad's a big-shot lawyer. Maybe it's because they don't see one another that they're still together.

Thinking about starting a YT channel of my own. I'd like to try some of your pranks just to see if I've got what it takes. It's a scary thought, but I've been practising a little.

Presentation, speaking – that sort of thing. I'm okay. Mum and Dad speak on camera a lot, and some of it must've rubbed off on me.

I really think I can become an influencer. Not in your league, of course.

I have a boyfriend. He's great, but he doesn't understand me wanting a YT channel. Something of my own. We're only sixteen, but he talks about the future like an old man. Kids –

WTF? He wants me to have sex with him. I love him but, the pressure.

I'd rather be like you.

Thanks for listening.

Hope to hear back from you. Even if it's just a word or two.

Oh, by the way, my name is Zara.

SEE YA!
Xxx

43

Excerpt from The Current Affairs Show

The Current Affairs Show *is a magazine-style TV show, beloved by the nation, and broadcast every weeknight at 7 p.m. For this particular segment, 'Ask the Public', presenter Carol Wood is strolling through central London on a sunny afternoon, interviewing members of the public about the rise in popularity of Hayley T. Prank, a controversial content creator who's become massively popular over the past year and a half.*

Carol begins by approaching a man in his fifties, dressed in a smart grey suit. No creases. The tie, perfectly knotted. He looks up from his phone, slightly red in the face, as Carol approaches with a microphone in hand.

CAROL: Excuse me, sir, we're asking members of the public what they think about Hayley T. Prank. Have you heard of her before?

MAN (*nods*): Yes, I've read about her in the papers.

CAROL: And? Are you a fan?

MAN: Good God, no. Bloody nuisance that one. Screaming for attention, but then again, aren't they all?

CUT to ...

Carol talking to a smartly dressed man in his thirties as he waits outside a shopping mall for a taxi.

BUSINESSMAN: Oh, Hayley. Yes, I know her. My daughter is twelve, and she loves those kinds of videos. I understand she's very popular with teenagers and people in their twenties. Just goes to show how big these internet celebrities can become these days, eh? Bigger than regular TV stars, you know? The last one, that lad Mickey ... something. Wonder what happened to him.

CAROL: Are you worried about the influence someone like Hayley will have on your daughter?

BUSINESSMAN: Nah. I mean, time will tell. Some of the things she gets up to, it's not nice, is it? But my daughter would never do anything like that.

CUT to ...

A twenty-something woman standing outside Pizza Hut. She has a labradoodle on a lead, which is sniffing at the pavement in search of crumbs. She talks and chews gum frantically.

YOUNG WOMAN: Yeah, I think she's brilliant. I pretty much live on YouTube, and right now, Hayley's stuff is some of the best-quality content out there. Like, I saw the first few videos, and they were funny but a bit amateurish, you know what I mean? Yeah, you stole a hat. You stole some clothes off a nudist beach. Not bad, yeah? But the quality has really improved over the months. She knows what she's doing.

CAROL: So, you're a fan?

YOUNG WOMAN: Yeah. It's all in the name, innit? It's just a prank. The people who get upset need to lighten up.

CAROL: What about the people she frightens? Or the people who are traumatised in the aftermath of her more daring pranks?

The young woman laughs nervously. The labradoodle stops sniffing for crumbs and looks up at his owner as if interested in the answer.

YOUNG WOMAN: It's just a prank, innit?

Segment ends.

44

New Year's Day
12.01 a.m.

Hayley is sitting on a long L-shaped couch in a gloomy living room. The living room is a massive space that belongs in a mansion or an ultra-luxurious apartment building. Slick avant-garde furniture, whirring fans overhead, yet a slight coldness that can't be glossed over.

Starry spotlights blink on the ceiling. The faint drone of a TV hums in the background – the sound of a lone piper playing the opening notes of 'Auld Lang Syne'. A choir joins in. The new year is underway.

Hayley's features are mostly hidden. On the wall behind her, the Lake District family photo can be seen. Blown up and framed. Twice the size of the original.

Her speech sounds slurred. Her voice, tired and husky.

. . .

HAYLEY: Happy New Year, everyone. I, umm, hope you all had a great time over the Christmas holidays with your friends and families. What a past twelve months, huh? Thanks for all your support. The way this channel has exploded ... wow ... it's beyond my wildest dreams.

Umm.

I've just been lying low over the holidays. I don't know. Christmas was tough this year, and ... I don't know ... it all feels a bit weird.

Look at that. Forty thousand people watching right now. I couldn't have imagined that when I was doing the hat-grab last year. Was it last year? Yeah, it was last year. I couldn't have imagined it. Just me sitting on a couch, talking shit to a screen. That's for you, Mum. Sorry I never got you to Australia.

She sips from a glass of wine.

HAYLEY: Alright, the live chat is blowing up here, so I'll answer a few questions. Just a few though, okay. It's late, and I'm tired.

Another sip of wine. Hayley mumbles to herself as she browses through the comments.

HAYLEY: Question from Jason P. Where do you get your singlets? Umm, that's easy – I'll put a link to the merch store down below once the live is finished.

She narrows her eyes, searching for the next question.

HAYLEY: Umm, Shauna5701 – thanks for the twenty-dollar tip. Shauna wants me to comment on copycats. Am I worried that it's getting out of control? Yeah, that's a big thing that people are talking about. Right, so for anyone who doesn't know, copycats are all the wannabe YouTubers out there imitating my pranks.

Okay. What do I want to say about this?

Yeah, so I wish people would come up with their own ideas. In an ideal world, we'd all be originals, right? While I always admired Mickey Morgan back in the day, there was no chance I'd ever copy his style. Good thing, too. His stuff hasn't aged well.

But creativity is hard.

So, what do I think? It's all good. Imitation is flattery, right? Am I worried that it's getting out of control? Not really.

The orchestra's rendition of 'Auld Lang Syne' reaches a powerful finale on TV. Hayley grabs the remote and turns it down.

HAYLEY: Umm. Yeah, copycats. Really, it's nothing to do with me. All I can do is work on myself, and this year I'm taking things up to the next level. Some of the ideas we're talking about here ... trust me, I'm only getting started. Bigger and better. I just wish—

Fuck.

I have to go.

Happy New Year, guys. Hug your family members. Hold them tight, and I don't care if it makes you feel weird or whatever – just do it.

Ah fuck.

Happy New Year ... bitches.

Video ends.

45

Message received through the Contact Form on Hayley T. Prank's official website.
Time: 11.12 p.m.

Happy New Year Hayley,

It's Zara, again.

It's okay. I don't expect a reply. I'm just a little worried about you. You seemed down on that NY Eve live. Something wrong? I really don't expect a reply, but I know you want to be intimate and friendly with your followers – unlike Mickey the Dickey. We're not just your fans, we're your *friends*.

But you're busy – I get it.

You don't have to reply.

Oh, I nearly forgot. Happy New Year. Didn't even say it, did I?

It was interesting to hear you talk about copycats, and I'm so happy you didn't diss us. I have tried to be original and come up with my own ideas, but they don't get views, not like the 'Hayley Tributes'. They *do* get views!

I've done quite a few now. You'll notice me soon enough.

Love,

Zara
Xxx

P.S. Your mum would be so proud.

46

HAYLEY T. PRANK – BREAKING INTO HOUSES

The video opens on a tranquil neighbourhood. Picture-postcard suburbia, a world of well-kept lawns, tidy pathways and two cars outside red-brick houses. Tall trees, trimmed hedges. The distant hum of traffic crescendoed by the roar of a truck.

Hayley is walking down this leafy suburban street, filming herself with a selfie stick. She strolls by the nice cars, a spring in her step. Her hair is long and blonde. She's tanned. Showing off dazzling white teeth when she smiles.

HAYLEY: Alright, guys, before we get going, a massive thank you to the sponsors of today's video – Lazer energy drinks.

CUT to:

A pre-recorded clip of Hayley talking for one minute, extolling the virtues of Lazer energy drinks (this one: raspberry flavour), letting her viewers know how much it helps with her creative energy. She tells them about the fifteen per cent discount offer if they bulk buy via the link in the video description.

CUT to:

Hayley in suburbia.

HAYLEY: Okay. I want to address the rumours about me and Mickey Morgan. No, there will NOT be any collaboration. You've got to be kidding – do you know how much of a dick that guy is? But yes, his people approached my people, and let me repeat – there's NO way it's happening. Shutting it down, folks, you heard it here. I can't handle that sort of neediness in my life, and to be frank, I don't have time to resurrect the career of a has-been.

Besides, Mickey was always a bit too safe for my taste. I can't believe I used to worship that guy.

Anyway.

Roll the credits.

CUT to:

Fancy intro/montage of Hayley clips. Professional, slick production with her own theme tune written by a well-known rock band.

CUT to:

Hayley walking down the street.

HAYLEY: And so on to today's prank. This one is called Breaking into Houses. What's that you say, dear subscriber? Why would I break into someone's house? Well, because it's a beautiful day, it's hot, and I need a drink. And besides, I'm not technically breaking in anywhere – I'm just going to find an unlocked door and let myself in. Boom!

She grins at the camera.

Oh, and by the way, I want to address something. These videos are getting millions of views, but a whole bunch of you – a whole bunch of you *bitches* – aren't even subscribed to my channel. That's rude. Subscribe. Do it now and stop freeloading. You don't get nothing for free in this world.

Then again ... do you?

That's what we're about to find out in my most daring prank to date –

Breaking into Houses.

A car pulls up behind Hayley. The driver's side window rolls down, and David's head pops through the gap. There's a coating of short fuzz on his face in an attempt to perfect the designer stubble look. He's got sunglasses on. A stud in his left ear – a gift from Hayley for all his hard work in helping the channel grow from nothing into the biggest thing ever on YouTube.

He flashes the peace sign at the camera as Hayley approaches. There's a second man in the passenger seat. Alex Garry is another of Hayley's assistants – slightly older than Hayley and David, in his late twenties. He gets out and limps over to Hayley on the kerb. The limp is a permanent reminder of a near-fatal motorcycle accident eight years prior.

Alex hands something to Hayley. She flashes it at the camera.

A gorilla mask.

HAYLEY: Just to make it more interesting, you know?

David and Alex watch while Hayley squeezes the rubbery mask over her head. It's a tight fit, and she has some trouble before it finally goes on.

DAVID: You're insane.

ALEX (*laughing*): How are you going to run with that thing on?

DAVID: Good question. This is stupid.

Hayley's voice is muffled under the mask.

HAYLEY: There he is. Doubting David.

DAVID: I mean it. How are you going to run with that thing on? It's a tight fit. It's not going to be easy to pull off.

HAYLEY: I run with my legs.

DAVID: I'm serious, Hayls.

Hayley mumbles something under the mask and then continues along the street. The video cuts back and forth between David's footage (from the car) and Hayley's (on the selfie stick).

She stops outside one of the red-brick houses. Unlatches the gate and hurries up the garden path. Her breath sounds noisy under the mask – like the sound of someone breathing under a gas mask. Hayley tries the front door – it's locked. She abandons the house. The next few houses are also locked, and Hayley speeds up, clearly aware that someone might be watching a gorilla trying to open people's doors.

HAYLEY: Man, it's hot in this mask.

The fifth door creaks open as Hayley pushes it forward. We go in, Hayley pointing the camera in front of her.

Voices from somewhere in the house. Muffled. Behind a door.

HAYLEY (*whispers*): Honey, I'm home.

A long, narrow hallway leads past a carpeted staircase. White walls – not a stain or blemish in sight. Shoe rack next to the door with the shoes lined up to perfection in a way that hints OCD is present in this household. A man's shoes, a woman's shoes and children's shoes.

HAYLEY: Here ... we ... go!

Hayley pushes open the door to her left and rushes into the living room, where a man and woman, approximately in their mid-thirties, are sitting on the floor, building a LEGO palace with two young children. The boy is about five. The girl, even younger.

The man leaps to his feet. His eyes bulging with horror.

MAN: What the bloody hell? What are you doing in my house?

Hayley can't hesitate. The power of shock is her friend here. Still filming, she rushes over to the dining-room table. Grabs an apple out of a crowded fruit bowl and sits down in a vacant armchair near the door. She waves at the horrified family and then pretends to eat the apple through the gorilla mask.

The man and woman are too stunned to move. The little girl begins to cry.

WOMAN: Who the fuck are you?

Hayley leans forward. She grabs the remote off the coffee table. Pushes buttons and turns on the TV. The sound of a daytime soap explodes, and now the boy's crying along with his sister. The house is a cacophony of children's tears and soap opera.

The man lunges at Hayley, but she's too quick. She's up off the armchair, running out of the living room. The mask allows her tunnel vision only, and she retraces her steps, clearly hoping she doesn't trip up on the way out. She has to be quick. Down the hallway, out the front door. The pounding of angry feet chasing after her.

MAN: Come back here, you little fucker. How dare you—

DAVID (*from the parked car outside the house*): Run!

Hayley runs down the path, hot and breathless in the mask. The engine idles as she leaps into the back of the car with the fake plates. The engine roars as David floors the accelerator. Down the street. The man chases the car for about ten seconds, then stops dead in the middle of the road. Watching them go. The look of disbelief still on his face.

Hayley pulls off the gorilla mask with great difficulty. Her forehead glistens with sweat. She looks at the camera, eyes shimmering with excitement.

HAYLEY: Kudos to the getaway driver.

DAVID: People are going to start pressing charges. This is some twisted shit.

HAYLEY: Yeah, because pressing charges went well for those who went after Mickey Morgan. Didn't it?

DAVID: Something bad will happen. You wait and see. Someone will come after us.

Alex turns around in the passenger seat. Flustered expression. Head shaking.

ALEX: You're crazy. That guy almost got his hands on you. What are we supposed to do if he does?

HAYLEY: Next one will be easier. I just need to get familiar with the routine. With the mask. It's all good, boys – relax.

DAVID: Alex is right. You *are* crazy. And he's right to ask the question – what do we do if someone puts their hands on you?

Hayley stares at the gorilla mask in her hand. Sweat drips down her face.

HAYLEY: Film it.

47

It's a windy day in Holy Family Cemetery. The cold is biting. Car fumes, drifting uphill on the wind from the main road, are a constant nuisance.

Hayley doesn't notice the fumes. She stands alone in front of two graves. Filming, of course. She traces the camera over the inscription on her mother's grave. Then over the inscription on her sister's grave. She does this over and over again. Slowly. Alice and Natasha Davies have matching headstones, two tall blocks of solid granite chosen to withstand the elements for decades to come.

White orchid plants have been placed at the foot of each headstone.

David, who's been waiting in the car, walks along the path. His face is creased up, and it's obvious that he's uncomfortable in a place like this – a place that reminds him of death. Of the certainty of death. He moves slowly, as if hoping that Hayley will notice and come to him. But she stays beside the graves, so he walks over, trying not to be too loud.

He stops beside her. Looks at the phone in her hand.

. . .

DAVID: Why are you filming? You're not uploading this, are you?

HAYLEY: Nope.

DAVID: Can't you do anything without filming?

HAYLEY: It's none of your business.

DAVID (*shrugs*): It's freezing. I have to get back to work soon.

HAYLEY: You know you wouldn't have to go anywhere if you'd just swallow your pride and work for me full-time.

DAVID: I don't want to become your employee, Hayls. That's not ... us.

He waits a few minutes while Hayley stares at the graves. He takes his phone out of his pocket, thumbs through a few pages and gives Hayley a soft nudge with his elbow.

DAVID: Are you paying attention to this?

HAYLEY: To what?

DAVID: They're still writing articles about copycats. There are *lots* of articles doing the rounds right now, and they're turning you into public enemy number one.

Hayley points the camera at David. He scowls. Almost gives her the finger but remembers where he is and lowers his hand.

HAYLEY: So?

DAVID: So?

HAYLEY: Yeah. So?

DAVID: It's getting worse, Hayls. It wouldn't be so bad if it was just us doing our thing, but these Hayley tributes keep popping up – they're everywhere. *Everywhere.* Hundreds of people dropping your name into their videos to get hits Most of them making a complete mess of the pranks, but one thing's for sure – you're pissing people off even when you aren't doing anything. As if you weren't getting enough bad press. People don't feel safe with this outpouring of pranksters everywhere. Everyone feels like they're a potential victim. A victim of you or your minions.

The wind moans softly, and it sounds like a sigh. All around Holy Family Cemetery, the trees sway, and the branches creak.

HAYLEY: It's Natasha's anniversary. I don't feel like talking about anything else.

DAVID: You're raking in the money, Hayls. Take a break. No one's going to forget about you if you lie low for a few weeks.

HAYLEY: Mickey Morgan did that, and look what happened to him. There's always someone else working to get noticed. Clawing their way to the top, waiting for an opening.

DAVID: Okay. Just take a week off, then. Can you do that? Unplug for a single week?

Hayley doesn't answer.

David lifts the hood on his coat, shoves his hands in his pockets and stands beside her as a light rain begins to fall.

48

Message received through the Contact Form on Hayley T. Prank's official website.
Time: 5.34 p.m.

Dear Hayley,

I did it. I just did Uninvited Guest!

(SCREEEAMMS!)

OMG, my hands are still shaking, and I'm fixing typos everywhere. I was only in the house for a few seconds and didn't upload to the channel because it's not long/good enough. Nobody saw it, but I'll try again soon.

FIRST STEPS, BABY!!

What a buzz. I've never felt more scared and alive in my life, and now I get you more than ever. I know why we do this.

I really hope you read this.

Love you.

Zara
Xxx

49

HAYLEY T. PRANK – PARTNER SWAP

We view the kitchen through a hidden camera in the wall. There's nothing unusual at first glance. It's an ordinary kitchen with mahogany countertops and a circular dining table in the middle of the room. A large steel fridge-freezer covered in magnets from a variety of global destinations, photographs and colourful, childish artwork.

A tall man stands at the counter, chopping vegetables at lightning speed like a pro. The blade is a blur in his hand. The frantic chopping sounds like some kind of weird percussion. As he works, a true-crime podcast plays on his phone, which sits on the window ledge.

He looks up at the sound of the front door opening. His glance lingers there for a moment. Then he goes back to chopping vegetables.

MAN (*calling over the podcast*): Is that you, Claire?

She answers from the hallway.

CLAIRE: It's me, babe.

MAN: How was your day?

CLAIRE: Oh my God, don't ask.

MAN: Why don't you come in and tell me all about it?

A pause.

CLAIRE: Matt?

The kitchen door opens. Claire walks in, takes one look at the man chopping vegetables and screams. Her back slams against the wall and hits the light switch. The room goes dark. She screams again, and there's a frantic clawing and scratching as she fumbles in the dark for the switch.

The light goes back on.

CLAIRE: Who the fuck are you?

The man stops cutting. He lowers the knife onto the chopping board and holds both hands in the air. The podcast is still playing – a serial killer being interviewed in prison talks about his reasons for eating his victims. He says there was no reason. He just ... liked it.

MAN: Honey?

CLAIRE (*shaking her head*): What's going on? What are you doing in my kitchen? Who ...?

She pulls her phone out of her pocket. Her arm moves slowly, as if expecting the man to charge. She looks back and forth between him and the knife on the chopping board.

CLAIRE: Oh God. Where's Matt?

MAN: Claire, calm down. Tell me, what's wrong?

CLAIRE: Where's Matt? Where the fuck is my husband? Tell me now, or I'm calling the police.

The man jerks back like he's dodging an invisible punch. At last, he turns off the podcast.

MAN: Is this some kind of joke?

Claire's panicky eyes probe the room. Penetrating every detail in the kitchen. Doubting everything she sees.

CLAIRE: Where is my husband?

MAN: Honey, it's me. *I'm* Matt.

CLAIRE: That's not funny. What have you done? What have you done to my husband?

The man takes a step forward. The light bulb in the kitchen makes a crackling noise, and Claire hears it and looks up. Begging with her eyes for it not to blow out.

MAN: No, it's not funny. It's not funny at all. Why are you doing this, honey? Don't you ... don't you recognise me?

They stand facing each other across the kitchen. Claire's back is still pressed tight against the wall, her face contorted into a horrified mask. The man doesn't move, yet it feels like the gap between them is closing.

CLAIRE: You're not Matt. Stop playing games.

MAN: Not Matt, am I?

CLAIRE: How did you get into my house?

The man wipes something from the corner of his eye. His voice trembles.

MAN: Oh honey.

CLAIRE: How the fuck did you get into my kitchen?

MAN: Listen to me, okay. We got married on the fifth of April, two years ago. That was your dream wedding – a beach ceremony in Hawaii. It's what you always wanted. You want children, but I'm not sure, and we've talked about it long into the night, both of us trying to find some sort of resolution. But we never have – at least not yet. You love books. You adore scary movies, especially those *Scream*-type films from the nineties. *I Know What You Did Last Summer*. That sort of thing. Right? There's a birthmark on your right leg. I think it's shaped like a heart, but you don't let me see it because you think it's ugly. I love that birthmark because it's a part of you.

Claire gasps.

He looks at her.

MAN: Remember the time we camped at Loch Fyne? Just the two of us. We saw a basking shark go right by the dinghy, and you thought it was going to eat us, even though I tried to tell you basking sharks are harmless.

Honey.

How could I remember that? How could I remember any of it if I weren't Matt?

Claire looks like she's sliding down the wall. Madness in her eyes.

CLAIRE: I'm ... I'm calling the police.

The man takes another step towards her, and Claire shrieks. She drops her phone, as if abandoning the idea of calling the police, and makes a run for it instead. She thunders down the hallway, calling for help. Her screams are deafening. She runs outside, still calling for help.

The man in the kitchen follows her outside. Yelling her name. Pleading with her to come back.

A moment later, the back door opens into the kitchen. Hayley T. Prank runs into the house with a man close behind her – the real Matt. Short, stocky and rugged. Nothing like the man in the apron who claimed to be Matt.

HAYLEY (*to the real Matt*): You'd better go after her, buddy. Looks like you've got some explaining to do.

She howls with laughter as a nervous-looking Matt sprints out of the kitchen. Claire's shrill screams out on the street can be heard inside the house.

50

Message received through the Contact Form on Hayley T. Prank's official website.
Time: 1.12 p.m.

Dear Hayley,

Wow!

Will these people ever realise? It's just a JOKE!

What made her drop the case in the end? Did she realise that she was being a GIANT spoilsport and that the whole can't-take-a-joke Karen look wasn't doing her any favours? I heard the publicity was grinding her down. That she feels stupid because she actually believed this other guy was her husband for a second.

Is it true she and her husband are separated now?

I don't get it. Why can't people lighten up?

Still, no court case. Nice! Like Mickey, you do have a knack of getting out of trouble, don't you? It gives me hope that I can keep pushing forward with my own plans. I have lots of ideas, but you keep raising the bar (TO PUT IT MILDLY!), and I'm still finding my feet with the Hayley tributes.

I'm going to try Partner Swap real soon. It's the best thing you've ever done, and for me, it's the ultimate test to see if I'm ready to step it up a level. Man, I'm scared, though. Walking into someone's house with a mask on. Being that brave?

I'll do a few more Uninvited Guest videos first. I've had a couple of close calls, and a man almost got his hands on me last week. But I'm getting good with the routine. And people are starting to notice me, I think?

Oh wow! I see you have a new video premiering soon.

CAN'T WAIT!

Can you just let me know you've seen this? A smiley face? A thumbs-up?

Love always,

Zara

51

WhatsApp group chat
Group Name – The Prank Execs (Hayley/David/Alex)

DAVID: More hate pieces in the *Mail* this morning. You guys seeing this? Time to dial it back for a while. We need to make an announcement for the production team and all the crew – tell them we need to take a break. Media is relentless, and this shit is getting clicks. They're making haters out of people who don't even know us. But they know your name, Hayls. Too many copycats doing tributes.

ALEX: Agree. An alternative would be to make 'safe' content for a few weeks. Nothing controversial.

DAVID: Doable. We can talk about that. As for tomorrow – cancel?

ALEX: Agree.

HAYLEY: Disagree. Tomorrow we're doing the biggest and best prank yet. Nerves kicking in, boys?

ALEX: I'm nervous. But not because of the prank. This hate they're stirring up – what does it lead to?

DAVID: Trouble.

HAYLEY: Relax. It's just nerves.

DAVID: No, Hayls. Feels like the media is turning on us, and the public is easily swayed. Don't like where this is going.

HAYLEY: We'll talk properly after tomorrow. The crew will be on site for 5 p.m., and everything is ready to go. This is too big. We've spent months prepping, so let's just get it done. It's going to be awesome!

DAVID: Hayls, you haven't stopped since your mum died. Think about calling it off. Rescheduling. No one else is going to come up with a prank like this. It can wait.

ALEX: I'm with David.

HAYLEY: Bright and early tomorrow. Will you guys be there, or is someone else getting a promotion?

52

The video begins with a wide shot of a suburban street at dusk.
    Slanted streetlights keep the approaching darkness at bay. Parked cars mount the kerb on both sides of the street, leaving only a narrow channel in the centre for traffic to get through. A stray traffic cone is toppled over at the edge of the road, most likely left behind after some recent maintenance work. Two rows of terraced houses sit on either side of the street, the curtains and blinds closed.
    Everything is still and quiet. The street and its inhabitants are settling in for a quiet evening.
    The camera sweeps across the neighbourhood slowly, then turns back to reveal a small group of ten people standing at the northern end of the street. They're huddled beside a tall, well-trimmed hedge. They have headsets on. Phones or two-way radios in hand.
    Hayley T. Prank turns the camera on herself. She speaks in a whisper.

. . .

HAYLEY: Hey, guys, welcome to another prank. I promised you something special tonight, didn't I? Well, I'm about to deliver the goods and then some. We gotta stay quiet because we're trying to be subtle here – at least for the moment.

Let me tell you, this one took a lot of work, and no amount of media harassment is going to shut me up. Don't believe what you read. Tell your family not to believe what they read. I will not be silenced.

She points to the other end of the street.

HAYLEY: This time around, we've got an entire neighbourhood working with us. Seriously, guys, everyone who lives on this street – except for one person – is in on this prank. And we've got people in the surrounding streets on our side too. Like I say, this took a *lot* of work.

So, what is going on? I'll tell you. After ... this!

CUT to:

A segment on today's sponsor, Vitality Protein Shakes.

CUT back to:

Hayley on the street with her crew.

HAYLEY: Here we are, standing outside number eleven. This is where a lady called Alison Jackson lives. According to her husband, Ricky, right now she's lying on the sofa, watching TV. He's upstairs, pretending to have an early night. For Alison, it's just another quiet Saturday night at home with her feet up. Nice and relaxing. A couple of glasses of wine.

But she has no idea what's coming next.

Hayley points to the southern end of the street.

HAYLEY: In about twenty minutes, my driver extraordinaire and partner-in-crime, David, is going to come racing down here in the stunt car. And I mean *racing*. It's going to be noisy. So noisy in fact that Alison's going to get up off the couch, go over to the window and have a look. She'll be shocked. She'll be frightened. Meanwhile, David's going to crash into the neighbour's fence across the street. See that black metal fence right over there? That one.

Don't worry – he knows what he's doing. No one will be hurt. There's going to be a lot of fuss, and all the neighbours are going to come outside, and we've even got a fake police car and ambulance showing up.

But here's the really fun part.

Alison is the only person who will remember the crash.

That's right. Come tomorrow, it never happened. Everyone on this street is going to deny what they've seen whenever Alison brings it up, including her husband. And we'll keep the prank going for a full forty-eight hours.

Crash. What crash?

I wonder how she'll take it.

How would you react?

Hayley touches her earpiece.

HAYLEY: Okay, I hear our girl Alison is dozing off on the couch inside number eleven. Might be a good time for to Mr Stunt Driver to start warming up the engine.

David, are you ready?

Hayley listens to a voice in her ear. She nods.

HAYLEY: Yeah, if you can go now, that'd be great. Alex, is everyone set on the street? They know when to come outside, yeah?

Alex limps towards her. Thumbs up for the camera. But his voice is a little flat.

ALEX: Ready to go.

Phone calls are made. Texts sent to confirm that the neighbours are indeed good to go – both the immediate neighbours and those in the surrounding area, all of whom have been generously compensated for the disturbance and for their promises not to alert the emergency services.

The car is coming.

Word reaches Hayley that Alison is up on the couch. Ricky, the husband, sends a text. 'She's heard it. She's on her feet. At the window.'

Hayley keeps out of sight with her team at the end of the street. They watch as David (along with two passengers) brings the stunt car in fast. The headlights are low to the ground, overpowering and fearless. Fast. Faster.

The curtains twitch at number eleven. A woman's face appears at the window, and a hidden camera across the street captures the moment. Alison is staring at the stunt car, a disbelieving look on her face.

HAYLEY: Here we go, ladies and gentlemen. Tomorrow, she'll wake up, and no one will remember a thing. And we'll capture every second of it for your viewing pleasure.

This is our biggest and best prank yet.

It's called ... Car Crash.

PART IV
HELEN (THE PROJECT)

53

A gentle drizzle starts to fall as the two women walk away from the open grave.

From there, they make their way onto the footpath. Heads down. It's the way you're supposed to walk when there's a teenager in the coffin behind you.

The family resemblance is unmistakable. Both women possess the same razor-sharp cheekbones, almond-shaped eyes and black hair. But it's not just looks that bond them. Both are highly driven individuals whose father instilled a strong work ethic from an early age after his and their mother's arrival from Pakistan. He would have been proud of their ambition and of their achievements. They've climbed high in their respective professions and will never have to worry about money again.

The rain picks up. Clouds have been threatening all morning but held off for the service at least. One of the big men in dark suits shadowing the two women opens an umbrella, stands close behind them and does his best to keep the rain off their heads.

Sadia, the older of the two sisters, takes a couple of steps, then hesitates. She stops. An agonising glance over her shoulder, one last look at the soaking wet hole in the ground where her daughter now lies. Full of dirt and flowers and now rainwater. Most of the mourners have dispersed, but a few remain gathered there despite the rain, staring down at the wooden box. Trying to make sense of the tragedy that brought them all together today.

'Goodbye, darling,' Sadia whispers. But her voice is lost in the rain.

She walks away with Helen, her younger sister, and the cluster of security personnel at their backs. They hurry towards the back exit where the car is waiting. Despite avoiding the main gate, there are numerous photographers, and they make no effort to hide their presence or intent. With all the subtlety of a sledgehammer over the head, they snap away as the two sisters walk towards the gate.

'Let's go,' Sadia says, walking faster.

They follow the path to the waiting car. A cold wind blows, and a grove of pines beyond the cemetery sways from side to side. In the cemetery, the piper begins the lament. Sadia hurries like she's trying to outrun the notes. She gasps. Winces as the rain hits her face.

Helen grabs her sister's arm, and they move even faster. To hell with the photographers. She's just as eager to put the cemetery behind her. Maybe it's the rain. Maybe it's the thought of her niece in that wooden box.

They clear the gate. The men in dark suits follow, their presence a subtle reminder for anyone watching not to get too close. And for the reporters not to get too brave.

'Very sorry for your loss,' a female voice calls out.

They reach the car without incident. In the back seat, Sadia unzips her bag and takes out her phone. She unlocks it, and the phone immediately opens on an article about Zara's death. Helen glances over while she dries off her hair with a towel kept in the luxury vehicle for just this purpose. She suspects there are dozens of tabs open on Sadia's phone with articles about her daughter's death. And Sadia will have read them all again and again. Studying the public response. She wants to know what people are thinking before she commits to Helen's idea.

Helen skims the article. She feels queasy at the sight of her niece's face smiling back at her. So alive. It's hard not to look at that face and think about the box in the muddy hole. The sound of rain splattering against the dirt. Zara was still pretty; most of her injuries were internal. But no matter how Helen frames it, her niece and that young, pretty face are rotting.

She drops the towel on her lap. Looks at the article again. Helen hasn't read this particular one, but she's seen many like it over the past week. She knows the narrative:

PRANK TRIBUTE KILLS HOME SECRETARY'S DAUGHTER

The daughter of Home Secretary Sadia Hassani has died after being struck by a car in East Pendleton. Witnesses claim that seventeen-year-old Zara Hassani ran out of a house and was struck while crossing the road. It's since been revealed by her partner that Zara was an aspiring YouTube pranker performing regular copycats of 'Uninvited Guest', a prank created and popularised by the noto-

rious influencer Hayley T. Prank. According to Zara's partner, Zara was 'obsessed' with becoming the next Hayley. And, tragically, her partner has also disclosed that Zara was eight weeks pregnant.

Helen stops reading there.

The car drives away from the cemetery. The photographers are still out there in the rain, taking their pictures, chasing after the car like hordes of zombies. Meanwhile, the spectators disperse. Walking away, their heads hidden under hoods and umbrellas.

'Helen,' Sadia says.

'Yes?'

'Talk to me again about this idea of yours.'

There's a partition between the sisters and the driver. It's closed, but Helen lowers her voice anyway. Makes sure the intercom is switched off.

'Well,' says Helen, 'it's like I said before. In terms of the plan itself, it's pretty much all laid out. We've been working on it for a long time. The problem isn't building a set. It's not even the legality of it – with your influence in parliament, we can always work in a law to support the Project. It's the court of public opinion. That's what'll make or break this in the long term. That's why we've been working with the press in recent months, well before Zara's accident. That's why we're trying to help them educate the public by emphasising how dangerous these influencers are.'

'Are the people with you?'

'We can't assume anything yet,' Helen says. 'But if pressed, I think so. Yes.'

'Really?'

'These influencers need an effective deterrent. An *effec-*

tive deterrent – not increased publicity from court cases. Not infamy. Not notoriety. The ordinary people they terrorise are no match for them financially or in court, and most people are too afraid to take action anyway.'

Sadia sighs. 'Let's not pretend, Helen.'

'What do you mean?'

Sadia takes the damp towel out of Helen's hand. She throws it onto the floor and looks at her sister. 'I know this is about more than Zara. You've always been ambitious.'

'Look who's talking.'

'You've been planning something like this for years, haven't you? Ever since these YouTube creators encroached upon your territory.'

Helen says nothing.

'Online influencers are a threat to network television,' Sadia says. 'You want to put them back in their place, and what better way to show the world what you can do than humble the biggest one of all.'

'She killed Zara,' Helen says. 'And your unborn granddaughter.'

Sadia shakes her head. 'Zara killed Zara. Or who knows, maybe I did? Maybe if I'd been a better mother—'

'No,' Helen says, cutting in. 'She never would've taken all those risks if Hayley T. Prank hadn't showed her the way. And it's not just Zara. There *will* be others.'

Sadia shrugs. 'I don't know, Helen. I don't know if we as a nation are quite ready for that sort of thing. It's extreme to say the least, and they'll call it personal revenge on my part. On your part, too.'

Helen doesn't push. At least, not now. Instead, she speaks to the driver through the intercom. Tells him to take a specific detour on the way back to the city.

'What are you doing?' Sadia asks. 'Why are we going *that* way?'

Helen puts an arm around her. Huddled together, the sisters feel the warmth of each other. 'There's no rush, is there? And besides, how many years has it been since we've gone home?'

54

The car drives through the lashing rain.

Black-tinted windows hide the sisters from the prying eyes of locals. Some people on the street, hurrying along under umbrellas, wave at the car like they know only too well who's taking shelter in there.

They're five miles into the journey, not far from the scenic countryside cemetery where Zara was laid to rest, when they reach the humble town where Sadia and Helen grew up as the children of immigrants from Pakistan. It wasn't a happy time, at least not to begin with. Their mother, Risha, died from a massive heart attack not long after their arrival in the UK. Their father pressed on, raising the girls alone. He was a strict but loving man, one who always instilled the values of hard work, entrepreneurship and loyalty. Even more so after the death of his wife. He knew that anything could happen at any time. He wanted his girls to be okay. To be strong and independent should something happen to him.

Helen had never forgotten his mantra.

Make something of your lives.

She saw the coldness in Sadia's eyes as, upon her request, the driver took them past the familiar streets of their youth. Down the street where their little semi-detached house once stood. Most of the houses (including the Hassani home) were long gone; now a small row of shops had taken their place.

Their primary school was still there, just off the main road, fresh and illegible graffiti scrawled all over the front gates. Clearly the quality of students hadn't improved much. Nearby, their local playground was intact. The swimming pool had been turned into a community centre. Everything appeared much smaller than they remembered.

There was no question of Helen or Sadia getting out of the car. It was too wet. And, in truth, neither sister wanted to get too close.

Sadia glares through the window. Her true contempt for this little shithole is there on her face, just as Helen knew it would be. Contempt for the town, its bullies and a long-standing racist core that had meant it never truly welcomed her family. Sure, they'd smiled. Said the right things, sometimes. But in their eyes there was always something distant, something that had left Helen and her family feeling 'other'. Like outsiders.

There was the 'hard' bullying – the outright, nasty insults, and God knows there were plenty of those tossed around at school. And there was the 'soft' bullying – microaggressions, they were called now – that was harder to pin down, to articulate, but in ways it was so much worse than being called a Paki bastard. Helen remembered the way that other men in particular spoke to her father whenever they went into his shop (the 'Paki shop' as it was known by such men) to buy their cigarettes, their booze and groceries. How they spoke down to him. Talked over him. And the way they laughed at him behind his back because he could be nervous around them. This town was full of bastards. Full of bullies. Always had been, always would be. The girls got out, but their father had stayed to the end of his days. Now he was buried in the same cemetery as Zara.

'Why are we here?' Sadia asks.

Helen shrugs. 'Thought you'd like to see it. That's all.'

'Today of all days?' Sadia's lips imitate a smile. 'You know me better than that, don't you?'

'I don't know what you mean.'

'This place,' Sadia says. 'You're trying to draw a parallel with the YouTube girl.'

'Hmm?'

'She's a bully. She terrorises innocent people. And here in this shithole, a long time ago, we put up with a different kind of bullying. I get it. You want me to be pissed off. You want me to be so angry at the sight of this place that I'll agree to get behind your mad venture.'

Helen falls back onto the seat. 'I never could get anything past you, could I?'

Sadia presses the intercom. 'Driver, we've seen enough here. Let's head back to the city.'

'Yes, ma'am.'

'Helen,' she says, 'I haven't been a very good sister to you, have I?'

'What are you talking about?'

'Growing up,' Sadia says. 'Neither one of us had many friends. I should've been there for you more. Dad told me to keep an eye on you, but I didn't. I hid from my responsibilities.'

'Who needs a little sister following them about everywhere, asking questions and slowing them down?' Helen asks.

Sadia shakes her head. 'We don't choose family. Zara didn't. Not in a million years would she have chosen Richard and me.'

'You loved her,' Helen says. 'She knew that.'

'Not so sure about that. I wasn't there for her either, just like I wasn't there for you. And look at Richard – straight from the funeral to catch a flight for a meeting in Manchester. Even today, he can't put work aside.'

'Maybe it's his way of coping. Or maybe the work just has to be done.'

Sadia looks at her sister. Her sunken eyes suggest that she's had little sleep over the past week.

'What you're talking about doing,' she says, 'is something truly revolutionary. You're talking about combining justice and entertainment in a way that's never been done before.'

Helen nods. 'I'm talking about an effective deterrent. These people …'

'Your competitors.'

'These people have too much freedom. There's no regulation, and they don't have the maturity to regulate themselves.'

Sadia doesn't speak for a minute.

'The criticism will be savage.'

Helen feels a sudden jolt of excitement. She senses that her sister might be with her after all. That they'll climb this mountain together. Her sister has the power and the connections to make it happen. To insert legality into the equation. And now, with Zara's death, terrible as it is, she has the motivation.

Two different types of revenge. Sadia would avenge her daughter, and Helen would strike back at those living it up in the wild west of the internet.

All she had to do was package the product wisely.

We have to stop influencers from killing our children.

Helen didn't want someone to have to die in order to get this thing up and running. Especially not her niece. But it was always going to take a tragedy to get the wheels turning. Zara had been a strange child, and they'd never really connected as people. Still, she was blood and so was her unborn child. The Project was both a private and public service, albeit an extreme one. Influencers were out of control and, yes, they were taking eyeballs and advertisers away from network TV. Killing themselves and others for clicks and digital validation from strangers.

This was necessary. Right-wingers would probably love it from the get-go. Everyone else would take some persuading.

'I wish Dad were here,' Sadia says, looking out the window at a vast expanse of rolling hills. Their hometown is far behind them now. The rain is still lashing down.

Helen can't agree on that one. Their father would be pleased with their bank accounts, but there are plenty of things he wouldn't approve of.

'Me too,' Helen says, even so.

Sadia looks at her sister. 'I'm sorry I wasn't there for you.'

Helen nods. 'We don't have to talk about this now.'

Sadia rests a hand on her sister's knee. 'How much have you planned out already?'

'Almost all of it.'

'Location?'

'We'd run out of the old film studios from the fifties – they haven't been used for decades, but the network owns the land and the building. We could build over it. If the financing is there, we could create something truly special.'

'Interesting.'

Helen takes a deep breath. 'What are you saying, Sadia? Are you saying you're with me on this?'

Sadia nods, but her eyes are distant. 'She was always a bit fragile, wasn't she?'

'I wish I'd known her better,' Helen says.

Sadia leans her head against the window. As the car joins up with the eastern motorway, the rain isn't letting up for a second. Water thumps off the roof of the car. The driver swerves into the outside lane and floors it.

'We'll have to arrest her.'

Helen nods. 'Not only that. We'll have to convince the public that we're doing it for the safety of their children. I guess that's what the media is for.'

Sadia's voice quivers with emotion for the first time since receiving the news that her daughter had been hit by a car. 'For the safety of our children.'

The two sisters sit in silence for a long time, listening as the world drowns in rain.

'Make your mark, Helen,' Sadia says eventually. 'Just like Dad wanted you to.'

55

Four weeks later

Helen's apartment feels lifeless. The cleaners have been in this morning, and although they've done their usual good job, the place feels sterile. Like a show home. Neutral, earthy shades that suck the joy out of the walls. Not enough colour in the soft furnishings. There's no personality here, but Helen's never home enough to notice how bland the place really is. And for the past month, she's been working harder than ever.

Today, she's staring at the massive TV fixed to the wall. The TV is so large it pretty much *is* the wall on that side of the living room. The twenty-four-hour news channel has been running over the same garbage for the past hour. War. Political corruption in Greece. Celebrity adultery like that's actually news. The same headlines scrolling back and forth at the bottom of the picture.

All that will change soon.

She paces the living room. From her luxury apartment in

the heart of the city, there are views of the cathedral in the distance. The river. Skyscrapers and world-famous monuments. Helen sees none of it. Instead, she walks back to the bar and pours herself another vodka. It's what she drinks when her nerves are shot.

Things have been moving so fast since Zara's death. It's like the Project has taken on a life of its own, and everyone, Helen included, is hanging on for the ride as it snowballs into something truly massive.

The housekeeper, Ariadne, has been dismissed. There are so many things to do, but Helen's put everything to the side because she wants to be on her own, watching TV as the news breaks for the first time.

Finally, it happens.

It starts with the headline.

BREAKING NEWS
Influencer Hayley T. Prank arrested

The glamorous blonde presenter is grim-faced as she elaborates.

Some massive news just in. The popular YouTube influencer Hayley T. Prank has been arrested. The content creator, real name Hayley Davies, was arrested at approximately eleven o'clock this morning after breaking into private property to film one of her infamous pranks.

Helen turns away. She hears the rest in snippets.

... she has influenced thousands of copycats ...

... responsible for the death of the Home Secretary's daughter

...

... breakdown of society ...

... people fearing for their lives even in the safety of their own homes ...

Her phone rings on the coffee table. That didn't take long. Without taking her eyes off the screen, she picks up. It's the American producer. He's been calling a lot recently, and already Helen is a little sick of his voice. But the man is good at what he does. And Helen needs the best if this thing has any chance of getting off the ground.

'Joel, what can I do for you?'

'Hey, you watching the news?'

'Sure am.'

'Now it's real, huh?'

'Yes. So what can I do for you?'

'Right, right. Just wanted to call and let you know things are progressing fast, and I mean *fast*. Where are we getting all these extra hands from?'

'That's not your concern.'

His laugh is low and gravelly. 'Must be nice having a sister with all that clout, huh?'

'Again,' Helen says, 'not your concern.'

'Fair enough. Anyway, the work is going great. This is going to be the best set I've ever been on – and I've been on some good ones. But this ... it's a town. Not just a re-creation of a town – it's a town, for God's sake. A town with hidden cameras, but, boy oh boy, it's impressive.'

'I'm glad you approve.'

'Damn right I do.'

Helen half listens while Joel bangs on about specifics in her ear. There's a lot of stuff she doesn't need to hear or that could be summarised in a fraction of the time. He talks while Helen watches the news. A young male reporter is interviewing one of Hayley T. Prank's crew members – a woman in her twenties with spiky blue hair. Looks like she hasn't showered in a month. The woman, named Terri according to the caption, is cursing (all bleeped out). She's coming off as a raving lunatic, so she's a good choice by the news crew.

Terri yells directly at the camera.

'It's a setup. This is all a setup. She said she was being followed, and we all agreed that there'd be no activity for at least a week. Now they're saying she's been arrested while breaking into someone's house in the west end. That's a f******g lie. It's b******t. They came for her. Don't fall for this—'

Bleep. Bleep. Bleep.

Joel is still talking specifics in Helen's ear: network and livestream broadcast setups, electricians doing final checks in Little Market, filming tests and organising extras and crew bonus schemes. There's more, much more, but it's aimed at a Helen, who's showing a rare lack of focus as she sips vodka.

I'm a pioneer, she tells herself. *I have to be brave.*

She checks her smartwatch. Her heart rate is through the roof, like she's coming to the end of a twenty-kilometre run.

The news report has moved on to interviewing selected members of the public and gauging streetside opinion on the matter. Most side with the idea of *effectively* punishing Hayley. That's the hope that Helen's holding on to, but she also knows the news channel isn't exactly impartial.

They're running an opinion poll, too. Text yes or no if you agree that influencers and content creators should face accountability for their actions. So far, a massive eighty-three per cent are in favour of 'accountability procedures'.

The media are warming up the public. That'll get them ready for the official announcement of the Project.

'About time,' a middle-aged man in a crumpled suit says on TV.

It's late afternoon, and he's being interviewed outside a busy train station. He doesn't look like a Hayley T. Prank fan.

He continues, 'It's absolutely ridiculous what these people have been allowed to get away with. I've heard all about this Hayley prank thing. Breaking into someone's house? Swapping their partner around for a bloody stranger? I mean ... what the hell? These aren't harmless pranks. This is obnoxious and juvenile behaviour from a generation of look-at-me morons. I'm sick to death of it. I've heard they're going to make an example of her, and that's a good thing.'

56

Three weeks later

Helen is the creator. As the creator, she was always going to have to answer questions about the Project. And it wasn't just questions she'd have to deal with. There'd be outrage. Accusations of all sorts that would target the work itself and Helen and her family personally. They had some of the media working with them, the bigger mainstream outlets mostly, but not all of them. She would have to manage the situation, and it was important to remember that there *were* plenty of people – ordinary people – on her side.

She stands in front of a wall of microphones. Reporters stand huddled around her in the hotel where they're hosting the official press conference to announce the Project. Outside, a protest of angry voices is getting louder. They've been there since the early hours of the morning, and a police barricade is the only thing preventing them from getting inside the hotel.

Helen isn't the public speaker that her sister is. Sadia never gets ruffled, at least not on the surface. But Helen believes in herself and is more than capable of weathering the storm. She's practised in front of the mirror for good measure. *Think like a politician,* that's her mantra. Neutral phrases. Generic language that might not specifically answer questions but that works well enough to get her out of a tight spot. Sadia has given her tips on keeping her cool in the face of media fire.

'Is this really going to happen?' a bespectacled male reporter asks. He sounds too angry to be neutral. 'Doesn't this seem like a misstep? Like we're veering off into some dystopian nightmare?'

Helen speaks in a calm voice.

'Nothing has been taken lightly. Not in parliament and certainly not within the network. Nothing was rushed. Every step of the process is listed in the official documentation, readily available to everyone online, free of charge. We want transparency here.'

Readily available. Those were Sadia's words. Two words that evoke openness and freedom and we're all in it together. *Say them,* she'd urged Helen. *Say them over and over again. Hypnotise them with repetition.*

'That's all very well,' the reporter persists. 'But let's call this what it is, shall we?'

He leaves a pause. Perhaps for dramatic purposes.

'This is state-sponsored revenge. Your sister is the Home Secretary, and we know what happened to her daughter and why it happened. Zara Hassani died because she was copycatting Hayley T. Prank. And now the Hassani girls are taking their revenge? Or is that all just one big coincidence?'

Helen clears her throat. She doesn't take her eyes off the reporter, not for a second.

'The Project has been on the table for a long time. In fact, it was being discussed before my niece's tragic death, and like I said, all the information is readily available online. I encourage you to take a look.'

Readily available.

'Fourteen hundred pages of documentation,' the reporter says, nodding. 'All to say just five words – we are now policing influencers.'

'Influencers are not being policed,' Helen says. Her voice remains calm although one leg is definitely shaking under the table. 'Deviancy is, just like it always has been and always will be by law-abiding citizens.'

'Are you confident that parliament is with you?' a female journalist asks.

Helen takes a sip of water before answering.

'Parliament is with us and for good reason. There is an ethical void in our society today, and our children are being exposed to online deviancy at a very young age. Cruelty in the name of entertainment is becoming the norm. Causing trauma to others is celebrated, and those responsible are rewarded with fame and wealth. They're perceived as heroes. Role models to our children. In reality, they're deviants, and it's irrelevant whether this deviancy takes place on a street corner or on a YouTube channel with ten million subscribers. In this country, there *will* be consequences.'

'Televised consequences?' another reporter calls out.

Helen nods. 'Putting these people in ordinary prisons will only turn them into martyrs. Crucially, it won't *change* them. I believe the Project will prove itself to be an effective deterrent against online deviancy. We put the deviants in their victims' shoes. They experience what it's like to be the victim of their own crimes.'

There are a few scattered outbursts of applause. The network has people in the room, and Helen assumes they're the ones clapping.

She waits for the clapping to die down, then continues.

'The Project has one overriding goal above all others. To make the internet a safe place for all of us. Additionally, we'll be hiring independent sensitivity consultants to oversee our decision-making processes, putting them on set, and we'll have at least one in the control room. And we *will* encourage them to make their voices heard.'

There's a sudden banging noise. Sounds like a door slamming shut. Everyone looks over that way to see a young woman standing at the back of the room. She's holding up a sign that says FREE HAYLEY.

So much for the police barricade, Helen thinks.

The woman yells in a Northern Irish accent, 'I guess if you've got power, you can legalise whatever you want. They're talking about drugs and hypnosis – in safe doses, apparently – but who's regulating this?'

'That information is readily available,' Helen says. She hears herself speaking in Sadia's cool, clipped rhythm. 'Anything still to be added to the official documentation *will* be added. Transparency is of paramount importance.'

The protestor's voice cracks with anger. 'This *cannot* happen. This *cannot* be allowed to happen. There are hundreds of people out there who can't believe this is even being discussed.'

She looks around the press room, pleading for support that doesn't come.

'We have to stop this. We have to get up, get out and

protest this dystopian nightmare. Not just from home. We need people on the street, mobilising. C'mon, people!' she urges.

'If you don't quieten down,' Helen says, 'I'll have to ask security to remove you. We want to talk about this, but—'

The woman waves her arms in the air. She's inching closer to the front, well aware that many people are filming her on their phones.

'This is what totalitarian control looks like. Soon we won't be able to post anything online without their say-so. Is this what you want? Is this what you want?'

Then security officers grab the woman and drag her away towards the door. She wriggles frantically in their grip. Continues to yell to the room.

'What about politicians like the Home Secretary? Will they be punished for authorising state-sponsored control in the name of personal revenge? We won't stand for it, let alone watch it. Do NOT watch this – that's what they want.'

Helen remains perfectly still except for that tremble in her right leg. She watches as the protestor is thrown out of the hotel, and then she hears it. The roar of the crowd as they greet the one who got inside and made her voice heard.

Amid all the hardship of the day, it's the sound of that roar that Helen will remember the most. All those voices coming together as one.

57

Less than a week after the press conference and all the sleepless nights that followed, Helen sits in the back of the car, being driven to the well-guarded set. That's where she, along with the entire crew, will be staying until it's over.

One month. Watching as the influencer experiences her own pranks as the victim. And when it's over?

Let's not get ahead of ourselves.

No more vodka for breakfast. She's thrown up more in the past few days than she can remember, and although she's excited, she's also terrified. Her gym routine has gone to shit as the Project has slowly taken over her life. She's seen pictures of the set but hasn't been able to visit for, according to security, safety reasons. One thing's for sure – it doesn't look like an old fifties film studio anymore. The new building is gigantic – several concrete mega-blocks joined together, and instead of building 'Kate's Town', as it's known, on the land behind the old studio as per the original plan, they've built the town inside. That way they can control everything – even the weather.

Helen knows there'll be protestors at the gates. It's okay; she'll get through it. And they'll get bored long before the month is over, go home and fight for some other cause. She won't be the only one working on the Project who's worried about protestors. She won't be the only one with doubts. But she has to give an impression of strength because she's the creator. Everyone, even a producer as experienced as Joel, will be looking to her for guidance.

The scenery whizzes past. Grey city turns to green countryside, yet there's no comfort to be found in the bucolic surroundings.

Poor Zara, Helen thinks as she stares at distant rolling hills. What would she have thought about all of this? The influencer was her idol, and now her mother and aunt are throwing her into the flames.

For love?

Or for glory?

Helen unzips her bag and pulls out a breath mint. She's been smoking all week after giving up the cancer sticks three years ago. It was stupid, but there's no doubt it helped her get through the past few days. Now the reek of stale smoke clings to her skin.

Helen pops a mint into her mouth and opens up her phone. She watches the official promo ad they sent her again. Hoping it'll stir her blood. The promo is minimal to say the least, and it features a throaty male narrator (think movie-trailer man) talking over an image of Lady Justice holding her famous scales.

Coming soon. The Project – is this what happens when influencers go too far?

Helen closes the ad. *I'm a pioneer,* she reminds herself. Nothing like this has ever been seen before, and surely Daddy would be proud. It's a public service. It's accountability.

All the information is *readily available.*

She sits back and closes her eyes. Despite her massive success in the television industry, Helen has always lived in the shadow of her older sister. When they were kids. When they left that shithole town. When they made something of themselves.

Not anymore.

The studio gates are less than a mile away, and already she can hear the protestors.

58

Three helicopters whizz through the air. Slapping blades, like machine-gun fire in the sky. The noise is deafening, and at first glance it looks like a scene from a war movie, but as the 24/7 News camera descends, we see the massive studio complex in the distance. Tall gates. A long road that leads from the gates to the studio entrance.

Somewhere inside that mega-studio, a town has been constructed. A small town with houses, streets, shops and a supermarket. No images of the town have been released yet, and the general public won't see it until the Project is live on air.

But it's not really the town that anyone wants to film today. All the media attention is focused on a large police van making its way towards the gate. The van is surrounded by patrol cars at the front and back. The convoy travels in slow motion, and everyone watching on TV knows that she's in the back of the van. Hayley T. Prank – the star of the show. They don't know if she's been drugged or hypnotised yet. Not all the information, it seems, is readily available on the official Project website.

The convoy passes the police barricade that shields them from a shifting, menacing crowd. The scene is heated. The crowd jeer and hiss. Hold up signs.

The gates swing open, and the van drives through, leaving most of the convoy behind at the gates. The crowd turn up the noise and somehow manage to drown out the helicopters.

On 24/7 News:

NARRATOR: Once more for anyone just tuning in, we're currently watching footage of the police van taking Hayley T. Prank into the studio that's been constructed for the sole purpose of her rehabilitation.

Isn't she a lucky girl? Not everyone gets a second chance, and we here at 24/7 News are with the government, with the network, and most all, we're with you, Hayley. We hope you find clarity in there.

59

Three days later

Helen watches from the control room as they carry her into the house. They take her off the stretcher and lay her down on the couch. They've dyed her hair. Put her in the sort of sad, faded clothes that Hayley T. Prank wouldn't be seen dead in.

From now on, no one in the crew is allowed to call her anything except Kate.

When she wakes up, the actor playing Tommy will call to her from upstairs. He'll say her name as often as possible in that first hour after awakening – that's what the crew in charge of hypnotic suggestion wants. *Reinforce, reinforce, reinforce.* That all-important first hour when her mind is trying to sort itself out.

No one has any idea if this is going to work. Or if it's going to be the most expensive flop ever. They'll soon find out.

Helen communicates with the heads of other departments. There are so many names to remember. Notes to pass on. Thank God for Joel – he might be a loudmouth who stinks of coffee and never stops talking, but he's handling the last-minute prep like a pro.

For her part, Helen is trying to maintain her composure. It's the illusion of calm. Let everyone else be nervous – they can afford to be scared and show it but not her. She's the rock. She's the foundation stone.

A sip of water. Wishing it were vodka.

The crew members are leaving the house. Leaving her there on the couch alone. The actor playing Tommy is upstairs, waiting for notification that she's awake.

Helen's legs shudder under the table just like they did at the press conference that day. She's grateful for the dim lighting and hopes it masks the fear in her eyes.

'Almost time,' Joel says.

A noise behind them. The padded door being pushed open.

The sensitivity consultant walks in, late. *That's not very professional*, thinks Helen. But what does she expect from this Gen Z or whatever the hell they call them nowadays? He's not much to look at – a skinny young man in brand-new clothes that make him look like a junior banker. There's a brief exchange of hellos, and then his awkward, Frankenstein-like walk takes him over to the couch.

Oh God, Helen thinks. Why did the network have to force the issue of sensitivity consultants down her throat? Apparently, it was non-negotiable that at least three of them would be on duty at all times.

She hears his laptop switch on at the back of the room where they put his couch. Right at the back of the room: out of sight, out of mind.

Hopefully he keeps his trap shut.

They run down the clock until showtime. Eventually, the lights on the ceiling dim. Final orders are given.

Helen sits back in her chair, wondering what her dad would think of all this. The answer provides no comfort. Meanwhile, it's Sadia who remains the voice of cold reassurance in Helen's mind. And even she's been distant lately. Then there's Zara, her beautiful young niece lying in a coffin. Dead girl. Dead baby.

A shimmering white glow fills the control room.

'We're live,' Helen says.

It takes longer than expected, but Kate wakes up on the couch. Dazed and confused.

'Okay,' Joel says, whispering into the headset mic. 'She's awake. Let's see if this stuff really works.'

Helen clears her throat. Speaks into the mic.

'Make sure the husband approaches within at least ten minutes of waking. Make sure he calls her Kate and starts reinforcing the programme.'

She falls back into her seat.

'So it begins,' she whispers.

PART V
ESCAPE

60

HAYLEY

My eyes open, and at first, I think the noises I hear are the remnants of some horrible nightmare that won't let go. Frightened voices. Shouting, loud banging and screaming. The sound of glass breaking and then more screaming.

I sit up too fast in a room I don't know.

My stomach lurches. I turn to my left and throw up over the side of the bed.

'Ugh.'

The room spins. My head is throbbing, and it feels like my insides are about to turn into my outsides. It's like being seasick, but I'm not on a boat, am I?

What's that smell?

Smoke?

'Oh shit.'

I get up and walk to the door on legs that feel like they might betray me at any second. There's a square of glass on the door, and looking outside, I see two men on the other side. Security guards by the looks of. They're talking to each other. Both are fidgety. Glancing along the corridor with fearful eyes.

More screaming. What the hell is going on out there?

I turn around. My legs throw a wobbly, and I pin my back against the door to ensure I remain upright. It still feels like the room is spinning. Maybe the spinning is just in my head.

God, I feel drained.

I look around. I'm in a small room with a single bed squeezed tight against the wall. Looks like some kind of medical room. White walls. The reek of chemicals. And of course, my freshly laid vomit on the floor.

A medical room?

I almost fall over as it comes back to me. They brought me somewhere just like this and then ... the sensation of being pushed so far back inside myself. The sensation of ... *disappearing*. I ended up trapped inside my own mind. There was a smothering feeling, yet I was in there all the time, kicking and pounding and trying to fight my way back through the fog. But I couldn't wake up from the dream. The dream of being this other person, Kate. Now I'm awake, and the dream is fading so fast it's like it never happened. The net has been ripped open, and my mind at last is running free.

My stomach lurches again, but I'm not sick.

Oh God, my limbs feel hollow. What have they done to me?

'Shit.'

What happened to David? What happened to Alex? I saw them in there, although the memories are cloudy. They got in somehow. They got in and tried to save me, yet I didn't recognise them. *Couldn't* recognise them. They took Alex away, and David ... he was in the car when the police chased us. I ran. What happened to David?

I face the door again. Turn the metal handle; it's locked. I hammer my fists on the door.

'Let me out!'

The guards ignore me. It's like I'm not even there, for God's sake.

'What's happening?

These people ... they turned my pranks against me. That was my punishment for the poor girl who died – the girl who got hit by a car. Zara – her name was Zara. I cried for her. The poor girl had a baby inside her, and they said she'd written to me and that I'd ignored her, but I couldn't keep up with all the messages I get.

You could've stopped her, they said. *You could've said something.*

Maybe it is all my fault. One thing I know for sure – if I could bring her back, I would. If I could swap places with her, I would.

'Let me out!'

I fall backwards, my lungs burning. The smoke is overpowering me, and I've no doubt that this building is on fire. With that comes the realisation that I might burn to death trapped inside this cell. At the same time, Kate's life continues to fade. I remember the things I did. The life I thought was mine or the half-life, as it turned out. I still recall her quiet despair and how it felt like mine. The frustration and fear of my best days behind me.

What did they put in my body?

Fuck. It feels like the walls are closing in all around me, and I have to get out of here. They've locked me up, but I'm not taking this shit. I rush for the door, and the room spins faster. I throw up again, but even vomit doesn't slow me down. I've still got the energy to pound the door.

I look outside.

The guards are gone.

'What the fuck? You can't leave me!'

The smoke is unbearable, and I'm sure it's heating up in here, but then again, maybe it's just me. There's a flurry of movement in the hallway. Five, six, seven people with face masks rushing past the door, possibly chasing after the two guards. It sounds like a train going past, and I duck out of sight before they see me.

I stare into space.

'What's happening?'

They've locked me up. They've locked me up and left me here. But something's happened.

I remember who I am.

Are they still messing with me?

I flop into a sitting position. Legs crossed, back against the door. My neck feels like it's forgotten how to support my head. I don't have the strength to get out of here, so I sink to the floor, my sluggish limbs drowning in quicksand. I ignore the footsteps outside until I hear the sound of a key turning in the lock.

I jump to my feet, backing away across the room as the door swings open.

'Leave me alone!' I scream. 'Leave me alone!'

61

JIMMY

Jimmy thinks that one of the guards must have left a key in the door. Maybe they did it on purpose so that someone else would come along and let her out. Or maybe they just forgot about it sticking out of the keyhole like that. Who could blame anyone for not thinking straight right now?

Jimmy wants to believe that someone did a good thing.

The studio is heating up in more ways than one. It wasn't easy getting down here from the control room. The corridors are flooded with protestors, and they're showing no mercy to anyone. Jimmy was smart to grab a tea towel from the canteen and wrap it around his face. They've left him alone. So far.

His heart is thumping. He spoke to Allie and Tina on the phone and promised them that he was on his way home. Right now, as fast as humanly possible. Easier said than done. Now he's trying to find a way out of the studio, but he couldn't just leave knowing that those fake cops dumped

Hayley in the third-floor medical room. Knowing that no one here really gives a shit whether she lives or dies.

But time is running out.

They're lighting fires everywhere. Spray-painting the walls and attacking security guards and crew members, most of whom have given up their posts.

HE'S three floors down from the control room. Having just avoided another train of protestors on the stairs, he's in a quiet hallway. Staring at the door, at the key hanging in the lock.

Jimmy lowers the tea towel and breathes in the smoke. His hands shake, but he manages to turn the key in the lock. Then he pushes the medical-room door open.

'Leave me alone!' a woman screams before he can even see her. 'Leave me alone.'

The door is fully open. There she is, standing in the middle of the room.

Hayley.

'Thank God,' he says. 'You're alright.'

It feels weird talking directly to her after watching her on a screen for so long. But that was different. And telling her she looks alright isn't the most accurate description. She's as white as a ghost. Her legs look unsteady, and there are two puddles of vomit on the floor, one of which Jimmy nearly slips on as he walks into the room.

'Who are you?' she asks.

'Jimmy. My name's Jimmy.'

Her eyes are still hazy.

'What's going on?'

'The protests spilled over,' he says. 'They stormed the

gates, the building, and now there's a full-blown riot in here. No one's safe.'

'How did you know where I was?'

He shrugs. 'There are cameras everywhere. But I guess you know that by now.'

They hear the sound of glass shattering from somewhere on the third floor. It doesn't sound that far off.

Hayley looks at him. Looks *through* him. At the same time, she reaches out to the wall for support. God knows what all those drugs have done to her. She's confused, weak, and she won't make it out without help. The way she looks now, Jimmy's not sure the protestors would even recognise her. Besides, the worst of the rioters are only here to burn the studio to the ground. Are they even looking for her?

There's no doubt – it's up to him. He has to get her out. Back to safety and far away from this place.

'Can you walk?' Jimmy asks.

62

HAYLEY

Feels like the world is on fire. The gigantic studio is burning behind us, and a merciless heat is descending upon our heads like a giant blanket.

Jimmy, the guy who got me out, runs beside me. He's holding my arm in case I topple over, but I'm getting there. The more I move, the more I feel my head clearing. Kate, or rather the dream of Kate, is almost gone now.

We exited through a fire door that had been left open at the side of the building. Jimmy gave me the damp towel he had on to wrap around my nose and mouth. He doesn't think I can take the constant smoke in my lungs, and he's probably right. Now we're outside, and it's like running into Hell. I inhale through the towel and immediately start coughing. Whatever strength I have left is dwindling fast, yet Jimmy urges me to continue.

Keep moving, keep moving.

'I'm trying,' I say through the towel.

It's carnage. Rioters everywhere. Puddles of blood on the

ground. Screams – there's always someone screaming. People running for their lives, begging for mercy.

We run past a car park, and every single car is on fire. There are dozens of rioters there, pouring petrol everywhere. Many of them are filming the action on their phones. The noise is like a hammer bludgeoning me into the ground.

'I can't do this,' I say.

Jimmy's grip is tight on my arm. 'Keep moving.'

I look around. This doesn't feel like it's about me anymore. There's no cause here, only chaos. This is just a bunch of people who've been waiting for an excuse to go crazy – and now here it is. They're robbing and looting, attacking the studio staff, most of whom haven't done anything wrong. They're simply working their jobs; they aren't responsible for what happened to me.

It feels like so many of us are trying to get to the front gate. Someone is directly ahead of us now. Limping. Staggering down the long driveway and swaying from side to side. He turns back to look at what might be chasing him. I scream.

'David!'

I wriggle free of Jimmy's grip, and my legs come alive. I sprint down the path, grabbing hold of David. His face is a puffy mask, and it's only because I've known him for so many years that I know it's him.

'Hayls ...'

He falls into my arms, and I wipe the damp hair off his face. I don't even realise I'm crying until I hear it in my voice.

'What did they do to you?'

He steps back from my embrace. Shakes his head, and for a second, I think he's about to topple over at my feet. He looks like someone who barely survived a war zone.

'We ... need to ... go,' he croaks.

'What about Alex?' I say. 'Is Alex still here?'

'No. They took him out.'

'Took him where?'

He can only shake his head.

'Alright,' I say. 'I'm going to get you out of here. We need to get away from all this, and then we'll figure it out.'

I look at Jimmy. I'm about to ask him what we should do, but he's staring at something, his face a picture of grim concentration.

'Jimmy! What is it?'

He points at something just off the path. At first glance it looks like an overturned golf cart. A four-seater with a long-necked steering wheel, white panels and a little sun roof at the top. It's a bit trashed at the front like someone's taken a club to it and then moved on to something else. Otherwise, it's intact.

'People drive them across the studio lot,' Jimmy says. 'They're supposed to be parked in the garage, but someone must have—'

He doesn't need to say any more, and anyway, no one wants to hear it. We're all imagining the rioters dragging some poor bastard out of the buggy. And instead of finishing off the buggy, they went after the driver and his or her passengers, if there were any. There are numerous people lying around dead or unconscious. It could've been any one of them.

'The keys,' Jimmy says. 'They might still be in the ignition.'

I'm holding up David as best I can under the circumstances. Thank God he's a skinny runt. I'm about to ask

Jimmy if he knows how to drive one of those carts, but he's off already, running off the path and towards the vehicle.

I drag David over there. Or maybe he drags me. It's hard to tell at this point.

'You're back,' he says, smiling.

I smile, sort of.

Jimmy's a long way from Hercules, but he does a good job of lifting the buggy off its side. He jumps on the driver's step. Stares at the ignition and throws me a thumbs-up. David and I hurry off the path, both of us nearly falling over one another. God knows how we're still on our feet. I shove him into the back – there's no time to be delicate. I jump in beside him, and Jimmy gets behind the wheel.

'Hold on!' he yells.

I scream back at him, 'Jimmy!'

A huge barrel-chested man in a dark balaclava is running towards us. Sprinting towards us. He's got a baseball bat in hand, and I don't miss the red smears all over it. His clothes are covered in blood too. I realise, too late, that by sitting in the buggy, we've marked ourselves out as studio staff in the eyes of the rioters. And the buggy's now pointing towards the exit.

'Jimmy!'

'I know!'

Jimmy's boyish face is a picture of confusion as he fumbles with the key. One hand grips the steering wheel, ready to go. He turns the key. The buggy coughs but doesn't start.

Balaclava Man sounds like an elephant charging straight at us.

'Jimmy!'

I throw myself over David and prepare for the bat to

come down on my head with enough force to split my skull open. In that split second that lasts for ever, I find myself thinking about Zara again. Wherever I'm going, will she be waiting for me?

The buggy coughs again, then staggers forward. We stop suddenly. David is almost thrown out of the back, and I hold onto him with all the strength I've got, which isn't much.

'Sorry,' Jimmy says, glancing down at the pedals. 'I've never driven one of these before.'

I yell at him, 'Go!'

The buggy cruises towards the path at fifteen miles per hour. That's top speed. The blood-soaked maniac is still chasing after us, the bat raised over his head. We reach the path, then cut onto the driveway that leads to the gate. Jimmy seems to have got the hang of it, and he weaves past burning cars. Baseball-bat guy seems convinced he can outrun the buggy. Maybe he can. It's hardly a Porsche. But he's not Usain Bolt either.

I hear wailing sirens in the distance. Beyond the front gate, I see the flashing lights of fire engines, ambulances and police cars. They'll be here in less than a minute.

I call over to Jimmy, 'Let's get to the gate before they—'

The first big explosion stops everything. It comes from inside the studio – a giant cracking noise that sounds like a rumble in the deep belly of the earth. I feel the scalding heat on the back of my neck. A glance over my shoulder and I see tidal-wave-like flames devouring the building. It's like watching the world collapse.

'Oh shit,' I say.

For some reason, Jimmy has slowed. We're almost at the gates, and I can't see the giant with the baseball bat behind us anymore. We have a chance, but if we don't go now, we'll be boxed in by the emergency services. All I want to do is get out of here. To run into the night, to get far away from this place.

'Jimmy!' I scream. 'Move!'

He's looking at something off the driveway and to the right. There are people in uniforms being attacked. Workers, dragged by their hair and beaten. It's horrific.

'Jimmy!'

But Jimmy's gaze is on one incident in particular. There's an older woman, brown-skinned, surrounded by a mob of about twelve people in masks. She looks familiar, but I can't put a name to the face. Jimmy seems to know her.

The mob strikes. I can't look. I can't. And when she lets out the worst scream I've ever heard, Jimmy floors the buggy, and this is it – our last desperate charge for the gates before we're locked in. But this piece-of-shit golf cart is so freaking slow, and I don't think we're going to make it.

I'm going to die.

The cart shudders. Another explosion from somewhere. Wild, high-pitched screams over the sound of incoming sirens. The atmosphere descends into something truly horrifying, and even some of the rioters are rushing towards the gates, afraid of their own mess.

That second explosion was a big one. I hear the sound of debris landing nearby. Massive chunks of studio flying all over the place.

But it's the third explosion – that's the biggie. I don't see it, but like everyone else there, I feel it.

The third and final explosion, the one that brings everything to an end.

63

ALLIE

Jimmy won't answer his phone. I've been trying to call his mobile at least every ten minutes. I've left voicemails and sent texts by the dozen.

Nothing.

Tina sleeps in my arms while I pace the living room. She should be in bed upstairs, but I don't want to let her out of my sight.

Oh God. I think we're in trouble. I think we're in trouble, and I don't know that I've ever been this scared in all my life. Waiting for confirmation that he's ...

No. Don't even think it.

We're at home. Jimmy's parents have come over, and they're sitting on the couch. Looking as sick as I feel. We're flicking between various news reports on TV. All of them showing the same footage of the riots at the studios where Jimmy was working. I've never seen anything like it. There were protests, sure. But it wasn't supposed to spill over. Now look at it. People being attacked by psychos in masks. People starting fires everywhere they can. And, of course, the explosions in the building itself. That massive third explosion was catastrophic, and while the firefighters are doing their best, theirs is a losing battle.

So many bodies. The fire. The smoke. There's no way that anyone inside the studio survived that final blast. Same with anyone who was too close.

He's dead, I tell myself. *And at some point, I'm going to have to accept it. And I'm going to have to tell Tina that Daddy isn't coming home.*

Jimmy's father, Craig, takes off his glasses and rubs something at the corner of his eye. He's a tall man with a slight stoop – apparently his early years in construction were tough, and they've affected his posture in later life. Craig is a good man – he worked hard for his family. Jimmy always says he was a tough but fair father.

His mum, Martha, a former primary school teacher, adores her son. They're alike in so many ways. The have the same eyes and smile. The same caring nature. I know this is hard for her. For both of them.

Craig and Martha hold hands on the couch. Like me, they're probably wondering about the best way for someone to die in this disaster. Better to go in the explosion than to be torn apart by the protestors.

I look at Tina, envying her peace. I brush a loose strand of hair off her face and think about how I used to love watching them play together. As well as being father and daughter, those two were great friends. No matter how tired Jimmy was, he always made time for her. Always.

'Cup of tea?' Martha asks.

I nod. Not that I want a cup of tea, but Martha's the sort of person who copes by doing things. She's already picked

Tina's toys up off the floor and tidied them away in the toy box.

'We don't know anything yet,' Craig says, unable to take his eyes off the screen despite the horrors being broadcast. 'We don't know anything.' Without Martha there to hold his hand, he balls it into a tightly clenched fist.

I look at him. He looks so old and small, but maybe I just never noticed it before. What good will denial do us in the long run? I'm waiting for that knock on the door. For someone in a police uniform to confirm the inevitable.

'Craig?' Martha says, poking her head through the kitchen door. 'Tea?'

But Craig doesn't answer because those footsteps have arrived on the path outside. He mutes the TV to confirm what we all heard. Yes, there it is. Martha gasps. It's almost like I summoned them, and now the news is here, happening much quicker than I expected. I feel sick. Dizzy. My world is about to turn upside down and so is my daughter's. I can barely hold on to Tina but I can't let her go. *Won't* let her go. The knock will come. I'll open the door and see two police officers with sympathetic expressions, and that's when my husband's death will become official.

Craig stands up. He's shaking.

But there is no knock on the door.

I hear a key scratching around in the lock. No one moves in the living room – we're paralysed with terror. Perhaps with hope too. I stand with Tina in my arms. Her gentle, oblivious, snuffling snores so at odds with the tension in the room.

I hate myself for daring to hope.

Martha makes a strange whimpering sound. Craig is

hunched over, trying to get to the door. But someone else opens it and walks into the living room.

Jimmy.

He's got minor but angry-looking burns on his face, and his hair is soaked with sweat. The boring shirt that I picked out for him (and that he hated) is torn at the front. Looks like someone tried to grab it at the breast pocket. There are small, scattered bloodstains on the shirt and also on his trousers and shoes. He looks like shit, but his eyes are clear. And he's smiling. Which makes him look a bit crazy right now.

'Hi,' he says. And then collapses onto the floor.

Craig, with all his physical limitations, hurries over to his son in the blink of an eye. So does Martha.

'Tina,' I say through the flood of tears I've been holding back all night. I watch as Jimmy's parents hold him tight. One on either side. Jimmy's still conscious and looking over at us. Somehow, he's still smiling.

Gently, I shake our daughter awake.

'Look, Tina. Daddy's home.'

EPILOGUE

The heat is merciless. And so are the flies. Lots of flies.

This red desert at the bottom of the world might as well be nowhere. But it's the Northern Territory, Australia. I've arrived at long last. Walking along what feels like the emptiest road in the world, nothing to my name except the clothes I'm wearing and a few odds and sods in the rucksack on my shoulder.

The silence is eerie.

Still, I don't mind. The further I walk, the further it feels like leaving civilisation behind, and that's what I came for. That among other things.

It's been three weeks since I arrived in Melbourne from the UK, and since then it's been non-stop lightning-fast visits to Sydney, Queensland and over to Western Australia before heading up here. This country is so big, and there are so many things to see and do. I've tried to see it all. I'm exhausted and exhilarated.

I keep going.

Every day, I imagine she's with me. Then I remind myself that she is. I have some of her belongings in the bag – her favourite pieces of jewellery and a few items of clothing. I even have a small clump of earth from her grave. And from Natasha's too. It's a very different family holiday from the ones I remember in the Lake District all those years ago, but it *is* a family holiday. It's the best I can do.

There's someone else here too. Before flying out of London, I hired a car and took a road trip to a rural cemetery out west. I visited Zara Hassani's grave and cried there. Spoke to her like the friend she wanted me to be. And took some earth for this trip.

Where to now? I don't know where this road leads. Probably to one of those remote outback towns with a pub and a hotel and the sort of quirky residents who were either born there or who came in from the outside to escape something somewhere else. The last bus dropped me off at what felt like a remote town, but I'm far north of that place now. This feels like disappearing, and perhaps that's the appeal of places like this. It can't be the heat or the flies.

I walk at the side of the road. The red sun will be setting in a few hours, its vicious heat easing to what I hope will be a soothing warmth. Whenever the wind picks up, I taste the sand that turns to dust in my mouth. And still the flies keep coming.

After about half an hour on this road, I hear a car behind me. I look back and see shimmering metal in the red sand. It's a white Ute, and it sounds like it's on its last legs. The lone vehicle passes scattered ghost gums at the side of the road. Pulls in just ahead of me.

I catch up and hear a comical squeak as the window is rolled down. The man in the driver's seat is probably in his fifties, but his haggard skin has seen way too much sun. He's wearing a chequered shirt, wide-brimmed hat and khaki shorts.

He touches his hat.

'G'day.'

'Hi.'

'Dangerous. Hitchhiking out here all alone.'

'I didn't put my thumb out.'

He laughs. 'That's very true. Where you heading?'

I point in the direction I hope is north. 'Isn't there a town up here somewhere? With a hotel.'

He looks at me like I've got a screw loose. Then smiles, turning his face into a map of wrinkles. 'Well, yeah, there is. But it's going to take you at least an hour on foot to get there. You need a lift?'

I look into the Ute. There's not much to see – an empty muffin packet, a bottle of water and an indoor gardening magazine sitting on the passenger seat. 'I don't know. Are you one of those outback serial killers?'

He smiles again. 'Don't know yet. Been thinking about taking up a new hobby.'

'Yeah, I've seen *Wolf Creek*. I know how it works.'

That gets him going. His laughter is the sort that makes you want to join in. He points a finger to the baking road in front of us. 'I work in the restaurant in that same town you're looking for. Population, thirty-four. The restaurant is also the hotel, where I assume you'll be staying, right?'

'As long as they've got vacancies.'

More laughter from the potential serial killer. 'Oh, bloody hell, love, we've always got vacancies.'

'How do you survive so far away from everything?'

He shrugs. 'Oh, we're survivors out here. Everyone you'll

meet up there has a story of survival. Maybe you'll fit in with the rest of us, eh?'

My smile fades.

'Guess I'll be staying at your hotel-cum-restaurant, then.'

'Don't expect the Ritz, and you'll be alright.'

'I won't.'

'You been walking all day in this heat?'

'Some of it.'

'Sure you don't want a lift? We're going to the same place.'

I shake my head. 'Nah, I'm enjoying the scenery too much. Besides, I'm still not sure if you're a serial killer or not.'

'Strewth. Well, don't dillydally on the road. It gets dark real quick out here, and trust me, this is *not* the sort of place you want to get stuck out at night. I can give you the hotel number if you want. You got a phone?'

I step back from the car, lift my head and listen to the wind in the rocks.

'Actually, I don't.'

'No phone? Bloody hell. Are you crazy?'

I look at him. Then I give a brief wave and start walking away from the car. I'm back to facing the horizon and the open road.

'No,' I call back to him. 'Not anymore.'

THANK YOU FOR READING

Did you enjoy reading *Fool Me Once*? Please consider leaving a review on Amazon. Your review will help other readers to discover the novel.

ABOUT THE AUTHOR

Mark Gillespie writes psychological thriller and suspense novels. He's a former professional musician (bass player) from Glasgow, Scotland who spent ten years touring the UK and Ireland, playing sessions and having the time of his life. Don't ask though. What happened on the road stays on the road.

He now lives in Auckland, New Zealand with his wife and a small menagerie of rescue creatures. If he's not writing, he's jamming with other musicians, running on the beach, watching mixed martial arts and boxing. Or devouring horror and thriller movies.

www.markgillespieauthor.com

ALSO BY MARK GILLESPIE

I Know Who You Are

The Lost Girl

Fool Me Once

While You Were Gone